by the Great North of Scotland Railway in 1891 and completely renovated, including the addition of electric lighting, which was seen as a total luxury by most of the people who booked rooms there.

Mabel Lassiter had been chosen for the simple fact that she was due to be in Aberdeen to perform in a show that would run for two weeks. No one would ever question why she had gone to Aberdeen because it was obvious. She had also been chosen because her beauty was far more important than her brain. Mabel was not very bright and could basically be told anything as she was unlikely to come back with any awkward questions. Her beauty, of course, would get her the attention he was banking on.

The chest that had been so successfully manhandled up to the room was to play a part in his plan; a plan that would unfold as the King and Queen visited Aberdeen on the twenty-seventh of the month to inaugurate Marischal College after its period of renovation. Mabel had been told about the chest and how it would fit in to a plan due to unfold over the time she would be in Aberdeen. She had listened to him, as they had sat together in a London pub, with indifference and a total lack of interest. In truth the only element of her part in the plan, that seemed to have any impact on her, was the fact she was going to be staying in a posh hotel while she was in Aberdeen. Dancers didn't usually stay in posh hotels.

Mabel had been shown to her room a little before lunchtime and had ordered room service to bring her a light repast, which she had eaten whilst looking out of the window across Union Terrace Gardens and the rail line that stretched out of view towards Inverness. She had been told to remain in her room until someone made contact with her and that was what she intended to do. She was not due at rehearsal until the following day so had plenty time to do nothing.

As per the plan he had waited until the early evening before making his way to the door of Mabel's room. After checking that there were no witnesses to him being there, he knocked on the door and waited for her to let him in. Mabel had been told that the purpose of the visit was to give her a little more information on the full plan and also to further check that everything had gone smoothly with her journey. The door opened and Mabel stepped back to let him enter.

She was already dressed in her nightclothes with a heavy dressing gown worn over the top. She was enjoying staying in a hotel, pampering herself in a way that she had never been able to do before. Just for a brief period in her life she felt like a proper lady, she felt as if she had made it in life and she intended enjoying every minute. As she moved across the room her dressing gown parted a little and he could see the swell of her breasts beneath. She noticed him looking and quickly covered herself again.

"Some place this," she commented with an expression similar to a child who had just been given the biggest bar of chocolate ever seen.

"Don't get too comfortable with the lifestyle," the man said quickly, "you'll not be here that long."

Mabel walked over to stand nearer to him. She looked at him and wondered what he might look like without the disguise. She had never seen him without the heavy whiskers covering most of his face and now that she could look really closely at him she could see the slight traces of stage make-up. This man was clearly a lot younger than the current image he was portraying to the world.

"It may just be for two weeks," added Mabel," but I have every intention of enjoying meself while I'm here."

"Myself, Mabel. If you're going to try and act like a lady then at least learn to speak like one. Now did everything go smoothly with the movement of the chest?"

"Of course," Mabel replied with a smile. "I had the young men buzzing around me like flies."

The man went over to the chest and pulled it open. Inside there was a small seat and around the outside of the chest small holes had been bored through to apparently allow air to pass in to the chest when it had been closed. The man studied everything and the stepped back, a broad smile on his face. He made his way over to where Mabel was standing and took her in his arms. He kissed her.

"What was that for? Mabel asked, though she had not put up a fight as he'd pressed his lips to her own.

"You've done very well, Mabel and I just thought that we might........"

He undid the dressing gown and let it drop to the floor. Her body was almost clearly visible through the sheer material of her nightdress and he felt himself harden as he looked at her. Mabel smiled. She knew what was about to happen and she wasn't going to do anything other than enjoy it. They went to bed and he made love to her with a tenderness that had rarely existed in her life before.

Once they had finished they lay in each other's arms for a little while longer. Mabel enjoyed having the arms of a strong man around her even though she had to put up with all those fake whiskers that had tickled her everywhere his lips had gone.

Suddenly the man looked at his watch, which was lying on the bedside table.

"Time I was going," he said and got out of bed.

He went across to the washing area and poured some water in to a bowl. He quickly cleaned himself, aware that Mabel was watching him from the bed. He looked at her reflection in the mirror. The bedcovers were pushed down and she was lying in full view, her naked body still covered with a light sweat after her exertions. He smiled at her and turned to walk towards the bed.

I also gathered a great deal of helpful information from the Handbook to City and University, which was produced by the University to mark the Quatercentenary celebrations of 1906. To have a book not only dealing with the subject of the celebrations but also written at the time was invaluable.

May I also add my thanks to the management and staff of the *Archibald Simpson*. I was not only sold an excellent cup of coffee every morning for nearly three years but also provided with a great deal of background information on the building, which they currently occupy.

One final point that may be of help to anyone reading this book; £1 in 1906 is equivalent to £100 today.

Eric R Davidson

Aberdeen – January 2014

About The Author

Eric R Davidson spent most of his working life in the Civil Service before having a second career with Grampian Police in Aberdeen. His role with Grampian Police came to an end in 2013, which allowed Eric to concentrate on his main passion, which was writing. The outcome of having more time to concentrate on his writing has led to the 1906 trilogy being conceived. *1906 – October* is already being written and *1906 – November* will follow as soon as it is completed.

Prologue

He had arrived back in Aberdeen that morning. Prior to this visit he had spent so much time in Aberdeen that it was now beginning to feel like a second home to him. He had travelled overnight from London on the same train as Mabel Lassiter. He had wanted to make sure that she carried out her part of the plan to the letter. She had no idea that she was being constantly observed but, to him, she was the only unknown element in what was a perfect plan to commit the perfect crime.

She had been chosen out of convenience; a matter of her about to be in the right place at the right time. He had spoken to her in London and explained that there would be a nice sum of money coming her way if she were to do a little job for him. He had made love to her, just to seal the deal and by the time he had left her in the morning he felt that she would have done anything for him.

He had told her what was expected of her but had said no more in terms of the content of the overall plan. There was no need for this woman to know any more than was absolutely necessary. She had a part to play, but in his mind it was a small part and there was little to be gained by wasting time by telling her more than she was ever needing to know. That had probably been just as well, he had thought later, as Mabel was not the brightest jewel in the box.

At Aberdeen's Joint Station that morning he had watched, with interest, as men buzzed around Mabel, all eager to help this poor, unfortunate young woman move a rather large chest from the guard's van up to her hotel room. He had smiled at how easy it was for a pretty face to attract such attention. Although mainly chosen for the fact she was going to Aberdeen, the part that Mabel would play in his plan would be made all the easier by the fact she was good looking; he knew she attracted attention and he wanted her to make an impression at the station. Had Mabel not been so attractive then there was every chance that, short of her offering a sizeable reward, she would have been left to struggle with the chest, at least until hotel staff, who had no other option, were compelled to offer assistance. As it was, everyone, at least every male, seemed to be falling over themselves to offer Mabel Lassiter all the assistance she required and in return all she had to do was smile sweetly.

The small army of helpers expertly manhandled the chest on to the lift and then upwards to the hotel room, stopping off in the foyer for Mabel to check-in. The Palace Hotel was ideally situated above the main platform of the Joint Station in Aberdeen. There was a direct link from platform to reception desk and as a result of such perfect geography The Palace Hotel cornered much of the market when it came to visitors arriving for the first time in the city. The building had been taken over

1906 – SEPTEMBER

Eric R Davidson

MYS
Pbk

Published by Edge60

Copyright (c) Eric R Davidson 2014

The Author thanks:

Firstly may I say that I have tried my utmost to be historically accurate, both in the geography of Aberdeen and also the speech and conduct of my characters, during the writing of this book. My thanks, therefore, to my wife, Heather, for her patient reading of the manuscript, her correction of my mistakes and her suggestions for improving the speech and conduct of my characters on the occasions where I drifted in to more modern terminology. Having said that, however, should you as the reader now pick up on something that we have missed I would be obliged if you didn't start a website highlighting such errors but merely put it down to the fact that this is a work of fiction.

My thanks also to my son, Adam, for the work he did to help create the cover to this book.

I am indebted to the content of The Diced Cap, which provided a detailed history of Aberdeen City Police and also to ex-colleagues at Grampian Police for providing me with further details on how the police may have operated back in 1906 as well as a clearer impression of the design of Lodge Walk.

This was the part of the plan that he had omitted to tell Mabel.

As he sat on the edge of the bed Mabel looked across at the chest. He could almost see her brain ticking over as she looked at the chest and considered its purpose. She was looking at the seat and then she had a thought about the air holes. He felt sure he saw the light bulb above her head go on.

"You're going back to London in that, aren't you?" she eventually said.

The man smiled down at her and let his hand, rather lazily, slide over the mound of her right breast. He let his thumb pass across her nipple and she shuddered with pleasure. "Why, Mabel, I do believe that little brain of yours has surpassed itself."

"But why?"

"Ah now there the thinking really will have to stop, it's not good for you."

"It's you the police will be looking for, isn't it?" Mabel then said, sitting up in bed.

He now moved a little closer to Mabel, his expression softening in to a warm smile.

"It really doesn't matter what the cargo is, Mabel, your part in the process will still be the same. It'll be nothing more than a pretty dancer returning to London with her costumes. There really will be no need for the police, or anyone else for that matter, to pay any more attention to you than to admire your beauty."

He moved ever closer, his lips seeking hers one more time.

"You really are very beautiful, Mabel," he added and his hand groped at her breast with a little more urgency.

"D'you think so?" Mabel said. They kissed.

"Oh Mabel," the man said, looking in to her eyes," I always knew it would come to this, only I was never completely honest with you as to exactly what part you would play in my plan."

The man's expression changed. There was an evil glint in his eye that Mabel did not like.

"What do you mean?" she asked.

However, what followed next was not what Mabel Lassiter had expected. In fact what followed next would have taken everyone involved in the plan by surprise as this was the part he had kept to himself. This was the part from which he would get no pleasure but it was essential that he carried it out. The main element of his plan was to create as much extra work for the local police as possible. It was essential that he diverted eyes away from anything he might be doing in the city. Mabel had never been anything other than a pawn in the game. She was to be a distraction, nothing more.

What followed next was nothing short of carnage.

He punched Mabel with a ferocity that caused her to slip down on the bed in a semi-conscious state. He then attacked Mabel Lassiter in as violent a manner as was possible. He hit her a few more times and then entered her with a force that only a rapist would bring to the sex act. As he came inside her his hands went around Mabel's throat and he choked the life out of her. By the time he was finished there was nothing more than a lifeless rag doll left draped across the bed. The attack had been deliberately violent as there could be no way that the police would ever think that Mabel Lassiter knew her attacker as well as she did. This had to look like the work of a maniac.

Having completed the deed the man arranged Mabel's body on the bed so that her open, lifeless eyes were staring towards the door. He thought that that might be a nice touch for whoever next came through the door and found her. He washed himself again and then dressed. He now let himself out of Mabel's room and hurried to the floor below, where he had another room booked for his own purposes. Once there he collected a travel bag and then returned to Mabel's room, all the time ensuring that no one was seeing him.

Once back in the room he put Mabel's clothes in to the smaller travel bag and then rearranged the chest so that it now looked perfectly possible for a man to sit in it and perhaps be transported around. He ripped Mabel's nightdress and left it lying on the floor by the bed. He looked around the room one last time, just to ensure that he was leaving no clues for the police that might set them on his trail. Satisfied that all was well he then moved back to the door, checked the hallway was clear and then hurried back to his own room.

Once inside he removed all traces of the whiskers and make-up. He also took off the clothes and put them and the whiskers in a bag, which he would dispose of later. He then adopted the image of a younger, slightly more debonair, man who wore a smart, expensive looking suit and heavy rimmed spectacles. He then checked the room to ensure he was not leaving any obvious clues that might point to his identity before wiping down the main surfaces and leaving. He placed the Do Not Disturb on the door handle, picked up the two bags, one containing the whiskers and old clothing and the other Mabel's clothes, then closed the door and made his way to the staircase.

He casually strolled down the stairs and out on to Union Street. No one had paid much attention to him and he felt confident that, if asked later, it was highly unlikely any of the potential witnesses would speak of his departure. He had thought of crossing the road and throwing the bags down on to the railway line, but the evening was still mild and there were too many people out walking the mile length of Union Street.

Instead he walked down Union Street, then down a short flight of steps on to Correction Wynd. He then turned right and went under Union Street and in to the Green. This had, at one time in the history of Aberdeen, been the main entrance route to the city. Now it was more a meeting place for traders. During the day it was a place where all manner of fruit and vegetables were sold. At night it was almost deserted but the traders left a lot of rubbish behind and the man found a suitable place to leave both bags. He knew that the rubbish would be collected and taken away so there would be no likelihood of anyone finding the clothes.

Feeling happy that the plan was very much on track he made his way through the streets of Aberdeen and back to the room he had rented from Mrs Bradshaw when he had last been in Aberdeen. She knew him as Lucas Spratt, a salesman from somewhere in England. That, of course, was not his real name; it had been so long since he had used his real name that even he was, by now, finding it difficult to remember what it was.

ONE

Wednesday 12 September - late morning and early afternoon.

It was not often that the city of Aberdeen, nestling as it did on the North East coast of Scotland, ever had much to smile about. Usually grey beneath the clouds that blew in from the sea or down from the much colder North, the city had finally been given a chance to shine, as the September of 1906 wore on, in weather that had brought both heat and happiness to the people of Aberdeen.

Not only was the weather bringing a smile to the city but there was a genuine feeling of joy at the fact the King and Queen were due to visit in a little over one week's time. To commemorate the day and to provide as many people as possible with the opportunity to see His Majesty and his popular wife, the Council had ordered an extra public holiday. This was further reason for the people of Aberdeen to be smiling.

With only one week remaining before the royal visit, Aberdeen had done much to smarten its image with an abundance of bunting and special lighting on show just about everywhere along the route that the King would take. Union Street and Union

Terrace in particular were looking very festive and along with the endless blue skies and late summer warmth, the city was most definitely looking at its very best.

However, for a small group of people standing in the Nellfield Cemetery, no amount of sunshine, bunting or extra lighting could have lifted the gloom that hung over them all. This small group of people had little thought for royal visits as they stood over the burial of a man who had been husband, friend or colleague to them in life but who now lay in an ornate box, the victim of a violent and as yet, apparently senseless crime.

To further compound the felony the victim had been a police officer, stabbed to death while going about his public duties. The magnitude of the crime had affected many Aberdonians as they had read the gory details in the local paper and there had been a general sense of outrage that something so terrible could happen to an officer of the law.

The dead officer had been Alexander Thomson, known to his family, friends and colleagues as Tommy. Standing around the grave were six people. The minister, solemn and quietly spoken, was in the process of concluding the short service. He had little to say beyond the 'dust to dust' as the main service had been conducted earlier at the St Nicholas Church on Union Street. It had been there that the vast majority of Tommy's friends and colleagues had gathered to pay their respects.

Next to the minister stood Mavis Forsyth, closest friend to the woman standing next to her, Mary Thomson. Mary had been married to Tommy for ten years and now stood, dressed in black, with a heavy veil pulled across her face to hide the tears that simply refused to stop running down her cheeks.

On the other side of Mary stood Inspector Jacob Fraser, known to absolutely everyone as Jake. At forty-three he was still what could be termed a handsome man, standing at a little less than six feet and retaining a physique where the muscle had yet to turn to fatty tissue. He maintained a clean-shaven image never taking to the idea of growing facial whiskers. His dark hair was cut short and receded slightly at the temples.

Jake had been a very close friend of Tommy's and was now intent on being a close friend to Mary. He had known Mary for as long as Tommy had, with both men at one time vying for her hand in marriage. It had been a mark of how close a friendship the two men had had that they never fell out over the fact they both loved the same woman.

It still remained the only time in Jake's life where he had even come close to thinking about marriage but he had been willing to commit himself to Mary had Tommy not won the day with his wit, charm and greater self-confidence. In the ten years they had had together they had been nothing short of the perfect couple and Jake held few regrets that his friend got the girl in the end.

Across from Jake stood Chief Constable William Anderson. Three years in the job, Anderson had already brought a lot of change to how the Aberdeen City Police functioned and he took a personal interest in everything and everyone covered by the remit of his post. Beyond the normal day to day issues that a Chief Constable would be expected to involve himself in, Anderson now had to plan for the royal visit. Yet, even in the midst of all this work, the Chief Constable had made the time to not only attend the funeral of a fallen officer but to also say a few words at the main service.

The only other person at the graveside was Roland Thomson, Tommy's brother. Roland and Tommy had never been close, mainly due to the fact there was a seven year age difference between them. After Tommy's birth his mother had miscarried twice before Roland was eventually born. Perhaps out of a sense of relief that a child had finally been born safely, Tommy's parents rather coddled Roland and that did little for how Tommy viewed his younger brother in later life.

Roland's childhood had never wandered far from his mother's arms and he grew up as a very immature, totally dependent on others, kind of human being. He had little idea how to look after himself and after his mother died he had felt like a sailor cast adrift on the ocean with no sense of direction whatsoever. He had never married and though he had remained in employment all his current working life, the jobs he had filled had been menial and boring.

Mary felt sure that Roland had only turned up at the funeral in the hope that he might hear of a small inheritance coming his way. Mary already knew that Roland was in for a disappointment if he imagined, for one moment, that his brother would think any more of him in death as he had done in life.

Jake's mind was in a million places as he stood listening to the final words from the minister. He had not been back to Nellfield Cemetery since the investigation of 1899 that had, effectively, led to his promotion to Inspector.

That had been another occasion when a sense of horror had permeated through the city as the details of the case became clearer. Starting as a civil case against the owners of the cemetery it had eventually developed in to a police inquiry which had, in turn, led to the Supervisor of the cemetery being charged and appearing in court to answer for the crimes of both himself and his staff.

As with so many crimes the main driving force for their actions was the need for financial gain. Bodies were being dug up and removed from their coffins so they could then be reburied in communal graves. These communal graves were unmarked so family members were never to know where their loved ones were actually lying. Plots were then re-used thus making more money for the cemetery and presumably, along the way, for the Supervisor as well.

Families and the good citizens of Aberdeen were appalled that anyone would treat the dead with such disrespect and it took some time before they once more had faith in the system for burials across the city.

However, the investigation had provided the then Sergeant Fraser with the opportunity to prove to his superiors that he had what it took to be an Inspector. The case had outraged him and he had thrown himself in to compiling the evidence that would eventually see the Supervisor have his day in court in the September of that year. By the time the Supervisor began his six month sentence Jake Fraser had been promoted.

The service eventually concluded and as the mourners stepped away from the graveside, four rather scruffy looking individuals appeared, as if from nowhere, to commence shovelling the soil back in to the hole. Although the men had waited until the party of mourners had turned to leave the grave, before moving in with their spades, Jake still had the feeling of being rushed at a time when speed ought never to have been a factor.

The mourners made their way to the exit on Great Western Road where Roland, sensing there would be no talk of wills today, bade Mary a fond farewell, though as he gave one last, rather unwelcome, embrace he did find the time to satisfy himself that Mary did know how to contact him.

He had couched it in terms of offering help but Mary knew full well that he was simply angling for an invitation to the reading of the will. Mary, of course, saw little need for Roland to be there as he did not appear in the will. She watched Roland head off along Great Western Road and a piece of her knew that she was unlikely to ever see him again.

Chief Constable Anderson once more offered his condolences and the help and support of Aberdeen City Police. He then provided Jake with the necessary permission to take some more time from his official duties so as to accompany Mary back to her home and to partake of some lunch with her and Mavis, as had been previously arranged. William Anderson then climbed in to the carriage that stood waiting for him and headed back to the Police Headquarters at Lodge Walk.

Mary, Mavis and Jake then climbed in to the other carriage that had been waiting by the gate. Pulled by two, large horses, each bedecked in black, the carriage now set off along Great Western Road before turning left on to Holburn Street and then onwards along Union Street and Rose Street to Esslemont Avenue, where Mary lived.

Esslemont Avenue was a relatively new street lined, in the main, with tenement blocks that now provided comfortable accommodation to a large number of people. However, these were not properties that were being made available to simply anyone. No, these were properties designed for someone of means and no one outside of the ever growing middle class would have had the money with which to afford such a property. Many of the properties were rented and the weekly expenditure required was well outside the means of the poorer classes.

The carriage pulled up outside the block in which Mary lived. Jake climbed down first and then helped the ladies alight, which was made all the more difficult due to the amount of material in their dresses. Everything had already been paid so the carriage set off again and Jake, Mavis and Mary went in to the building. Mary lived on the ground floor and she already had the key in her hand as they approached the door. Moments later they were all inside and Mary was showing her guests in to the large, rather disorganised front room.

It seemed to be a room where far more furniture than was necessary had been almost shoe-horned in, leaving little space in which to actually move around.

Mary asked her guests to sit down and then left them while she went through to the back room to finish off the work she had started earlier. Jake sat in one of the easy chairs situated by the fireside and Mavis, having now removed her hat, sat on the settee. A silence hung over them both for what seemed like an eternity.

Jake had always thought Mavis to be a very attractive woman and he always felt rather embarrassed to be alone in the company of a woman to whom he was attracted. She was thirty-three, the same age as Mary and was still unmarried.

Just for a second Jake wondered what Mavis's family thought of her still being single at such an advanced age. To not have found a husband by the age of twenty-three was worthy of scorn in some quarters so to still be single at the age of thirty-three would most certainly have raised eyebrows. It was certainly a mystery to Jake especially with Mavis being so attractive.

However, it was but a passing thought for Jake did not judge anyone on the way they chose to live their lives and if Mavis had not seen fit to get married then that was her business and nothing to do with him or anyone else.

Jake glanced across at Mavis and they nervously smiled at each other. With her hat removed and her hair hanging more freely Mavis looked even more attractive in Jake's eyes and with that growing sense of attraction came an even greater difficulty in finding the right thing to say. Eventually it was Mavis who finally broke the uncomfortable silence.

"It was a lovely service."

"Yes it was," agreed Jake. "It was very considerate of the Chief Constable to find the time to attend when everyone is so busy at the present moment."

"I can imagine, especially with the King and Queen coming in just over two weeks' time."

Silence descended again for a little while and Jake looked around the room whilst thinking of something else that might be discussed. It was all very cluttered with a dark and sombre three-piece suite filling much of the space. Against one wall was a large sideboard on which sat a clock and a variety of photographs, most of which, Jake already knew, were of Tommy.

Above the fire was a shelf on which sat more photographs, only this time they were mainly of Mary. There was also a small table, which sat in such a position as to allow the occupants of the three-piece-suite to lay down cups and saucers that may have been offered to them during their time in Mary's company. The sight of the photographs brought to mind something he had heard regarding the royal visit.

"Apparently there will be a company committing our King's visit to the new format of film," he said.

"Really?" said Mavis.

"Yes, there will be shows in some of the halls around Aberdeen and I'm led to believe they will also be going to Peterhead and Fraserburgh."

Mavis looked a little surprised. "It's hard to imagine being able to see the visit on film just a couple of days after the actual event. I'm just coming to terms with photographs and now they can already make those pictures move."

Jake smiled. "I think the idea of filming major occasions is a good one. Apparently the company covering the King and Queen will be able to have shows over a period of time at which the general public will be able to see the day unfold. I imagine it will be of special interest to those who will not be able to be in Aberdeen for the actual event. It all sounds very exciting."

Mavis almost shivered. "People moving on a screen doesn't seem right to me. It's not natural."

"Perhaps," added Jake, finding Mavis's reaction amusing but not daring to show her that.

Mary came back in to the room and noted that the only sound she could hear was the ticking of the clock. She crossed the room and placed the cake stand, she had been carrying, on the small table by the fireside. Jake noted with some pleasure the number of different home-baked delicacies there were on the three-tier stand.

Mary stood up and looked down at her guests. "You are allowed to talk you know," she then said with a smile. "I'm sure Tommy won't mind you having a conversation on the day of his funeral."

Mavis and Jake smiled. "I'm sure you're right, Mary," added Mavis.

"We had been talking," Jake then said, probably quicker than was necessary.

Mary almost laughed. "You don't have to defend yourself, Jake, I didn't mean to accuse you of anything."

Mary made two more visits to the kitchen area at the back before they could all be seated with cup of tea in hand and sandwiches and home-baked cakes on offer. Mary invited her guests to help themselves to the food, which they started to do with some relish. Jake had always known that Mary's talents in the kitchen were legendary and Tommy had often waxed lyrical about some of the food he had gone home to, particularly on a Sunday.

"My but you have been busy," Mavis commented.

"It kept me busy and stopped me thinking about the obvious," explained Mary who had, by now, removed her veil and combed her hair in to a more casual style. Like Mavis she now looked prettier than ever with her hair slightly loose although the redness around her eyes was still very evident. Once they were all seated and eating another silence descended upon the room and once again it was Mavis who spoke first.

"I was just saying to Jake that it was a lovely service, especially at the church."

"Yes, it was lovely," agreed Mary. "I think Tommy would have been pleased with the turn out."

"He was a very popular man," added Jake. "Had we not been required to keep some officers on duty I feel sure that everyone would have been at the church to formally pay their respects."

Mary seemed to ponder on that comment for a few seconds before she spoke again.

"I always thought him to be popular with his colleagues and yet, in the last few weeks of his life, he more than once said something along the lines of wanting to distance himself from some of the lads at work."

"Really?" said Jake in a tone that was heavy with disbelief.

"I thought it was a rather strange thing for him to say but I never asked for an explanation. I didn't see that it was my place to pry."

"Did he ever speak of any particular lads at work?" Jake then asked.

"No, he just made the odd general statement about things at work not being quite as they were. Tommy seemed under pressure these last few weeks and was definitely prone to outbursts of anger that were not usually in his nature."

"He shouldn't have been under any more pressure at work; certainly no more than usual at any rate. I can always ask around the muster room in case there were issues that we weren't aware of because anything that we can uncover will be of help to Sandy Wilson's investigation."

"I shouldn't do that," Mary said quickly. "I wouldn't want to have Tommy's colleagues think ill of him now. It was clear, from the turnout today, that his colleagues did not appear to have any issues with Tommy, so please don't give them reason to believe that he may have had issues with them."

Jake thought for a second. "I'll let Sandy know about this anyway and leave it up to him as to what, if anything, he does with it."

Jake had another cake and as he ate his mind turned over a few issues as if, perhaps, trying to make some sense of what had happened.

Although not directly involved in the investigation in to Tommy's death, which had been allocated to Sandy Wilson, Jake was still interested in how the case was going. After all, there had been no closer friend to Tommy than Jake himself. Even the Chief Constable had recognised the fact that Jake would find it next to impossible to stay outside of the case altogether and had asked that, should Jake think of anything relevant or uncover anything further from Mary, then he was to inform Inspector Wilson at once.

The problem with this case, however, was that it seemed no matter which direction the information took them it met with nothing but brick walls and ever increasing mystery. There seemed to be no answer to the one burning question that lay at the very core of the investigation:

Why had Tommy been singled out for what seemed more like an execution than a murder?

On the night in question Jake had met Tommy at the corner of Union Terrace around the time they were both due to complete their shift. They had met, quite by chance, beside the statue of William Wallace, which had stood over them, arm outstretched in the direction of the new theatre that was due to open later in the year. As they chatted they suddenly heard screams coming from Rosemount Viaduct and both men had hurried to see what the problem might be.

They had found a young woman standing outside one of the tenement blocks, her clothing in a dishevelled state and weeping into a handkerchief. The handkerchief had covered most of her face, which would make identification almost impossible were anyone to link her to the murderer.

The woman had made a point of standing in the way of Jake's progress and had started to tell him of her ordeal. She had explained that a strange man had grabbed her and that when she had screamed he had run in to the tenement block outside of which she now stood. Jake had remained to take note of the woman's story and Tommy and gone in to the building in search of the assailant.

Tommy had not reappeared and after assuring himself that the young lady would be okay in his absence, Jake then entered the building only to find Tommy lying on the first floor landing with a fatal knife wound to the heart.

When Jake had come back out of the building he found that the young woman had now disappeared and was never to be seen again. Enquiries then made within the building came to nothing with all the occupants satisfying the police that they had nothing to do with the crime. The working theory, at least for the moment, was that the assailant committed the crime then made good his (or her) escape out of the back door and over the wall on to Jack's Brae. From there the murderer would have had a choice of escape routes.

Which basically left the investigation team with nothing. There was no evidence, no eye-witnesses and no obvious reason as to why anyone would want to kill Tommy. The manner in which the young woman had prevented Jake from following Tommy in to the building clearly indicated the desire, on someone's part, to ensure the intended victim entered that building alone.

When speaking to a variety of people later, Jake had made the point that no one could have known that he would be there as it had been quite by chance that he had bumped in to Tommy that evening. Wilson had offered the opinion that it hadn't mattered to the killer whether Jake had been there or not; it simply meant that the young woman had to do a little bit more than simply direct Tommy in to the building.

It certainly made sense that the woman would have had to have been there anyway so as to ensure that Tommy went in to the right building. Seeing two men running in her direction simply meant that she had to ensure that only one of them went in to the building immediately. Thinking back, Jake had to admire the young lady's acting skills for she had, most certainly, managed to detain him in a manner than in no way raised his suspicions. Such was Jake's high opinion of the lady's acting ability that Wilson had even checked out touring companies and local drama clubs in the hope that she might have been identified there. Again there was nothing.

Jake was still thinking to himself if they would ever get to the bottom of this crime when it struck him that he had been quiet for a very long time and that his actions may well be construed as being impolite in the extreme. However, when he re-focused on the two ladies in the room, he found them to be lost in their own conversation and were showing no sign of missing his input.

Jake checked his watch and decided that this might be a good time for him to leave. He stood up, making his apologies as he did so. He said goodbye to Mavis and thanked Mary, once more, for the home-baked cakes.

Mary walked him to the door and they made arrangements for Jake to call on her on Sunday for some lunch. Jake had only recently been given time off on most Sundays and was still coming to terms with having time to call his own. To be offered the opportunity of eating a good meal in the company of an attractive woman was too good to refuse. They arranged for Jake to call around midday and after giving Mary one last, comforting embrace, he set off back to his work.

TWO

Wednesday 12 September - mid afternoon

Jake did not go directly back to the office. He was still dressed in his best suit and did not want to risk damaging it, in any way, by wearing it for the remainder of his shift.

Instead he took a slight detour from the Upperkirkgate, through the Guestrow until he reached the property block in which he owned a couple of rooms. The Guestrow had, at one time in the history of Aberdeen, been a well-established street occupied by people of means. It had once been a well sought after thoroughfare that offered good accommodation in a location situated so close to Union Street.

However, the passage of time had not been kind to the Guestrow. Those people of means moved to newer, more upmarket locations as they were built around the city and the Guestrow became a place where those much further down the social ladder now took up residence.

Many of Jake's immediate neighbours had crossed paths with him in the course of his daily duties. It was a street now better known for its criminals and prostitutes than anything else. Even in the block in which Jake lived there were rooms above him that were occupied by a young prostitute by the name of Alice. Jake had pretty much taken her under his wing and kept an eye out for her, particularly when it came to the way she was treated by her pimp, an obnoxious, weasel faced little man by the name of Scroggins.

Scroggins had taken the view that Alice was his property and that he could do with her as he pleased. Jake had shown her compassion and understanding and in return she had confided in him that Scroggins beat her and generally mistreated her, especially if she was perceived as not earning enough money from her trade.

A friendship had arisen with Alice, even though there was a twenty-five year age difference between them. Jake provided Alice with the father figure she had never known before and in return for him simply being there when she needed him, she had taken to sharing his bed. However, with Jake it was never business it was only about two people sharing a true affection for each other.

For Jake, Alice provided the only physical contact he had with women. It had been many years since he had had a relationship with a woman as his job had always managed to get in the way. When the vast majority of Jake's waking time was taken up with work that included dead bodies and violent crime it made it next to impossible for him to switch in to wooing mode when, on those rare occasions when it might occur, he was to find himself in the company of a woman. As a consequence of this lack of regular contact with the female of the species Jake had developed a crashing lack of confidence in their presence, as had been so clearly illustrated when left alone with Mavis earlier in the day.

It was different with Alice. He didn't feel he needed to impress her in any way and he now felt that, over the months they had been fostering their friendship, he had come to think a lot of Alice and his desire to protect her had strengthened as well. He might even have admitted, though only to himself, that there might just be an inkling of love developing between them even though that would have been perceived, by many, as being wholly unacceptable given that he was a senior police officer and she was a lady of the night.

Jake would not have chosen to live in the Guestrow. He knew it for what it was and had it not been for how circumstances had unfolded he would never have considered having a property of his own anywhere, let alone in a street occupied by a growing number of low-life characters.

It was also highly uncommon for police officers to be granted permission to live in accommodation that was not approved by the Chief Constable. Anderson had certainly not approved of Jake living in the Guestrow but given that the property was bequeathed to him by a close friend, who had died in a shipwreck at sea, the Chief Constable had, rather grudgingly, agreed to Jake living in the property rather than letting it out to someone else. The idea of a police officer making money from anything other than police work was even more abhorrent to the Chief than having an officer occupy a property in an undesirable area of the city.

Jake's friend had used much of his money made at sea to purchase the two rooms with the intent of living there himself when his days at sea were over. He had also, rather surprisingly, taken time to have a will lodged with one of the local solicitors in which he left everything he had to Jake, seeing as Jake was the only living person he knew and trusted to look after the property.

There had been no one more surprised when a representative of the solicitor's had arrived at Lodge Walk one day with news of both his friend's death and his inheritance. He had then discussed the situation at some length with the Chief Constable and they agreed that it was best that Jake lived in the property himself but that he look for an opportunity, in the not too distant future, to find a new owner.

Jake opened the door and entered the building. He was immediately hit by the strong smell of stale urine in the hallway and when he reached the first landing he found a prostitute and her client in the middle of completing a bit of business that had obviously been agreed and paid for prior to Jake's arrival.

Neither party paid much attention to the fact that someone was passing them as the man, trousers down around his ankles and little buttocks wobbling, continued to pump himself into a frenzy between the thighs of the not so young woman whom he had pinned to the wall with her legs wrapped around him. There was much grunting, groaning and other noises to accompany the physical action but Jake did not hang around to witness any conclusion as he opened the door to his property and went in.

He went through to the back room, which served him as both bedroom and kitchen. The front room was essentially for Sunday best and was used on very rare occasions. The two rooms were sparsely furnished as Jake's friend had never found the time, nor the money, to put much in the way of furniture in to his home.

In the corner of the back room was a wardrobe in which Jake kept what little clothing he had. The only change he had made to the place after moving in was to remove his friend's clothes from the wardrobe and replace them with his own.

He now hung up his good suit in that wardrobe and then put on his working suit. He checked his appearance in the mirror and then made his way back out of the property. The coupling on the stairs had been completed and both parties had now moved on. Jake slowly made his way down to street level and back out in to the sunshine. He had little desire to return to work.

As he passed another street sign of Guestrow he pondered, as he had often down, on the name and why any street in any town should be called Guestrow. Who had been the guests? It was a question he would never know the answer to as he cut through on to Broad Street. He paused to look across at the Marischal College. This would be the centre of attention on the twenty-seventh when the King would visit to complete the inauguration of the building. For just a second he marvelled at the fact the King and Queen would be along this very street in just two weeks' time.

A great day for everyone but the police who were going to be very busy indeed.

Jake crossed Broad Street and continued along Queen Street, A little way along there was a break in the buildings, which was the opening to Lodge Walk. The police building was along this road on the right hand side.

Lodge Walk had been a purpose built police office, opened in 1895, which now stood on the site of what had been a prison. It was a two-storey building with a parade ground area at the back and beyond that a separate building that housed the mortuary.

Jake walked in through the front doors. To his left was a set of stairs, which led up to the Court rooms on the second floor and to his right was the public counter. Jake paused at the counter, which was today, like so many other days, manned by

Sergeant Bill Turnbull, a big, bull of a man with face whiskers and a stern expression.

He looked a very imposing character but, in truth, Bill was a police officer whose bark was considerably worse than his bite. He had been a police officer for twenty years and in that time had seen just about everything there was to see by way of police work. He was now the occupant of the front desk due to his natural ability to bring calm to any situation. It could get quite heated at that front door and it was essential that the Desk Sergeant was not as volatile as some of his customers could be.

Bill looked up as Jake walked in. "Ah, Jake, best not take your jacket off, there's work to be done at the Palace Hotel."

"Somebody run off without paying the bill again?" suggested Jake for it would not be the first time were that to be the case.

"A young woman has been found dead in one of the rooms. We were notified about two hours ago and Sergeant Mathieson is already there. He said he'd wait there until you arrived as he expected you'd like an update."

"Very good," Jake concluded and he turned and went back out of the building. He now turned right and walked to the Union Street end of Lodge Walk where he passed under an archway and on to the pavement of Union Street. He turned right again and walked up Union Street, once again enjoying the warm sunshine. He passed over the Union Bridge and immediately came upon the hotel which was on the left side of the street.

He walked in through the front doors and paused, almost immediately, as his friend, Eddie, who was one of the main doormen, was standing there. Eddie Ralston looked resplendent in his uniform and his face lit up at the sight of his friend.

"You'll be here about the dead woman," Eddie said, more by announcement than asking a question. "Nasty business from what I'm hearing."

"And what are you hearing, Eddie?" Jake then enquired.

"Just that a lovely, young woman in room twenty-one appears to have been murdered by some maniac."

"Strong words indeed, Eddie. Have you been anywhere near the crime scene?"

Eddie scoffed. "Of course not, Jake, they wouldn't let the likes of me anywhere near a young lady's room unless, like yesterday, it was to help manhandle her luggage up to the room for her."

"Did she have a lot of luggage?"

"Just one big bugger that took four of us to shift. I heard she was here to dance at Her Majesty's and by the size of that chest she must have taken enough costumes for the entire cast."

"Have you heard anything else?" Jake then added.

"Nothing beyond Mr Hardy being well shaken up seeing as he was the gentleman who found the body."

"Okay, Eddie, thanks for that. I'll maybe see you later," and with that Jake pushed open the inner door and made his way in to the reception area of the hotel.

"Good afternoon, Inspector," a voice announced just inside the door to Jake's left.

Jake turned to face the man who had spoken. "Well, well, what are you doing here?"

The man stood up. "I'd heard there had been an incident."

"Whoever told you that?" asked Jake.

"Now, now, Inspector, you know that a good journalist never discloses his sources."

"Goodness me, Alan, whoever told you that you were a good journalist?"

And without waiting for a reaction Jake continued on his way. Although they occasionally exchanged some healthy banter, Alan MacBride was a man whom Jake would never fully trust. MacBride was always on the hunt for a story and cared little for the whole truth at the end of the day.

As with so many journalists it was all about getting the story printed and it mattered little if the facts became a little blurred along the way. Misquoting was another habit of MacBride's which irritated Jake and had led to him ensuring he gave the young journalist no opportunity to quote him.

In fairness to MacBride, however, there had been times when he had been able to help the police with their enquiries. It was often the case that people were happier to talk to the Press than they ever would be with the police.

Jake made his way over to the reception desk where he was greeted by a tall, young man with a spotty chin and wearing spectacles that betrayed exceedingly poor eyesight. Jake had hardly had time to introduce himself before the young man was hurrying around the counter and heading for the lift, which was situated to the left of the main staircase.

"Come with me, Inspector," he was saying in his wake and Jake hurried to catch up.

A young boy was operating the lift. As the doors closed he did not wait to be told the floor as there could only be one destination for anyone on a day such as this. When they reached the first floor the boy opened the doors and Jake departed. The other two returned to the ground floor. Jake walked along the corridor to a door, outside of which stood a stern looking police constable. The constable stood to attention as he noticed Jake approaching.

"Sir," he said.

Jake hated being called 'sir.' As far as he was concerned he was Jake to everyone, however the general protocol did not allow for junior members of the Force to refer to senior members by their Christian names.

"McGill," Jake replied. The constable seemed pleased that he had been recognised. "Is Sergeant Mathieson still in the room?"

"Yes, sir and I'm told it's not a pretty sight in there."

"I'm sure it isn't," added Jake and opened the door to enter the room.

Inside was a scene of general tidiness. In seventy per cent of the space it was as if the cleaner had just left. Everything in its place; neat and tidy. However, the remaining thirty per cent was a scene of pure carnage. The area around the bed looked like a bomb had gone off. The bedclothes were thrown everywhere and the bedside table had been knocked over. What had once been covering the woman's body was now ripped and lying around the floor.

The woman herself lay diagonally across the bed her open eyes staring in the direction of the door. She was on her back with her legs spread at an angle that did not look possible. There was a hint of blood visible just below her pubic area and also what looked like a large patch of semen was visible in the same area. She was bruised all over and scratched on the inside of her thighs and across both breasts.

Jake looked a little closer and felt sure that there were bite marks around her left nipple. Whoever her attacker had been he had been in a mighty frenzy when he launched himself at her. This attack was borne out of pure hatred, either for the individual or for women in general.

Jake looked around the rest of the room and found it hard to believe that everything else looked so normal. "Do we have a name for her?" he then asked.

By the time Jake asked the question Mathieson had moved across the room and was standing beside him. Sergeant Richard Mathieson had been working directly with Jake for the last year and they had forged a successful partnership in that time, putting away more than their fair share of criminals. Mathieson checked his notebook.

"According to the register her name was Mabel Lassiter...."

"And she was here to dance at Her Majesty's," Jake added in a matter-of-fact tone.

Mathieson was briefly taken aback at how his superior could have known that, considering he had only this minute come in to the room and did not even know the woman's name. However, time working with Jake had taught Mathieson one lesson and that was never question how he acquired his information. Jake was a good detective with many contacts to call upon and he had a habit of being one step ahead of his colleagues. Mathieson chose to move on without further comment.

"Miss Lassiter arrived yesterday morning on the train from London. She made a bit of an impression on everyone as she needed to get that chest up to the room. As you can see, sir, it's a hefty bugger."

Jake went over to the chest and inspected it closely. Apart from a few remaining items of clothing within it was nothing more than an empty chest. At least it would have been nothing more than an empty chest had it not been for the seat that had been so carefully placed within. "What do you make of this?" Jake then said.

Mathieson moved a little closer. "It looks like this chest was designed for someone to sit in it, sir," he then replied. "I noted some air holes as well."

Jake looked closer and he too noted the holes in the chest. He looked again at the seat and then he looked around the room.

"Any sign of this woman having any other clothes than the few still in the chest?"

"Yes, there's a travel bag over here," Mathieson said producing a bag from the other side of the bed.

"Would it really be possible for someone to travel any distance in that?" Jake then said, though it was more by way of thinking aloud.

Mathieson moved over to the chest and sat on the seat. He could only just get his whole body inside and it would have been grossly uncomfortable had he been there any longer than the few moments it took to test it. Mathieson unfolded himself from the chest and stood up to his full height once more.

"So, if someone did travel to Aberdeen in there," Jake observed, "then they would have needed to have been smaller than you."

Mathieson was relieved to be able to stand up properly again. "But why would someone feel the need to come to Aberdeen squashed in to a chest rather than sitting on a seat on the train like everyone else?"

"Only if you were someone who did not want to be seen," added Jake, "though who that someone might be is beyond me just for the moment."

"And was it that someone who attacked this poor woman?" asked Mathieson.

"That also remains to be seen," Jake replied. "Whether he was in the chest or whether he came to her room later, it would appear that this woman knew her killer as there is no sign of forced entry to the room. However, if she knew her killer then why would he have attacked her with such ferocity? I mean this looks like the work of a madman and it seems beyond comprehension that she would have transported a man in to her room knowing that he was likely to attack her."

"It does seem highly unlikely," agreed Mathieson.

Jake made his way back to the bed. "I'm told Mr Hardy discovered the body; would that be correct?"

Again Mathieson was momentarily struck dumb by the ability of his boss to uncover information before anyone else.

"He did indeed," Mathieson eventually said. "Apparently Miss Lassiter was expected at Her Majesty's Theatre this morning for a rehearsal and when she hadn't turned up by mid-morning they sent someone here to find out what might have happened to her. Mr Hardy is one of the assistant managers and he came up to check that everything was in order with Miss Lassiter. When she did not reply to his knocking he thought that she might have made off without paying for her night of comfort so he let himself in to the room only to find this horrifying scene laid out before him."

"Has the Police Doctor seen the body yet?" Jake then asked.

"Not yet, sir," replied Mathieson. "The Doctor was informed but returned a message that he did not have time to attend the scene and asked that the body be removed to the mortuary as soon as possible so he can carry out an examination there."

Jake thought for a moment. "Very good, arrange for the body to be removed immediately and I want you and Constable McGill to take some time over this room once the body has been removed. I want you to look for any useful evidence concerning the man who was in here with Miss Lassiter. Every indication from this room is that this poor woman's attacker was allowed in, either in that chest or by the friendly gesture of her opening the door. Had she thought for one moment that this man was likely to bring violence upon her then surely she would never have allowed him to enter her room. It also raises the question that if she did know this man and the reason for him being here had been something quite inconsequential then why would he suddenly turn on her with such savagery?"

"Perhaps the murderer was overcome by pure lust, sir? She was a very attractive woman."

"You may well be right, Mathieson, some men have been known to turn to violence if their advances are not met favourably. Was anyone seen in Miss Lassiter's company after she arrived yesterday?"

"The Manager was of the opinion that Miss Lassiter did not leave this room. She certainly did not go down for an evening meal."

"Then perhaps she was dead by then? I'm sure we will make more sense of things after we receive the Doctor's report. Now, where can I find this Mr Hardy?"

"I believe he may have gone home, sir."

"What?" Jake said in sheer disbelief. "He's a material witness so why the hell did you let him go home?"

"I didn't, sir, he was already gone by the time I arrived. The Manager, a Mr Bainbridge, had made the decision as he thought Mr Hardy was in shock."

Jake shook his head. "Very well, where can I find Mr Bainbridge?"

"He has an office to the left of the reception desk."

"Right, well you get the body removed to the mortuary and get started on that check of the room I asked for as well. I'm going to have a word with Mr Bainbridge."

Jake left the room and made his way to the staircase. He took that route to the ground floor in case there were any signs of useful evidence there. There was nothing. As Jake approached the front desk the young, spotty-faced, youth positively jumped to attention.

"Is Mr Bainbridge here?" Jake asked.

"Yes," replied the young man.

A silence hung in the air for a few seconds and Jake realised that the young man had no intention of saying or doing anything further with prompting of some kind. Jake could wait no longer.

"Could I see him then?"

The young man jumped again. "Oh, sorry, of course. Please follow me."

He led Jake to the door, which Mathieson had described and knocked loudly. A very severe sounding gentleman's voice bellowed through the door informing them that he did not want to be disturbed. The young man was about to convey his apologies when he was pushed out of the way and Jake opened the door and walked in.

Bainbridge was seen to be rapidly putting something in to his top drawer. He clearly looked flustered but now his expression was one of anger as he leapt to his feet and started to walk round his desk.

"I said I did not want to be disturbed," he snapped at the young man," and yet you deliberately disobey me and enter anyway."

"I was the one who chose to disturb you, Mr Bainbridge," Jake interrupted, showing his warrant card as he did so.

Bainbridge's expression changed immediately and the slight bend he seemed to permanently have to his tall frame seemed to get even more pronounced as he almost bowed in Jake's direction.

"Oh, I do apologise, Inspector," Bainbridge said in a tone of reverence and a slight wringing of the hands. "My name is Cecil Bainbridge and I am the General Manager." He then swept his arm in a dramatic gesture towards a chair that sat on the opposite side of the desk from his own. "Please have a seat."

As Jake sat down Bainbridge ushered the young man from the room and closed the door. He then returned to his own seat and leaned forward. "Now how can I help?"

"Why did you let Mr Hardy go home?"

Jake's opening question had probably not been what Bainbridge had been expecting. He saw himself as being a major player in this enquiry and would have expected to be asked something more pertinent to the victim. As it was, the question had caused another momentary flap from Bainbridge until he had composed an answer in his mind before speaking.

"He was in a severe state of shock so I told him to go home and to arrange to see a doctor."

"But he found the body, Mr Bainbridge, so would it not have seemed perfectly obvious to you that we, the police, would wish to speak to him as soon as we got here?"

Bainbridge did not react like a man accepting he had done anything wrong. "But you can speak to him anytime, Inspector, I'll give you a note of his address."

"And if Mr Hardy had been the one to commit the crime then there would seem little chance of us, or anyone else for that matter, finding him at his home address, would there?"

Bainbridge looked shocked and not a little outraged at such a suggestion. "Inspector, my staff are not murderers, especially Mr Hardy. I will have you know that Alf Hardy fought for Queen and country against the Boers. As a result of his injuries received in that conflict he now walks with a limp and carries a useless left arm. However, he has never allowed those injuries to prevent him from creating a normal, hard-working life for himself. I can assure you that Mr Hardy is a fine, upstanding gentleman and I, on his behalf, take great offence at your comments."

"Perhaps," added Jake, caring little for Bainbridge's feelings. "Anyway, did you know anything more about Mabel Lassiter other than she had travelled from London and was to be dancing at Her Majesty's?"

"Nothing. No one in the hotel had any need to speak to her for I feel sure she never left that room after her arrival yesterday morning."

"I believe her luggage caused a few problems?

"Indeed it did, I must admit we were all very suspicious of that chest when she arrived."

"Suspicious?" prompted Jake.

"Well you know, Inspector, it would not have been the first time that a young lady had attempted to smuggle a young gentleman in to her room."

"Is that what you thought she was doing?"

Bainbridge shifted in his chair; he was finding this very uncomfortable.

"She was young and attractive and being a dancer it was always possible that she might have tried to get around the hotel policy of no men in unmarried women's rooms."

"You use the word dancer, Mr Bainbridge, but the tone of your voice reads prostitute. Is that what you think of these young women?" Jake asked and Bainbridge squirmed even more in his chair. His feathers ruffled again and that look of indignation returned to his face.

"I can assure you, Inspector, that that was not my intention but even you must admit that women who work in the theatre are often of lower morals than, shall we say, better bred young ladies."

Jake could hardly believe what he was hearing. This pompous man actually seemed to believe that he belonged to a better class of person than many others and it took Jake a few seconds to calm down inside before he could speak again. He wanted to tell Bainbridge what he really thought of him but knew that that would not be acceptable behaviour for a senior police officer.

Having settled himself he then continued.

"Was it normal practice for dancers from Her Majesty's to stay at this hotel?"

"Certainly not," came the almost instant reply. "I have to admit that Miss Lassiter probably would not have been staying at this hotel had the period she was due to be in Aberdeen not already been paid by her booking agent."

"Paid for in advance?" Jake asked, finding that a bit strange.

"Yes."

"How?"

"By cash. A man came from Her Majesty's last week and made all the arrangements."

Jake sat forward, finding this all very interesting. "Did you see this man?"

"I didn't. I think it would probably have been Mr Scott who would have dealt with the transaction as I believe it took place around midnight and he would have been on the front desk at the time. The man said he'd been involved with the show that night and apologised for arriving so late."

"Did this man have a name?"

"I'm sure Mr Scott will have noted all the details when he took the booking. If you would just give me a moment I'll see what I can find out for you."

Bainbridge stood up and left the room. Jake sat for a moment and then a thought struck him. He felt sure that Bainbridge was putting something away, when he had abruptly entered the room earlier. He began to wonder what that something might be so he took the opportunity of moving around to the other side of the desk and opening the drawer in question.

Sitting on top of a pile of papers, all with the hotel's name on them, were some photographs. Jake did not need to look beyond the first one or two to quickly realise what Bainbridge had been looking at and why he had reacted with such haste and apparent panic.

The photographs were of young women; more importantly naked, young women. Each photograph had been artfully posed in a studio somewhere but no matter how much anyone tried to defend these pictures as art they were still nothing more than blatant pornography.

Men would always get pleasure from looking at naked women and as long as these men were prepared to pay for photographs of that kind then there would always be someone else happy to produce them. Jake knew that these pornographic images were becoming all the rage, especially amongst gentlemen of means who would keep their collections locked away only to be taken out for their own personal pleasure.

Jake closed the drawer and returned to his seat. Bainbridge may have been a pompous, little man with designs above his station and views about certain women that were questionable at best but beneath the surface he was nothing more than a sad individual who liked looking at pornographic pictures. On the one hand he had the audacity to question Mabel Lassiter's morals when he actually had few of his own.

Bainbridge came back in to the room clutching a piece of paper. He sat down again and began scanning the paper. Jake was tempted to say something about the photographs but, of course, he knew that he could do nothing as he should never have been looking in the drawer in the first place.

Bainbridge eventually started to read from the paper.

"The man gave his name as Martin Bagshaw of the Fritton Booking Agency in London. He paid for the full fortnight that Miss Lassiter was to be here and also warned that she would be arriving with a large chest and that she would appreciate some help in moving that up to her room."

"Someone wanted that chest well looked after," mused Jake as he wrote down the details of Mr Bagshaw. Changing the subject slightly, Jake then said, "I believe it was someone from Her Majesty's who called this morning looking for Miss Lassiter?"

"Yes, a young woman," Bainbridge said, starting to look down his nose again. "I think she may well still be in the Coffee Room."

"I'll speak to her in a moment. In the meantime could you provide me with Mr Hardy's address?"

Bainbridge opened a box on his desk in which he had cards neatly filed. He flicked through them and eventually took one out of the box and placed it on the desk in front of him. He then took a piece of paper from a drawer (Jake noted it was not the one with the pornographic photographs) and wrote some details on to it. The paper was then passed across to Jake.

"My thanks, for just now, Mr Bainbridge," Jake then said, standing up. "I may need to speak to you again."

"You know where to find me, Inspector," concluded Bainbridge and Jake left to try and find the young lady who had called from the theatre.

THREE

Wednesday 12 September – late afternoon

He found her, as Bainbridge had thought, still sitting in the Coffee Room enjoying a large plate of food, the like of which she would have rarely seen any other day. At first she hardly responded to Jake's arrival at the table but she did drop her cutlery when he sat down. Her first thought was that this was hotel management coming to check on why she was still eating, considering it had been some time since she had been asked to wait in the Coffee Room.

"I am Inspector Fraser from Aberdeen City Police and I'd like to ask you a few questions about Mabel Lassiter."

Now safe in the knowledge that this was not hotel management, the young woman resumed her attack on the food lying before her. She stabbed a piece of meat with her fork and pushed it in to her mouth. She was quite a pretty woman with striking eyes and a mane of blonde hair. Eventually those eyes settled on Jake and she swallowed the food.

"Don't know nothing about Mabel Lassiter," she then said and stabbed at some more meat.

"You came here looking for her?" prompted Jake.

"I was sent to make sure that she had arrived, that was all."

"Are you another of the dancers?"

"If you'd seen me legs you'd know I wasn't one of them dancers. I'm also blessed with two left feet so dancing is most definitely not for me."

"Then in what capacity were you asked to come here and check on Miss Lassiter?" Jake enquired.

The woman looked at Jake for a few seconds of silence and then eventually said that she hadn't understood his question.

"What do you do at Her Majesty's?" Jake repeated in simpler terms.

"Make the tea mostly, though I sometimes get important jobs like sweeping the floor backstage."

"Maybe we could get some of the formalities out of the way," Jake then said, "starting with your name?"

The woman looked at Jake as if he had just insulted her. She had a look of complete surprise on her face.

"What the hell has my name got to do with anything?" she then said, forgetting the food for a moment.

"This is a police enquiry," Jake said softly, "I need to have a record of everyone who has been interviewed."

The woman gave what Jake had just said some thought but still seemed unsure about whether, or not, to give this man her name. Eventually she seemed to come to a conclusion but took another mouthful of food before saying anything.

"Stella Grainger."

"Thank you, Miss Grainger," Jake added and wrote her name in his notebook. "Do you have an address in Aberdeen?"

"Yes."

Jake soon realised that, without further prompting, it seemed unlikely that Miss Grainger would tell him anything more.

"Would you mind telling me what that address might be?"

The last of the food disappeared from the plate and Jake had to sit a little longer and watch while the last mouthful was chewed and swallowed. Only then did the young woman say anything further.

"Nelson Street; number fifteen."

Jake thanked her and wrote the address in his notebook before continuing.

"Was Miss Lassiter due at the theatre this morning?"

"She was supposed to be there for rehearsals but when she didn't turn up Mr Shearer sent me to find out what had happened to her."

"Who's Mr Shearer?"

"Jasper Shearer, he's the show's Director."

The rest of the interview did not last very long as it seemed perfectly clear to Jake that Stella Grainger knew absolutely nothing about Mabel Lassiter. Had it not been for her capacity to eat an endless supply of food it seemed highly likely that she would have gone back to the theatre hours ago. She also seemed the type who would not have taken kindly to answering any stupid questions that some copper might have to ask her.

Just before Jake left Stella to make her way back to the theatre he asked her one last question. "Have you ever heard of a man called Martin Bagshaw?

"Can't say I have," Stella replied.

Jake took that as his cue to leave. On his way out of the main door he stopped for a final word with Eddie. Jake was interested in having someone other than the management having a quick word with Mr Scott about the night Martin Bagshaw had called to book Mabel Lassiter's room.

"Who might Mr Scott be? Jake had asked.

"Paddy Scott is one of the staff on the reception desk, "Eddie had said." He does the night shift so he won't be on duty until around seven this evening. Do you want to have a word with him about something?"

"I would appreciate it if you did that, Eddie. There seems no point in me speaking to Mr Scott if he doesn't actually know anything that helps in anyway. Just ask if he remembers anything about the night Martin Bagshaw paid for Mabel Lassiter's room. A description of the man would help"

"I'll speak to him when he comes on duty."

"Excellent. Would you be up for a pint in the Saltoun Arms tomorrow night after work?" Jake then asked.

"Only if you're paying," quipped Eddie.

"See you then," concluded Jake and he left the building and set off up Union Street towards Holburn Junction. Mr Hardy's lodgings were at the Holburn Junction end of Holburn Street so it was no distance to walk. Within a matter of moments Jake was standing at a door, on the second landing, waiting for someone to respond to his rather loud knocking. Eventually the door opened and Jake was met by the sight of a rather dishevelled looking individual, dressed only in dirty underwear and looking as if he would have benefitted from a good wash himself.

"Yes?" the man said in a tone that betrayed the fact he had not been best pleased to be disturbed.

"Mr Alfred Hardy?" Jake said.

"Only my mother calls me Alfred."

"I'm Inspector Fraser from Aberdeen City Police. I'd like to ask you a few questions about the death of Mabel Lassiter."

"You'd better come in then."

Inside the property there were rooms coming off from the entrance hallway. The door to a bedroom lay open and the other two doors were closed. Mr Hardy opened one of them and showed Jake in to a large, public room that overlooked Holburn Street itself. Jake was invited to take a seat, which he did and Hardy went off to put some clothes on. When he returned he sat opposite Jake and awaited the questions to begin.

There was actually very little that Mr Hardy could tell Jake and it was also obvious that with such a useless left arm it would have been impossible for him to have strangled anyone.

Mr Hardy said he had spoken to Stella Grainger when she came asking about Miss Lassiter. They had then gone up to Mabel Lassiter's room to check if she had, perhaps, been taken ill or was in need of assistance for any other reason. He had knocked on the door quite a few times and when she had not responded he had decided to use his management key to open the door.

"Before you continue, Mr Hardy, what was your opinion regarding a dancer staying at the Palace Hotel?"

"It was highly unusual. Dancers don't get paid enough to afford the Palace for two weeks. I had wondered if some rich gent had set her up in the Palace so they could meet in private, if you know what I mean."

"Do you all seriously believe that a dancer is little better than a prostitute?" Jake asked with dismay.

"I didn't mean it that way, it's just that some of these girls do have men friends who like to spend money on them. We often see rich gentlemen booking rooms for themselves and their lady friends and some of those lady friends I know, for a fact, work in the theatre."

"Were you aware of Mabel Lassiter ever being at the Palace Hotel before?"

"I certainly hadn't seen her before."

Mr Hardy then went on to say what happened when he had opened the door. He had immediately seen her dead body lying on the bed and had then turned to stop Stella Grainger from seeing anything. He had locked the door again and hurried down to reception to arrange for the police and Mr Bainbridge to be notified of what had happened.

Mr Hardy could say no more about Mabel Lassiter.

Jake took a note of what little had been said and then suggested that Mr Hardy get some sleep and to try and forget the image of what he had seen in that hotel room. Mr Hardy had thought for a moment before replying to Jake's comments.

"I have fought in battles, Inspector and I have seen some terrible sights as a result of warfare. I have seen blood and I have seen gore but I have never seen anything as horrific as the look on that poor woman's face when I opened that door today. I fear there is no way that I will ever forget that image."

Jake left the building and started to walk back down Union Street. It was nearly six o'clock and Jake pondered on returning to the office. He eventually decided to go down to Her Majesty's Theatre first and check on the possibility that someone there might be able to tell him a little more about Mabel Lassiter.

It was ten minutes past the hour when Jake arrived at the theatre on Guild Street, situated across the road from the main railway station. The theatre had been rebuilt as recently as 1897 and had become popular for variety shows that were performed there. Jake had not been in the theatre for a while and this had been the first time that he had been required to visit on official business.

An unshaven looking gent wearing a flat cap and smoking a Woodbine was standing at the door when Jake arrived. Jake asked to see the manager so the flat-capped gentleman took a final drag on his cigarette and flicked the butt in to the gutter. He showed Jake up a few flights of stairs and along a couple of corridors until they finally arrived at a small room in the very top of the building.

The door to the room was already open and inside Jake found a small, balding man with round spectacles perched on the end of a rather hooked nose. HIs shirt was minus its collar and his trousers were shiny with age.

"Policeman to see you, Mr Young," flat cap announced and then left.

"Inspector Fraser," Jake added.

"And I'm Percy Young. Please take a seat."

There was just enough space in the cramped room to allow for a desk, two chairs and a filing cabinet. The room was lit from the light coming through the small window set in to the roof of the building. Both men sat down and the conversation began.

"Have you heard what has happened to one of your dancers?" Jake began.

"I had heard that one of them failed to turn up this morning, though that in itself is nothing unusual."

"In that case I'm sorry to have to inform you that the young lady in question has been found murdered at the Palace Hotel."

"At the Palace?" Young added with a tone of incredulity in his voice. Jake was of the opinion that Young found it a bigger shock that the woman had been at the Palace Hotel than the fact she had been murdered. "My goodness, our dancers don't usually take rooms at hotels of that quality."

"The booking agency had apparently paid for it," Jake said.

Young looked every bit as surprised at that news as he had been about everything else spoken about so far. "The booking agency doesn't pay for the dancers' accommodation," Young then said. "Part of their wage is to cover that and the girls choose their own accommodation when they are here."

"How are the dancers booked?" Jake then asked.

"The booking agency gets them the work but nothing else. We deal with pretty much the same agencies every time and as a result we get many of the same girls every time as well."

"Which agency was Mabel Lassiter booked through?"

Young got up and made his way over to the filing cabinet. He opened the third drawer down and took out a large folder, which was crammed with papers. He took this back to his desk and opened it. He flicked through some of the pages until he found the one he had wanted. He then ran his finger down a column of names until he stopped.

"Yes, here it is. Mabel Lassiter came to us from the Masterton Agency and they are based in London."

Jake checked his notes.

"Not the Fritton Agency?"

Young looked back at the page in front of him. "No, it's definitely the Masterton Agency. Just a minute," he then added as he started to flick back through previous pages until he stopped again. "Now that I think about it I do actually remember Mabel being here before because she rather made a fool of herself with the leading man at that time. Yes, here we are. No, it's definitely the Masterton Agency."

Jake looked a little surprised. "The hotel were told that it was the Fritton Agency that was paying Miss Lassiter's bill and the man who went there to make the payment was called Martin Bagshaw."

Young thought briefly. "I've never heard of a Martin Bagshaw nor, for that matter, a Fritton Agency."

"You said Mabel had been here before and that she had made a fool of herself with the leading man. What was the story behind that?"

Young sat back in his chair. "She was here about nine months ago performing in a show called *Girls Don't Just Sing*. The show was booked to run for six weeks but we nearly had to stop everything after four because Mabel had started getting too close to the leading man and the leading man's wife was none too pleased. As all three were connected to the show it nearly brought the curtain down permanently."

"Who was the leading man?"

"Sammy Gill."

"Never heard of him," Jake added quickly.

Young smiled. "I'm sure Mr Gill would be disappointed to hear you say that. He is, in fact, one of Scotland's top performers though I would accept he is better known on the west coast."

"And what about Mrs Gill?" Jake prompted.

"Ah the lovely Sadie. She is still at Sammy's side as she really has nowhere else to go. Poor Sadie has the face of an angel, the most shapely body imaginable but, alas, the brain of a gnat. It's not as if she even has much talent in the song and dance department and I'm afraid without the surname of Gill she would not be gaining employment in the world of entertainment."

"Was Sammy Gill prone to being over familiar with the chorus line?"

"The man's a menace. He has a pitch perfect voice, great stage presence and hands that sometimes seem detached from his body. I have seen him touch the bottom of one of the dancers from a distance that would seem impossible. I've no idea how he does it but he certainly does it far more that he should."

"I presume Sammy Gill is not in this show?"

"No, he's performing in Glasgow at the moment. The current show, *Legs Legs Legs* has been booked for two weeks and then, after that, there will only be a couple more shows before the theatre closes for a refurbishment."

Jake was surprised. "But wasn't this theatre refurbished just a few years ago?"

"Indeed it was but with another theatre about to open in Rosemount it was felt this might be a good time to refurbish again."

"What are your thoughts on the opposition?" added Jake, slightly digressing from the need to ask questions about Mabel Lassiter.

"Aberdeen will have a larger and some might say better theatre in which to stage its plays and musicals. We will hopefully continue to cover the variety show when we re-open. There is some talk of us changing the name as well as it might be too confusing for the good people of Aberdeen to have a Her Majesty and a His Majesty's theatre. It would be such a pity if we do have to change the name; after all we were here first. Anyway, I'm sure you didn't come here to hear me moaning about the changing face of Aberdeen."

"Would it be possible for me to speak to the current cast of you show in case any of them knew Mabel Lassiter?"

"That poses no problems if you come back during the day when they are rehearsing rather than try to catch them in the evening when they are getting ready for a performance," replied Young.

"Is there a time, during the day, that might be preferable?"

"Around two o'clock would catch them all at the end of rehearsal, which would not lose them any working time."

"In that case I'll come back at around two o'clock tomorrow." Jake stood up and thanked Percy Young for his time. Young then stood up and said he would show Jake back down to the front door as it was all too easy to get lost in a building that had so many corridors.

As they reached the front door and just before Jake left the building he turned to face Percy Young once more. "You mentioned Mabel Lassiter got too close to Sammy Gill. Were you aware, when she was here the last time, of her having any other admirers?"

Young gave the question some thought. "To be honest, Inspector, the chorus girls always attract a lot of attention wherever they go. By the very nature of their work they tend to show more flesh than most young ladies and this often leads to men getting slightly over-excited, if you get my meaning?"

"But no one, as far as you can remember, was particularly keen to impress himself upon Miss Lassiter?"

"I have no recollection of anyone other than Sammy Gill being in her life at that time."

"Did they all stay at the same hotel?"

"Oh no, Sammy and Sadie were at the Douglas Hotel, which is where they always went when they were in Aberdeen and Mabel would have been with the other dancers in rooms somewhere. It really is most out of the ordinary that she was at the Palace Hotel for this visit. However, if you would like to check on any of the landladies who provide rooms for the girls then I can provide you with a list."

"I'll maybe be back for that, Mr Young," Jake said, "but for the moment it's the fact someone booked her in to the Palace Hotel that I find the most puzzling."

"Perhaps this Martin Bagshaw was paying for her to be at the Palace Hotel in return for particular favours?" suggested Young.

Jake had not considered that possibility. "I was speaking to someone else, earlier today," Jake then continued," who also thought that dancers and prostitutes were one and the same thing."

Young looked outraged. "My apologies, Inspector, I did not mean to infer that all dancers were free with their favours, I was merely trying to find an explanation for someone paying for a young woman to stay in an upmarket hotel."

"And I do understand your thinking, Mr Young. Would you have believed Mabel to be free with her favours?"

"She certainly seemed free with Sammy from all accounts."

"Well, thanks again for your time. I will see you again tomorrow."

Jake left the building and made his way along Guild Street then up Market Street. The harbour area was as busy as ever with a constant coming and going of carts delivering and removing items from the boats tied up at the quayside.

Once back at Lodge Walk Jake actually managed to get to his office, which lay towards the back of the building. Through the wall from his office was situated the cells and occasionally Jake was distracted by someone throwing a fit in their cell. It was incredible how much noise one person could generate when they were annoyed.

Before finishing for the day, Jake went to see Sandy Wilson. Sandy was in the room next door and Jake found him sitting back in his chair reading a rather large report. He seemed genuinely relieved to be able to put the report down and discuss something else.

Sandy was interested to hear that Tommy had suggested to his wife that there may have been issues at work with his work colleagues. Sandy had not been given that impression from anyone that he had spoken to so far on this investigation. No one in the muster room had had anything to say about Tommy other than that he'd been a great friend and ally to them all.

They concluded their discussion and Jake returned to his own office to clear up for the day. Jake couldn't help but feel that he was surrounded by puzzles at the moment and he worried that he may not have the ability to solve them all. It was with a heavy heart that he made his way home that evening.

FOUR

Thursday 13 September - early afternoon

Jake returned to Her Majesty's Theatre at a little after two o'clock. Percy Young was waiting at the door to take him down to the stage and introduce him to the show's director, Jasper Shearer.

When they arrived on stage there was a man flitting about like a butterfly from chorus girl to chorus girl. It was immediately obvious to Jake that this man's interests in the girls would be purely musical. He had seen men like this before and they all had shown little interest in anything that a woman could provide on a sexual level.

"Jasper," Percy Young said and the young man ceased his flitting and spun to face them. "This is Inspector Fraser from Aberdeen City Police. He would like to ask you and the rest of the cast some questions about Mabel Lassiter, the dancer who was so cruelly murdered. Inspector Fraser this is Jasper Shearer who is the writer and choreographer of our show."

"Thank you," Jake said and waited until Percy Young had left the immediate area before turning to speak to Shearer. "I presume you have heard about Miss Lassiter, Mr Shearer?"

"It's terrible, absolutely terrible," was all that Shearer could say, leaving Jake free to assume that Jasper Shearer had indeed heard about Mabel Lassiter.

"Did you know Miss Lassiter from previous productions?" Jake then asked.

"I prefer to remember faces rather than names. As I didn't see Mabel on this occasion I can't be sure that I'm thinking about the right girl but I'm fairly sure that I did work with her once before, though that would have been in Glasgow."

"Would Sammy Gill have been in that production as well?"

Shearer looked surprised that Jake would have known that. "Well, yes, he was as a matter of fact. Sammy and Mabel appeared to know each other and he had been very keen to get her in to the production. Mind you I don't think he wanted her for her dancing skills, if you know what I mean?"

Jake smiled. "And was Sadie Gill part of that production as well?"

Shearer's look of surprise deepened. "My but we are well informed aren't we? Yes, Sadie was also in that production but then if Sammy was doing a show it was inevitable that Sadie would be there as well. I seem to recall the two women rarely spoke and were rarely even seen together. What may, or may not, have been going on outside of the show is anyone's guess of course."

"But for this production there is no Sammy or Sadie?" Jake then enquired.

"None whatsoever. Our lead man is Delphont Trueman who, as far as I am aware, has never worked with Sammy, Sadie or Mabel in the short-lived career that he has had to date. Delphont is a wonderful song and dance talent who can also, thankfully, be trusted to keep his hands to himself."

"Thank you," Jake then said. "Would it be possible to address the whole cast now?"

"But of course," replied Shearer who then skipped around the stage, clapping his hands furiously and rounding up all the cast in the same way that a dog might collect sheep in a pen. Once everyone was gathered centre stage he then introduced Jake to them and then stood back.

Jake kept what he wanted to say in very general terms. Two of the girls broke down at the mention of Mabel being dead. Jake noted their reaction as this was not the first time they had heard of Mabel's death and yet it still cut deeper with them than it seemed to do with the others.

No one appeared to know Mabel that well, although a few did admit to having worked with her in previous productions. The two who had shed the tears were standing towards the back of the group as Jake made his way round collecting any snippets of information that might have been forthcoming. Jake deliberately left them until last but eventually he was standing in front of them.

They were both slightly shorter in height than Jake and wore their long hair tied back off of their faces. They were very pretty and their costumes left little to Jake's imagination. Everything was covered but there was more than a hint of the womanly charms that lay below.

"How well did you know Miss Lassiter, Miss.......?" Jake began, deliberately leaving the lack of a name floating in the air. The girl quickly filled the gap.

"Grant. Helen Grant. I had worked on a couple of shows with Mabel. She was a lovely girl though perhaps a might too quick to fall for the smooth tongue of an apparently nice, young man."

Jake turned to the other woman. "And you, Miss.......?"

"Abbot. Myrtle Abbot. I too have been in a couple of shows with Mabel and Helen is right; Mabel seemed to fall in love with every man who showed her even the slightest bit of attention. She seemed incapable of seeing through the lies that these men will tell you simply to get you alone with them in a room."

"How old would Miss Lassiter have been?"

"Most of the girls lie about their age, Inspector. We're generally a lot younger than we might claim. That being the case I should have thought Mabel would have been eighteen, perhaps nineteen."

"Or she could have been as young as fourteen or fifteen," added Helen Grant," as she did come across as being very immature. She was a pretty girl with a mature body, which I suppose makes it all the more difficult to guess her age. She attracted men wherever she went but she didn't seem able to cope with the interest shown in her. She could walk in to a room and every man in that room would be looking her way. There was a magnetism to the girl that you don't often see. We all get attention from men after the shows, Inspector, but most of us turn that to our advantage by getting our admirers to buy us a meal or a few drinks. Mabel never seemed able to do that and as a result it was the men who took advantage of her."

Myrtle Abbot seemed to come out of a deep thought. "There is little doubt, Inspector, that Mabel was badly treated by the men who visited her. She was a gullible girl who was far too easily led astray."

"Do you remember if there was ever one man who paid her more attention than others?" Jake then asked.

"You mean more than Sammy Gill?" added Helen Grant.

"Yes."

Both girls thought for a moment. "I can't think of anyone in particular," Myrtle Abbot said. "However, there seemed to be men buzzing around her all the time so it's perfectly possible there could have been one regular in amongst the masses and I just missed him."

Helen Grant added that she could think of no one either. Jake continued.

"Do you believe she was ever in love with any of these men?"

Both girls scoffed, but Helen Grant actually put something in words. "I'm sure Mabel thought all those men were in love with her. However, the truth is that love can never really find a place in the life of a dancer who is moving in circles that are way above her station. Mabel might have been delighted to have been in the company of men who had money and who probably bought her gifts but she would have been very stupid indeed if she had ever thought for one minute that love ever came in to it."

Jake suddenly felt a deep sadness for Mabel Lassiter. It seemed the more he heard about her the more pathetic she became. She had been a young woman trying to better herself in whatever way she could. She had nothing but her looks and her womanly charms but armed with those she had tried to get the best out of life. Her killer may well have known her but given the life that she lived and the many men that she had been in contact with, identifying that one particular maniac might prove to be even beyond the investigative skills of Jake Fraser.

If the killer had been someone from Mabel's past then there seemed little chance that he would ever be caught. Jake had this image of a young man, besotted by this pretty young dancer, hearing about her coming back to Aberdeen and somehow hearing that she was living at the Palace Hotel. Maybe this young man had been the mysterious Martin Bagshaw.

Anyway, this young man had visited Mabel. He would have been confident of receiving some sexual favours after spending money on her and yet he had found a woman desperate to defend her honour rather than throw it away. This young man would have become violent at being rejected and so he attacked her and vent his lust in the most despicable and violent manner. It certainly all made sense had it not been for the chest.

What was the point of the chest?

Jake thanked Helen and Myrtle for their help and then went over to Jasper Shearer to thank him for making the time for Jake's visit. They were just saying their final farewells when a handsome young man with short, black hair and a pencil moustaches breezed on to the stage.

"I heard there was a policeman here asking questions about one of the dancers?" the young man announced in a very and unnecessarily loud and theatrical manner.

"Inspector Fraser," Jasper Shearer said, "this is our star Delphont Trueman."

Trueman held out a hand in the offer of a handshake. Jake did not take up the offer. He simply asked Trueman if he had known Mabel Lassiter and when he said he hadn't Jake simply turned and walked away, leaving the star of the show looking more than a little deflated.

***

Sergeant Turnbull was waiting for Jake as he walked in through the main door. Jake could tell from Turnbull's face that all was not well.

"A dirty faced, little brat ran in here about half an hour ago and threw this at me," Turnbull said handing Jake a piece of paper, the creases of which made it clear that the paper had been scrunched in to a ball at one time. "The little bugger ran out again before I could say a word so I know nothing other than what is written on the paper."

Written, in neat though rather small writing, was an address in Marischal Street and a suggestion that the police may want to visit it.

Jake looked up. "And there was nothing else?"

"No, sir. As I said it all happened rather quickly. The wee bugger ran in, threw the ball of paper at me and ran out again."

"Did you recognise him?"

Turnbull thought for a few seconds. "I've seen the face around the streets but I couldn't put a name to him, sorry."

"Not to worry," added Jake, "I'll deal with it."

Jake went through to the office and found Mathieson pouring over some paperwork connected to the Mabel Lassiter case. Jake asked Mathieson to accompany him and they then stopped off at the muster room to collect a couple of Constables. Jake also dispatched a third Constable to warn the Police Doctor that his services might be needed once more. Jake had a bad feeling in the pit of his stomach that they were not going to find this property empty.

The small group of police officers then made their way through on to Union Street and then across the road and down Marischal Street. They continued down the left hand side of the street until they reached the number written on the piece of paper. They then climbed to the second floor as, again, instructed by the writing on the paper.

They were now presented with two doors, one to the right and one to the left. The paper did not make it clear as to which door they were now supposed to turn. Jake decided to try both doors and found the one to his right was unlocked. He decided to venture further and if they found irate occupants then he would apologise and suggest, that in future, they locked their door.

One of the Constables remained outside on the landing and the other three went in to the property. As with many of these flats there was essentially two main rooms but in this case the kitchen, though small, was separate.

Jake led the way through to the back room first. Here they found the naked body of a woman lying on the floor. She was lying on her back and it was clear from the marks around her neck that she had been strangled. She looked to be in her late thirties, perhaps early forties and her body looked undernourished and in general need of a good meal.

"That's Jessie McGill," the Constable announced at once. "She used to be a prostitute down at the harbour but I haven't seen her around the streets in months. I'd heard she was trying to better herself in life."

"Maybe she had a fall out with her pimp?" Mathieson suggested.

The Constable shook his head. "As far as I know, sir, Jessie never had a pimp she always worked for herself. This may sound daft but Jessie always seemed to be different from the other prostitutes; that bit more intelligent you might say. I got the feeling that she didn't have to work in that trade but that she chose to do so anyway."

"It looks as if the trade has been the death of her, though it's very unusual for prostitutes to use their own homes for work. Home is usually the one place they can forget about the life they live."

As Jake spoke it was a vision of Alice that formed in his head rather than the reality of looking down on Jessie's body. He then looked around the rest of the room. It was generally very tidy with only a few, what might be called personal, items lying around.

"See if there's any sign of her clothes in here, or the kitchen," Jake then said. "I'll check the other room."

Jake went through to the front room and was surprised to find the body of another woman, only this time she was laid out on the bed as if she had been grabbing a few hours precious sleep. She was fully clothed and apart from the tell-tale marks around her neck it would have been impossible, at first glance, to tell if she were dead or alive. The way in which this body had been posed was in direct contrast to that of Jessie McGill who looked as if she had simply been dropped to the floor and left there.

"Constable!" Jake called out.

"Yes, sir," came the almost instant reply.

"Come in here for a moment."

The Constable came in to the room and reacted at once at the sight of the second body.

"Do you know this one?" Jake then said.

The Constable looked closely at the body. "I don't recognise her at all, sir. If you don't mind me saying so she doesn't look like your average whore."

"I agree, Constable. Now get back to Lodge Walk and ask the Police Doctor to attend. Tell him we have two bodies that will require his attention."

"At once, sir?"

The Constable went out the front door and Mathieson joined Jake in the bedroom. Jake was looking closer at the second victim. This woman was younger by many years and prettier as well. Although she was wearing a dress made from very poor material her general appearance was of someone who had lived a healthier life than poor Jessie lying in the other room. This woman's hair looked clean and well-kept as well. It seemed clear to both Jake and Mathieson that this young woman had been able to maintain an appearance far higher in standard than would have been expected from a prostitute.

"Do you reckon these murders are connected to the death of Mabel Lassiter?" Mathieson then asked.

"Doubt it," was Jake's instant response. "Neither of these women look to have been attacked with the same violence as that which visited poor Mabel. They've obviously been strangled but unless he took the time to dress this woman again, I'm guessing we'll find no sign of sexual interference. Having seen the sexual violence suffered by Mabel Lassiter I would find it hard to believe that that man, were he to kill again, would not also rape again."

They continued their search of the property. They found a bag, which belonged to Jessie but they found nothing that might be connected to the second woman. They also did not find any items of clothing that may have come from Jessie, not unless the killer took time to hang everything in the wardrobe.

"Perhaps this was a robbery gone wrong," Mathieson then said. "The killer maybe thought the property was empty and when he found the two women he had to silence them. There seems to be at least one bag missing so he could have taken that to sell the contents?"

Jake thought for a little while. "It's possible, but that wouldn't explain why the killer took time to lay this woman out so carefully and yet was happy to dump poor Jessie on the floor. It looks as if the killer somehow cared more for this one."

"She's younger. Maybe he has a daughter of his own and he was stricken with remorse after he'd killed her."

"You may well be correct, Mathieson," added Jake as he continued to look around the property.

Around fifteen minutes later the door opened and the Police Doctor came in. Jake met him in the hallway and thanked him for coming. Doctor Symon was a man in his mid-thirties; handsome of face and sharp of mind. He was only assisting the Police during the absence, on ill-health, of the usual and long standing Doctor.

"Thank you for coming so quickly, Doctor," said Jake.

Symon smiled. "Not at all; where would you like me to start?"

"Front room first, please, she's puzzling me more than the other one."

The Doctor went in to the room and made his way over to the bed. He began to examine the body so Jake and Mathieson left him alone and went to check the rest of the property for any clues that might help them find the killer.

It was only a matter of minutes later that the Doctor came through to the back room looking for Jake. As he walked in to the room his eyes glance down at the second body lying on the floor.

"I'll get to that in a moment," he said, pointing down at the corpse," but for the moment, Jake, could I ask you to accompany me back to the other room."

Jake went through with the Doctor and found that he had lifted the hem of the young woman's dress to allow a more intimate examination. With the hem lifted the young lady's undergarments were now in full view and it was obvious, even to two men with limited knowledge of women's underwear, that the quality of her underwear was far higher than that of the dress.

"This is a new one for me," the Doctor then said. "I've seen a better quality dress worn over poor underwear but never this way around."

"I just can't believe that this woman is a prostitute," Jake added. "They rarely bother with underwear as it gets in the way of business and even if she had saved enough money to buy herself a wee treat then it would, almost definitely, be a dress as that can be seen by everyone"

The Doctor looked across at Jake.

"If this woman was a prostitute then maybe she had a special customer who bought her the treats?"

Jake continued to look down at the body. "I say again, Doctor, this woman was definitely not a prostitute."

"You're probably right. Certainly, judging by this woman's overall condition, I would say the underwear was more in keeping with her lifestyle than the dress. It looks of very poor quality and probably slightly small for her as well."

"The other woman has been identified as Jessie McGill who lives here so it's possible this dress belongs to her, though why she would be lending it to someone else is beyond me."

"I'll maybe learn more once I've had a look at them both down at Lodge Walk," the Doctor then added.

"Would you offer an opinion as to when these murders took place?"

"No earlier than twenty-four hours ago. They've been dead for some time."

"Thank you, Doctor that gives us something to work on, I'll get Sergeant Mathieson to arrange for the bodies to be brought to the morgue."

"Thank you," concluded the Doctor who then set off to examine the second body.

Jake was almost out the front door when he remembered something that he had meant to ask the Doctor. He went through to the back room where he found the Doctor kneeling beside the body of Jessie McGill.

"Sorry to bother you, Doctor, but did you get an opportunity to examine the body of Mabel Lassiter?"

The Doctor looked up. "I did find time for a preliminary examination but you'll really need to wait for my report."

"I appreciate that, Doctor, but would you at least be able to rule out any connection between that murder and these?"

"I wouldn't rule out anything until my examinations are complete," the Doctor replied rather curtly. "However, I would say that, from the visual evidence at least, there would seem to be no obvious indication that the same madman who attacked Mabel Lassiter also attacked these two women. The ferocity of the attack on Miss Lassiter seemed excessive whereas the crime committed here has a different signature to it altogether. At least in the case of the woman through in the other room the killer has shown compassion in how he has arranged her body. The man who killed Mable Lassiter would not be capable of showing compassion to anyone."

"Thank you, Doctor, we seem to be agreeing on what the evidence is telling us. Unfortunately that means we are now hunting two killers and a time when we can least afford the manpower."

"I'll get my report on all the murder victims to you as soon as I can," the Doctor then said and returned his attention to the body of Jessie McGill.

Jake thanked him for his help and left the property. He went back to Lodge Walk and actually managed to get back to his office without being intercepted by the Desk Sergeant. However, he had only been at his desk a matter of minutes when he was informed, by a young Constable coming in to the room that the Chief Constable was wanting to see him at once

FIVE

Thursday 13 September – mid-afternoon into early evening

Jake made his way along the corridor and up the stairs feeling a little like a naughty child who had been summoned to the Headmaster's study. He wondered whether he should, perhaps, have put a large book down the back of his trousers before taking to the staircase.

Jake reached the door of the Chief Constable's office, which was pretty much situated above Jake's own office and knocked lightly before stepping back and awaiting some form of invitation to enter. A muffled voice was heard through the door and Jake took that as being his invitation to enter so he opened the door and stepped in to the room.

The Chief Constable's office was not particularly grand with the only slight nod towards his position in the community being the large picture of the King hanging on the wall behind him. The furniture was fairly basic and the Chief sat behind a desk that was positively straining under the weight of paperwork awaiting his attention.

"Ah, Jake, in you come and sit down," the Chief said and Jake took heart from the fact the tone appeared to be quite cheerful.

Jake sat down and the Chief leaned forward putting all his upper body weight on to his arms. He looked at Jake with an expression of growing intensity and some small measure of concern.

"Do we have some kind of lunatic on the loose in this city?" he then said.

"I take it you are referring to the murders, sir?"

"Indeed I am," added the Chief, sitting back in his chair. "Three murdered women in the space of twenty-four hours is not the kind of news any Chief Constable would want to hear, but it sounds particularly bad in a city like Aberdeen where murders, thankfully, don't happen that often."

"The murders are not connected," Jake then said, with some confidence. "The murder at the Palace Hotel was carried out with extreme violence, whereas the murders at Marischal Street were committed by someone who actually seems to have shown remorse towards one of his victims. Obviously we'll know a lot more once I receive the Doctor's report on both crimes but, for the moment, I am confident in saying we are looking for two killers."

"The death of this dancer seems particularly nasty," the Chief then said. "Do we have anything on which to build a decent investigation?"

"Not much meantime, sir. There is the rather puzzling issue of the chest that the young lady took with her from London," Jake then continued. "It is very large and has been adapted, it would appear, to accommodate someone sitting inside it."

"You mean she smuggled someone in to Aberdeen?" the Chief said sitting forward in his chair with concern written on his face.

"It may have been designed to look like that, sir, but I can't believe that that was actually the case. There is no reason for anyone to want to sneak in to Aberdeen in fear of being recognised by the Police. We have no major criminals on file at present and certainly none that might be visiting our city. No, sir, whatever the reason for the rather elaborate changes that have been made to the chest I don't believe it was to bring someone to the city."

"Maybe the idea was to take someone *away* from the city, Jake?" the Chief then suggested and as soon as the words had been spoken Jake could see, immediately, that that certainly made more sense.

Someone intent on committing a serious crime in Aberdeen might then sneak out of the city inside the chest. At least that may have been their plan but now that Mabel Lassiter was dead and the chest was in police custody there was no way that the chest would play any part in a criminal plan.

"That would perhaps make more sense," Jake finally said in agreement, "and if the plan had required them to sneak out of Aberdeen then the crime they intend to commit must be fairly significant."

The Chief's face seemed to drain of blood.

"The royal visit, Jake; my God, someone is going to do something to the King and Queen!"

Jake held up his hand. "If the chest had been meant to go back to London with Mabel Lassiter then it would not have left Aberdeen until a full week and more after the royal visit. I can't imagine that someone would attack their Majesties and then hang around Aberdeen for another week waiting for a giant chest to transport them to God knows where."

The Chief sat back. "You may well be right, Jake, but we daren't take any risks with the security of the monarch. Maybe the plan is to lie low in Aberdeen until the initial police activity calms down"

"Perhaps." Jake did not sound convinced.

"We really are being stretched to the limits. It is imperative that these new developments are not allowed to distract us from our main objective and that is to protect the King and Queen at all costs. To that end I cannot afford to take anyone away from the teams already allocated to the Inspectors. I'm sorry to say, Jake that you will have to investigate these murders pretty much on your own."

"I understand, sir. Mathieson and I can deal with most of what will be required in the early stages of both enquiries but we could be doing with another officer to carry out some door to door enquiries for us."

Anderson thought for a moment.

"We do have Detective Smith who has recently been given permission to retire from the Force, but not until after the royal visit. I will arrange for him to report to you and apart from the twenty-seventh, you may use Detective Smith however you may choose."

"My thanks, sir. Alex is a good man and I'm sure he'll be a great help to us. May I ask, sir, how the main preparations for the twenty-seventh are coming along?"

The Chief Constable brightened a little. He had spent much of his time preparing for the day and felt that most of the arrangements were now in place even though these murders and the mystery chest did put a spanner in the works.

"I believe everything is slowly falling in to place. Other Forces have been very generous in their offer of help on the day and I estimate we'll have somewhere in the region of nine hundred police officers in Aberdeen by the time the King and Queen arrive. I'm happy that those officers will be deployed to the best effect. However, as if checking that we yokels out in the Shires are truly capable of protecting the Royal couple, I am being visited on Monday by Detective Superintendent Harris, from Scotland Yard. He, apparently, is at Balmoral at present overseeing the security of the Royal Family while they are there."

"I do hope Superintendent Harris is not coming here to try and tell you how to do your job, sir," added Jake with a smile.

The Chief smiled in return. "He may try but he will not succeed. Anyway, returning to our murders for the moment, might I ask that you make every effort to get a quick result on these. I really would prefer to not have two unsolved murders hanging over the city whilst the King and Queen are here. It might detract from the good news that comes from their visit and the smile it seems to be putting on the face of the City as a whole."

"I appreciate that, sir, and I will do all that I can to bring someone to justice as fast as I can. However, at the moment, there is very little to go on. At present we have no motive and very little evidence so we have some way to go before a killer is apprehended."

"Well, do what you can and keep me informed of developments," the Chief then said, in a tone that almost added 'and shut the door when you leave.'

Jake took the hint. "I will do, sir."

And with that he left the office and returned to his own room downstairs.

***

Jake had caught up with much of his paperwork as the afternoon slipped in to evening. He had a half notion to head for the Saltoun Arms and catch up with Eddie and had got as far as putting his jacket on when the door opened and Sergeant Turnbull walked in to the room.

"Sorry to bother you Jake, particularly as you seem to be leaving, but I have a Doctor Samuels in the interview room and he'd like to report his daughter as missing. I don't know if it will be connected to your current enquiries, but I thought you might want to speak to him."

Jake paused for a second or two and then started to take his jacket off again. "Yes, of course I'll speak to him."

"As I say, he's in the interview room."

Jake collected his notebook and pencil and went through to the interview room where he found a very serious looking gentleman with white hair and heavy whiskers covering much of his face. He sat very upright in his chair and exuded an air of someone who had had a military upbringing. He was dressed in a three-piece pin-striped suit and there was a top hat and coat lying on the table.

He showed little reaction to Jake entering the room and remained very still in his chair whilst Jake sat down and opened his notebook.

"My name is Inspector Fraser and you, sir, would be?"

The man seemed lost in a trance for a few seconds. Eventually he appeared to snap out of it and focus his attention on the fact that someone had not only come in to the room but also appeared to be talking to him.

"Sorry?"

"Your name, sir, I was asking you what your name was?"

"My name is Doctor Nathaniel Samuels and I am here to report the fact that my daughter, Julia, has gone missing."

"Why do you think she is missing?"

Doctor Samuels' expression changed to one of incredulity. "Because she is not at home, Inspector."

Jake realised at once that he might have phrased the question a bit better. He tried a slightly different version of the same question in the hope that he would get a more thoughtful response.

"What makes you think that she is actually missing and not just visiting friends?"

"My daughter has no friends," came the rather blunt reply.

Jake was slightly taken aback by such bluntness and he took a little while to compose himself enough to proceed with the questions.

"If we could, perhaps, begin with some details concerning your daughter, Doctor Samuels. You said her name was Julia, is that correct?"

"It is."

"And how old is Julia?"

"Nineteen. She will be twenty in one month's time."

"Could you describe her for me please?"

"A little over five feet in height, blonde hair, blue eyes and though I am speaking as a proud father, rather pretty I should think."

Jake realised at once that the Doctor had just described the young woman found earlier on that bed in the Marischal Street property. He tried to continue as normal, asking his questions in measured tones.

"When did you last see her?"

"We had breakfast on Tuesday morning."

"Tuesday morning? Have you been away, Doctor Samuels?"

Doctor Samuels looked at Jake with some disgust. "No, Inspector, I have not been away. I was at a medical dinner on Tuesday night, which required me to stay over at The Douglas Hotel. Last night I worked late and did not get home until after eleven. When I found the house in darkness I assumed my daughter had retired for the night."

"Would you not have expected to see your daughter at breakfast this morning?" Jake then asked.

"My daughter did not always come down to breakfast before I left the house."

Jake made a couple of notes in his book before continuing.

"Could I please have a note of your address?"

"My home is at Number Seventy-Nine, Hamilton Place."

"Does anyone else live there apart from yourself and your daughter?" Jake then asked.

"I have a housekeeper who lives with us, that is all, but she will be of no help to you in this matter as she is currently visiting her sister in Elgin for a few days."

"Is your daughter in employment?"

"She carries out charity work on a Tuesday, Wednesday and Thursday at the Sailors' Institute in Mearns Street."

"Is your daughter happy at her work?"

Doctor Samuels looked slightly perplexed. "As far as I am aware she is very happy, Inspector, but as I do not reside inside my daughter's head I cannot answer truthfully as to whether, or not, she enjoyed her work."

"Was your daughter in the habit of wearing the same clothing to her work or did she wear different dresses for different days?"

"My daughter was most certainly not the type to wear the same dress every day," came the emphatic reply. "She has a vast array of clothing to choose from and she takes a pride in her appearance at all times."

"So you haven't actually seen Julia since Tuesday morning?"

"I believe that is what I said," Samuels snapped.

"How did you get home from work last night?

Samuels looked puzzled. "What a strange question, Inspector. My surgery is on King Street so I was able to hail a cab as I came out."

"And this was just before eleven?"

"Yes," Samuels said with some annoyance.

"Do you employ any other staff beyond your housekeeper, Doctor Samuels?"

"There is a man who tends the garden once a week, but there are no other live-in staff if that was what you meant?"

"And there was no indication in the house as to where your daughter might be?" Jake then said.

Samuels looked exasperated. "Inspector, would I be here if I had any inclination that my daughter was simply having tea with a friend? I said, before, that my daughter does not have friends nor does she ever do much in her life beyond going to her work and being at home with me. Apart from the few occasions that we may go out together to a show, or something, I cannot think of the last time that Julia was out in the evening. That was why, Inspector, I knew that something was definitely wrong when I arrived home this evening and Julia was not there."

"So she has never been missing before?"

"Certainly not," snapped Samuels.

"When you last saw your daughter did you detect any change in her manner, any sign that she was unhappy about something?"

Samuels was now struggling to contain his ever growing temper. He momentarily looked as if he might explode with anger but he seemed to pull himself together and eventually managed to answer the question.

"No, Inspector, there were no signs of unhappiness. In fact Julia has been in particularly high spirits of late and gave me every indication that she was extremely happy with her life. It is not in her character to simply go missing so would you please stop asking me all these stupid questions and simply get out there and find my daughter."

Jake considered asking the Doctor to go with him to the mortuary to confirm that it was poor Julia lying there. It was still possible she might not be Julia Samuels and he decided against putting the Doctor through more pain, for the moment, by perhaps presenting him with the dead body of his lovely daughter.

"Very well," Jake did eventually said," I will get on to this immediately and of course, I'll keep you informed of any developments."

Samuels stood up. He was not a tall man and he looked slightly out of proportion when he placed his top hat on his head. Nothing else was really said between the two men as Jake showed the Doctor to the front door. Jake stood for a few seconds longer than was necessary just watching him disappear down the street.

As Jake went back in to the building Turnbull looked up from some papers he was reading on the counter.

"Do you think it's his daughter we've got in the mortuary?"

"I am some a-feared it might be," Jake replied and continued on his way back to his office. He tidied his work away and set off for the Saltoun Arms.

Twenty minutes later he was sitting in the corner of a very busy bar enjoying his first pint with Eddie. Eddie was able to tell Jake that he had spoken to his colleague but had not learned anything that appeared to be helpful in any way. Apart from confirming that the person who had paid for Mabel Lassiter's room had been a young man, the rest of the description amounted to little more than Mr Average.

They were still deep in conversation when Alan MacBride came sidling over to them. Jake noticed him coming and was talking almost before he arrived at their table.

"Not just now, MacBride. I'm off-duty and enjoying a drink with my friend."

"I'm not here to disturb your evening, Inspector," MacBride said, his eyes scanning the rest of the bar for familiar faces who might bring him a story. "I'm just here to ask that you keep the Press informed of developments seeing as there have now been three women murdered in this city in the last twenty-four hours. I mean, if there is a madman on the loose in Aberdeen then the people need to know."

"There is no madman loose in the city," Jake responded.

MacBride grinned. "Can I quote you on that?"

"You can quote my arse, MacBride," snapped Jake. "Now get the hell out of my way before I arrest you for harassing a police officer."

"Won't you give me something to pass on to our readers?" MacBride added.

"You can tell your readers that the City Police of Aberdeen are on the case and quite frankly, that is all they need to know at the moment."

MacBride sensed that he would get nowhere and he didn't want to push his luck and perhaps permanently damage what was a useable relationship with Jake Fraser. He reluctantly backed away and lost himself in the general mass of bodies that was crowded around the bar.

Jake and Eddie resumed their conversation only this time they talked about anything and everything that did not have connections with dead bodies.

SIX

Friday 14 September - mid morning to mid afternoon

Jake went across to the mortuary. It was a short walk across the parade ground to the single storey building at the back. It was a little after ten in the morning as Jake pushed open the front door and entered the building.

As usual, the first thing that struck anyone entering the building was the overwhelming smell of cleansing fluid. Every room was spotlessly clean and it was to one of the main rooms that Jake now walked.

As he entered he found Doctor Symon busy working on the body of Jessie McGill. He looked up as Jake walked in and sighed audibly. He recognised the need for police officers to gather information as quickly as possible but they, in turn, had to realise that providing medical information, with any remote chance of accuracy, was not a five minute job and that he really needed to be given both the time and the space to get on with his job rather being constantly interrupted by impatient detectives.

"You'll get my report as soon as it is written," Symon said.

Jake drew closer. "I appreciate you have a lot to do, Doctor Symon, but I would be forever in your debt if you could provide me with some early thoughts on both crime scenes and victims?"

Symon stepped back from the body of Jessie McGill and turned to point towards the body of the young woman stretched out on the other slab. Jake looked across and couldn't help but think that anyone working in the world of dead bodies would surely lose all feeling for the living.

If this was indeed Julia Samuels then she had been reduced to a discussion point, her once lovely body now cut in various places as the Doctor sought confirmation of the exact crime committed upon her. This was no longer the naked body of a beautiful woman this was simply another cadaver.

"That young woman was definitely treated more kindly by her killer than the other two and as you already know, Mabel Lassiter was the one treated most brutally. Her attacker took out a great rage upon her body and every action seemed to have been made with the sole intention of doing as much damage to her body as was physically possible. Jessie McGill was strangled but there are no signs of anything else being done to her body. There's certainly no sign of recent sexual activity with Jessie and given her previous profession then I would, perhaps, have expected things to be different. Going back to the young woman there seems little doubt in my mind that she was very carefully arranged on that bed and that she was wearing a dress that I'm guessing belonged to Jessie. The killer appears to have taken the young woman's dress away with him, which again seems strange."

"He took her bag as well, Doctor, which means that both items must have some particular significance to the killer," added Jake. "Are you still happy, therefore, to contend that we are looking for two different killers?"

"Oh I'd stake my profession on that assumption," Symon said. "One killer has a sadistic streak in him and the other may almost have killed in error. The bodies in the Marischal Street property were definitely treated with greater respect than that of Mabel Lassiter. I mean the young woman over there is still a virgin, Inspector and I feel sure that if she had fallen in to the hands of our sadist that would definitely no longer be the case."

"My thanks, Doctor," Jake then said. "I look forward to reading your reports once I've given you a chance to write them."

Symon smiled. No matter how he tried sometimes he just couldn't bring himself to ever be truly annoyed with Jake. He went back to his work as the door swung shut and Jake made his way out of the building.

Instead of going back across to the main building, Jake walked around and out on to Lodge Walk. He then turned right and walked along to Union Street. Horse drawn carts clip-clopped passed and a tramcar slid sedately down the middle of the road. People were crossing at all points, oblivious it seemed to the different modes of transport that came and went all the time.

Jake knew that there were regular incidents of pedestrians being hit by moving vehicles but, thankfully, the majority of them tended to be minor. However, there had been one incident, just the previous week, when a man had been knocked unconscious in Market Street when he had hit his head on the road after being hit by a horse and cart. The Police Ambulance had been called to take the unfortunate man to the Infirmary.

Jake crossed Union Street and carried on down Marischal Street. He was heading towards the Sailors' Institute where he hoped to learn a bit more about Julia Samuels. Jake had a feeling that the girl described by her father was not the girl that other people might have known. It is often the case that the parents are the last people to really know their offspring as there would always be some secrets kept from them. It was often a case of sparing their feelings or simply being too embarrassed to take them in to your confidence.

A casual stroll along Regent Quay took Jake to the Institute on Mearns Street. He had noted how quiet the harbour area had been with many of the fishing boats currently out at sea. Aberdeen had quite a mix of vessels plying their trade in the German Ocean and beyond.

The Institute was a stone built, depressing looking building that offered a temporary home to seamen passing through the city and with nowhere else to go, It also provided food and shelter, on a daily basis, for those seamen who were simply wanting away from the boat for a little while. The restaurant was an integral part of the building and provided food and beverages for more than just the sailors. It was a building in which Jake had not been before.

Jake entered the building and was met, just inside, by a reception area not unlike that of most hotels. Behind the desk stood a man whose face was clean shaven apart from a splendid moustache that had clearly been cultivated over many years of careful growth and grooming.

"Can I help you?" the man enquired.

Jake showed him his identification and then said he would like to speak to someone about Julia Samuels.

"That sounds like something Mrs Gifford would deal with," the man then said. "If you would care to follow me."

They went through a door behind him, along a short corridor and then right in to an area that had been laid out with tables and chairs. Jake reckoned that around forty people could have eaten at any one sitting within this space. In the wall to his left was an open serving hatch through which could be seen the kitchen area.

The man led the way to the kitchen door and shouted through, presumably to someone working there, though Jake could see no immediate sign of anyone.

"Mrs Gifford, there's an Inspector Fraser here to speak to someone about Julia."

The man then left, obviously satisfied that he had done enough for the moment. Jake stood for a little longer, still not totally convinced that there was anyone else actually there.

Eventually a tall, elegant looking woman with attractive features came out of the kitchen. She looked to be in her late thirties, perhaps early forties with dark, curly hair. Jake might have expected this woman to wear her hair tied up in a tight bun, however she had chosen to keep it loose and fall to her shoulders. She shook Jake's hand and introduced herself with a little more formality.

"I'm Margaret Gifford. I believe you want to talk about Julia, has something happened?"

They sat down.

"Her father has reported her missing and I'm hoping that you might be able to tell me a little about Julia in terms of her work and how she seemed to you of late?"

"I did wonder why Julia did not come here yesterday. She has never missed a day before."

"Did you not miss her on Wednesday as well?" Jake then enquired.

Margaret Gifford looked surprised. "Julia hasn't worked here on a Wednesday for the last month and more. I would have thought her father would have known that."

"Apparently not as he told me that his daughter worked here on a Tuesday, Wednesday and Thursday."

"Which she did for the best part of a year but, as I said, that all changed around the beginning of last month when she announced that she had agreed to do some hours at the Fishermen's Friend Charity along the quay every Wednesday."

"So the last you saw of Miss Samuels would have been Tuesday?"

"That would be correct. By the way, Inspector, would you like to join me in having a cup of tea?"

"That would be very nice, Mrs Gifford."

"Oh, please, call me Margaret."

Margaret Gifford returned to the kitchen area but, on this occasion, Jake could still see her through the serving hatch as she filled a pot with water and tea and set out some cups and saucers. Jake found himself watching this highly attractive woman as she worked and when she turned around and asked if he would like milk and sugar he jumped in the manner of a young child being caught with its hand in the cookie jar.

"Yes please," he replied. "Milk and two sugars."

He forced himself to look away until Margaret returned to her seat carrying a tray on which the tea and some biscuits. As she walked over to the table Jake couldn't help but notice that this woman curved in all the right places and that her beauty was something that simply could not go unnoticed. He wondered what such an attractive woman was doing working in what was predominantly a male domain

Once Margaret was seated and comfortable Jake continued with his questions.

"Did you notice anything different about Julia on Tuesday?"

Margaret thought for a moment. "Not that I can recall. She has certainly been generally happier of late but that change of mood goes back some weeks now."

"Was there any obvious reason for this happiness?"?

"Julia never said anything. Of course I never pry in to the private world of any of the people who work or attend here. Should anyone wish to confide in me then I'm here for them but, beyond that, people come and go from here safe in the knowledge that no one will question anything that they do."

"But you reckon Julia had been happier for around the last month?"

"Something like that."

"Which would coincide with her starting work with the Fishermen's Friend Charity?" Jake then suggested.

Margaret Gifford pondered on that statement for a few seconds.

"I hadn't actually thought of it in those terms but, now that you mention it, there has been a more cheerful side to Julia's nature since she changed to working here only two days a week. Perhaps she had not been as happy here as I thought."

"You make it sound like she was a very unhappy person before; was that really the case?"

"Julia has always been a very serious, young woman. I think her father keeps her on a very tight leash. She had few chances to meet with other young people and spend time talking about young people's things. I know he disapproved of her working here because it was a place full of men, but the job was arranged through a friend of the Doctors who happens to be on our management board. Both men had agreed that it would be good for Julia to meet other people and also to learn the meaning of doing a job of some kind. I think they thought this was a good place for her to work as I would always be here to keep an eye on her."

"Do you think it bothers Julia in any way to be working in a place that is pretty much men only?" Jake then asked.

"She has never said, nor done anything to make me think that working here made her feel uncomfortable though, obviously, she is very popular with the men as she is so young and pretty and maybe that attention was beginning to bother her."

"Was there ever an occasion where someone in particular acted in an Inappropriate manner towards her?"

"Good heavens, no. The men who come here know better than to do anything that would get them banned. This is the closest thing to home for many of them and they would never put that one piece of luxury in jeopardy."

"I hope you are treated with the same respect," Jake added and the warmth on his face told him that he was blushing.

Margaret Gifford smiled. "Why, Inspector, it is very nice of you to spare a thought for my well-being. I can assure you that I am always treated with the utmost respect around here and I have never, in all the time that I have worked here, had any man act in an inappropriate manner towards me."

"How long *have* you worked here?"

Jake knew that he was straying slightly from the point, but this woman had spirit and a personality that was every bit as attractive as her facial features. Jake felt a need to simply talk to her rather than ask police related questions.

"I have been here nearly five years now. We had another girl who worked here before and when she left, Julia started."

"If you don't mind me asking," Jake then said, "but what does your husband think of you working in a place full of men?"

Margaret Gifford smiled and leaned forward slightly in a conspiratorial manner.

"Between you, me and these four walls, there is no Mr Gifford. I suppose that I called myself Mrs Gifford in the early days as a means of protection from some men who may have got the wrong idea about me. I admit that when I started working here I had the same misconceptions as you appear to have and presumed that all men would find it difficult to control themselves in my company. I, of course, was flattering myself in thinking that men would even find me attractive, let alone try to suggest anything inappropriate."

Jake was blushing again. "My apologies, I did not mean to pry in to your private life."

"But you weren't prying, Inspector, you simply asked a perfectly obvious question. I'm sure, had I been married, that my husband would have been less than enamoured with the fact I worked in a man's world."

"Is it possible that Julia could have been attracted to one of the men attending here?"

"Obviously a romantic attraction would not have been out of the question. Some of the men who come here are very close to Julia's age and quite handsome. However, I would have to say that Julia has always struck me as being a very insecure young woman who lacks the self-confidence to talk to these men about anything other than general chit-chat. Perhaps, more importantly, she would have been terrified of her father ever finding out about her having a relationship of any kind with someone so low in the class system as a man of the sea."

"Did you get the impression that Julia would have lived in fear of her father?"

"Fear may be too strong a word, Inspector, but I firmly believe that she would never have knowingly done anything to displease her father. I'm assuming you have already met the man so you will know that he is someone who lives his life with almost military precision. His daughter would have been part of that perfect little world where everything had its place. Anything that might have adversely affected the world he had created, would incur his wrath. I also had the impression, on the few occasions on which I met him, that he would be a man with quite a temper on him and that that temper was never far from the surface of his emotions. To be honest I am pleased that he is not my doctor as I would not wish a man like him to have access to my every personal detail. There is certainly something slightly unnerving about him, if you get my meaning?"

"I believe I do, Margaret," Jake said, finding it strange to be using her first name when he didn't really know her. Jake paused for a second.

His line of questioning was about to move closer to details concerning the murder. Jake felt that with Margaret Gifford being a very intelligent woman, she would quickly link what he was about to say to the piece that had been in the morning paper.

Alan MacBride had not been able to say much in his report but he did refer to a murder occurring in a Marischal Street property. He had also, as Jake had rather jokingly suggested, added the fact that the Aberdeen City Police were throwing as much resource as was possible, at the investigation. Yes, it seemed likely that Margaret might link the next question with the murder story, however there seemed no other way of trying to tie Julia Samuels with Jessie McGill without simply asking a question.

"Were you ever aware of Julia being friends with anyone who lived in Marischal Street?"

Margaret Gifford's expression changed immediately and her face was now etched with concern. This change of expression confirmed to Jake that she had, indeed, read the morning paper.

"Did the paper not say something about a murder in Marischal Street?" she asked.

"There was something in the morning paper to that effect," Jake agreed. "However, we have one or two investigations underway at present and the disappearance of Julia Samuels is just one of them. With that in mind would you please be good enough as to answer my question, Margaret?"

Pleased to hear him using her first name all the time, Margaret Gifford relaxed a little once more and gave the question a little thought.

"Another of our volunteers has a property in Marischal Street, though I would not have thought that she and Julia would have been in contact beyond their time at work."

"Could I have the name of this other volunteer?"

"Jessie McGill."

Jake felt a chill pass through his body at the mention of Jessie's name. Until that moment there had still been a very small part of him hanging on to the faint possibility that Julia Samuels was not the young woman they had found dead in Jessie McGill's flat. However, it now seemed a certainty that Julia Samuels had died by the same hand as Jessie.

"Could you tell me a little more about Jessie McGill?"

"Jessie is a very special woman, Inspector, who has turned her life around and I am very proud of her."

"In what way has she turned her life around?"

Margaret paused for a second and poured some more tea in to their now empty tea cups.

"Jessie was a prostitute in her early days. Some women have to make their money by whatever means they can and I will not judge her. However, in the last five years she has been working here and I have been paying her a small allowance for the work that she does. I believe she also did some part-time work for a bakery in the Castlegate. With the money that she was earning through legitimate employment she has been able to give up the need to prostitute herself."

"Were Jessie and Julia friends at work?"

"I would have said that their relationship was no more than that of colleagues. I would not have expected Jessie and Julia to have any reason to be in each other's company outside of work. However, beyond Jessie living there, I cannot think of any other reason to connect Julia with Marischal Street."

"On which days did Jessie work here?" Jake then asked.

"Jessie varied her days each week to accommodate the needs of the building."

"Did she work on a Wednesday?"

"No, that was always her day off. Forgive me for asking, Inspector, but I thought you were here about Julia so why all these questions about Jessie?"

She had no sooner asked the question when the story from that morning's paper came back in to her mind. She felt, more than ever now, that something terrible had happened, not only to Julia but to Jessie as well.

"As I said, "Jake replied, "there are a few lines of inquiry concerning the disappearance of Julia Samuels that we still need to address. The more we know about a person's usual movements the quicker we can identify something that may seem out of place. It is often that one out of place piece of evidence which helps us to solve the crime, if indeed a crime has been committed."

"Inspector, do you think that Julia is dead?" Margaret Gifford then asked with a look of horror on her face.

"There is a possibility that she may be dead, but there is also a possibility that she may be sitting have tea with a friend somewhere" Jake answered, hoping that his ability to lie, when it suited an investigation, had not left him.

Jake now jotted down some notes prior to leaving. This allowed him to identify that Margaret Gifford had a flat in Rosemount Viaduct and she was thirty-nine years of age.

Throughout the questions of a more personal nature Jake felt sure that Margaret was teasing him. She had a smile on her face at times and it seemed the more he reddened with embarrassment the more she teased.

Jake could have sat there all day talking to Margaret but there was work to be done elsewhere.

Jake put away his notebook and after removing it from his waistcoat, he glanced at his silver pocket-watch, "I really must be going. Thank you for your time, Margaret and thank you for the tea as well."

"Not at all, Inspector........."Margaret began,".....surely I can't keep calling you Inspector while you call me Margaret?"

Jake blushed yet again and Margaret found that strangely endearing.

"My name is Jake."

They both stood up and Margaret held out her hand for a handshake. "It's been nice speaking to you, Jake, it is just a pity that it could not have been in less upsetting circumstances."

"I may need to speak to you again," Jake then said shaking her hand.

"You have my address should you wish to call there and of course, Monday to Friday, you will always find me here."

Jake noted the suggestion that he call on her at home should there be further need to seek information from her. He was sure that there would be a further need; he would certainly think of some reason to see her again but whether it would be appropriate to call on her at home was something he still had to decide.

"Thank you again for your help today."

Jake found his own way out of the building and walked back along Regent Quay to where the Fishermen's Friend Charity building was located. He walked in to the reception area where he was greeted by a rather nervous looking young girl who became even more nervous when Jake said that he was a policeman.

"I'd like to speak to your manager if that is at all possible?"

"If you would like to take a seat," the young woman said, "I'll let Mr Tait know that you are here."

Jake sat down and watched the girl head off down a short corridor that was situated behind her desk. Off of the corridor came four doors and the girl knocked, then entered, the door furthest away on the left.

Moments later the young woman was back in the corridor and walking towards Jake. A few steps behind her was a gentleman, dressed in a pin-stripe suit and leaning heavily on a stick, which seemed to compensate for him walking with a severe limp. The man looked to be quite old with a shock of white hair that belied his years.

"My name is Patrick Tait and I am the manager of this establishment, Inspector. If you would care to follow me we can talk in my office."

Jake followed Tait back to his office and once they were both seated he asked his questions about Julia Samuels. It was a short interview as it soon became obvious that Julia Samuels had never worked there. In fact, Mr Tait was fairly certain that there was no connection, whatsoever, between his establishment and Julia Samuels.

"Would you happen to know a Jessie McGill?" Jake had then asked.

Tait gave the question a moment's thought "Again that is not a name that brings anyone to mind."

Jake saw no reason for asking any more questions so he thanked Mr Tait for his time and left the building. Outside the sky was blue once more and the sun shone down with a heat that was beginning to make Jake feel a little uncomfortable having to wear his working clothes.

Jake arrived back at his office where he found Sergeant Mathieson talking to Detective Smith.

Jake offered his hand to Smith. "Welcome, Alex, to our little team."

"Nice to have a proper job this close to retiring, sir," Smith replied.

"Okay, gentlemen, if you would like to take a seat I'll update you on where we are with the Marischal Street inquiry."

Jake spoke about his visit to the Sailors' Institute and also the Fishermen's Friend Charity. He told them that he was now confident that the body of the young woman in the mortuary was that of Julia Samuels but he had to admit that the motive for such a crime was still escaping him.

He reiterated the fact that it seemed certain that the killer of Julia Samuels appeared to show some remorse towards her and he still felt sure that the killer knew her in some way. He still had no explanation for why Julia Samuels had taken to lying to her father about every Wednesday and why, on that day, she should be found in the property of Jessie McGill. "

"Surely Julia Samuels was not making money as a prostitute?" Mathieson asked, though the possibility of the answer being yes was beyond belief even to him.

"Jessie McGill was no longer a prostitute, Mathieson," Jake said. "She had been away from that line of work for a few years now and there seems no reason for her, let alone Julia Samuels, slipping in to that profession. It was interesting today," Jake then continued," that the woman I interviewed at the Sailors' Institute was firmly of the opinion that Julia Samuels would never knowingly do anything that might incur the wrath of her father. Now visiting an ex-prostitute is not something that Doctor Samuels is likely to condone so Julia must have had a really strong reason for going to Marischal Street and for lying to her father about it."

Smith then spoke.

"I remember my daughter, just after she started work, telling me a few untruths about her time-keeping. I eventually found out that she had been spending that time with a gentleman friend she had met at work. That gentleman friend is now my son-in-law but for that brief period in our relationship my daughter was, most certainly, telling me lies. We fathers can sometimes be over protective towards our daughters."

"Margaret Gifford, at the Sailors' Institute, didn't seem to think there was any likelihood of a romance forming with anyone at the Institute and Julia's father claimed, rather bluntly I have to add, that his daughter had no friends, no friends at all. Having said that, I agree with you Alex that the strongest reason for lying about not being at work on a Wednesday was that she was meeting someone and that that someone was almost definitely never going to meet with her father's approval."

"Which brings us back to the Institute and the possibility of her meeting a seaman," added Mathieson.

"It does seem to be the only place that she was ever likely to meet someone," agreed Jake.

"So who's the domineering father?" Mathieson then asked.

"Doctor Nathaniel Samuels; a very prim and proper gentleman with military bearing who would quite clearly disapprove of his only daughter showing even the slightest interest in a man well below her station. I can well imagine the good Doctor would very quickly lose his temper were he to find out that his daughter had been visiting the property of an ex-prostitute let alone that she was there to meet with a seaman. Anyway, would you both go back to the properties around Jessie McGill's flat and see if anyone has remembered anything since they were spoken to the last time. Alex would you also check with the cab companies that one of their drivers definitely picked up a fare from King Street around eleven on Wednesday night and took that fare to Hamilton Place. I'm going to speak to the Police Doctor again."

Jake went across to the mortuary where he found Doctor Symon sitting at a small desk writing reports. Symon sighed again as Jake walked in though Jake was quick to tell him that he only had one question to ask and then he'd be on his way again.

"When we last spoke you told me that Julia Samuels was still a virgin. Have you since identified any marks on her body that might indicate sexual activity that fell short of actual penetration?"

Doctor Symon sat back from the papers strewn across his desk with the air of someone who was actually glad of the excuse to break from such a tedious task.

"I'd be fairly confident that Julia Samuels was sexually innocent at the time of her death. There is absolutely no indication from examining her body that she had been touched in any way, although obviously without excessive force marks are not always left on the body."

"Thank you, Doctor, what you have just told me may prove to be very helpful indeed."

And with that Jake left the mortuary and after picking up his jacket, he left the building and set off for home.

SEVEN

Saturday 15 September - early morning to early evening

Jake awoke at a little after half past six on a morning that promised another warm and sunny day. As his foggy brain cleared of sleep he became aware of the fact that there was someone else in his bed. Slowly the memories of what had happened started to return, though they were slightly impaired by the number of beers that he had drank in the course of the latter part of the previous evening.

He had got home from work around eight and at a little after ten there had been a knock at his door. He'd opened it to find Alice standing in the hallway, clutching some bottles of beer.

They had drunk the beer and discussed the fact that Scroggins was beginning to annoy and disturb Alice with his actions towards her. She was once more fearful of what Scroggins might do and she wondered if there might be something that Jake could do to help her once more.

Jake had agreed to help. He had not needed much persuading to help Alice particularly when it came to Scroggins who really was a man for whom Jake felt nothing but loathing. They had finished the beer and then one thing had led to another and before too long they were in bed together, making love. It had been a beautiful experience for them both.

Jake felt slightly guilty afterwards, as Alice had cuddled closer to him, as he had been having thoughts of Margaret Gifford during their love-making. They had then fallen asleep in each other's arms and for Jake the guilt soon passed.

Sleep had been deep and peaceful and the struggle to waken up in its aftermath was proving more difficult this morning than most for Jake. He finally pushed himself free of the bed and stood up. His head spun slightly and there was a dull ache imbedded in the centre of his brain. Alice rolled over on to her back and the blankets dropped away from her breasts. Jake stood for a moment looking down at her.

This allowed him to achieve two things; one was the obvious appreciation of Alice's lovely, young body and the other was to give his balance a few seconds more to sort itself out.

Jake moved away from the bed and crossed to where he could pour some water in to a bowl and have a quick wash. As he shaved he looked back at Alice as she moved once more in her sleep. He didn't feel particularly comfortable with the fact that he had sex with Alice knowing that their relationship could never move to a different level. No one would sanction a Police Inspector and a prostitute having a life together.

He felt that guilt return. He knew that, at least in the eyes of others, he could have a life with Margaret Gifford and no questions would be asked. That could never be the case with Alice; she would always be remembered as a prostitute.

He turned back and finished his shaving. He washed his body quickly and started to put on some clothes. As he was dressing there was more movement from the bed and a voice spoke to him.

"Good morning."

"Good morning," added Jake, looking down at Alice with a smile.

"Sometimes I don't want to leave here," Alice then said. "I feel so warm and safe and wanted when I'm here. There is nowhere else where I feel so safe."

Jake went back across to the bed and sat on the edge of it. Alice sat up and Jake kissed her.

"I'll deal with Scroggins," he said.

"It's not just Scroggins, it's everything," Alice added. "My life is just one man after another. I am nothing more than a moment's release to them. Only you make me feel like a woman, Jake."

Jake put his arms around her and held her tight, probably tighter than he had ever held her before. They sat like that, in total silence, and let the clock tick around for another few moments.

"I'll see what I can do for you," he then said," but, for the moment, I need to finish getting ready for work."

"Can I stay here a little longer?" Alice asked.

"You can stay as long as you like."

Jake then finished dressing and as he did so he made a cup of tea for both himself and Alice. He found some bread in the bread bin that was just the right side of edible and sliced and spread enough for both of them. Having completed what had passed for breakfast he left Alice still tucked up in bed and went off to work.

Lodge Walk was relatively quiet as he walked through the front door at a little after seven. He bade the desk Sergeant good morning and then went straight through to his office where he started to sort out the various items of paperwork that were lying there. He was pleased to find reports from Doctor Symon concerning both murders and he sat down to read through them.

The report on Mabel Lassiter spoke of multiple injuries, especially around the pubic area. She also had severe bruising on her breasts and inner thighs and the Doctor also formally recorded that Mabel had been strangled. The report further spoke of the severe violence that had been brought to bear on Mabel's body and suggested it had been inflicted by a calculating sadist who might be capable of any form of violence. This was most certainly a crime committed by someone who enjoyed what he was doing.

The report on the murders of Julia Samuels and Jessie McGill was completely different. Both women had been strangled but neither body showed any sign of sexual interference. Outside of the bruising around the neck of both victims there was no other indication of violence and as such there seemed no obvious motive for the attack either. The report also commented on the fact that the young woman's dress had never been found and the Doctor could only surmise that, for whatever reason, the killer had taken it with him.

In terms of murder scenes; one had been a scene of chaos and turmoil and the other one of organised calm. The Doctor also formally recorded that in his opinion these murders were definitely the work of two, different people and that there was nothing to link the crimes in any way.

Jake sat back in his chair. He now felt that he had enough evidence with which to approach Doctor Samuels and ask him to formally identify the body of the young woman across in the mortuary. He knew that once the Doctor Samuels had identified the body there would follow a barrage of questions regarding what his daughter might have been doing there in the first place. Jake also knew that most of those questions would have, at least for just now, to go unanswered.

He did some more work around the office until nearer ten o'clock before he left the building and made his way through to Union Street, where he caught a tram that would take him to Fountainhall Road. From there it was a short walk from the tram stop to the Doctor's house.

It was a large, semi-detached property on three levels. There was a driveway at the side of the house and at the front were a large, bay window and the front door. Jake walked up the front path and knocked on the door.

There was a brief period where it looked as if nothing was going to happen before the door opened and Doctor Samuels stood before him. Jake assumed that the Doctor's housekeeper was still in Elgin.

"Inspector Fraser, do come in," said the Doctor stepping back to allow Jake to enter the hallway.

Inside the hall stretched away in front of him with two doors going off to his right and a staircase on his left. There was clearly more in the way of rooms through the back. Doctor Samuels opened the first door on the right and led Jake in to the large, front room.

"I'm sorry to bother you, Doctor Samuels," Jake said as he accepted the invitation to sit down," but I may be the bearer of some bad news."

Doctor Samuels had sat down opposite and his expression changed little after what Jake had just said.

"Is it about Julia?" he finally said.

"I'm afraid that it is. I think we may have found your daughter," Jake replied, watching the Doctor's face for any sign of emotion.

There was still no real change of expression and what Doctor Samuels said next was delivered with a coldness that Jake found quite difficult to cope with.

"Is she dead?"

Jake was all for the stiff upper lip attitude of the British but there was a time and a place where all that should be forgotten and some real emotion shown. Surely the possible death of your only daughter would be one such time?

"I'm afraid we have reason to believe that she might be," Jake eventually said. "We do have the body of a young woman down at Lodge Walk but until you, or someone else, makes a formal identification we cannot say, categorically, that it is the body of your daughter."

"But you believe that it is her?" pressed Samuels.

"I do," replied Jake with some honesty.

"Do you know what happened?"

"Not at present. The investigation is still in its early stages and so far we have very little to go on."

"Where did you find her?" was the next question asked in the same flat tone of indifference. It really was as if this man was talking about someone he'd never met before.

"I'd rather not discuss the matter any further until we have had a formal identification, if you don't mind Doctor Samuels."

Samuels suddenly sprang to his feet. "Very well, we had better get any formalities out of the way. I will just get my jacket and we can go down to Lodge Walk immediately."

Half an hour later they were both in Jake's office in Lodge Walk. Jake had asked one of the Constables to go over to the mortuary and ask Doctor Symon to prepare the young woman's body for formal identification. As soon as the Constable returned with news that that had been done he then took Doctor Samuels across.

The two Doctors acknowledged the fact that they had met before, though neither could remember exactly where. Doctor Symon led Doctor Samuels across to the slab where a large, white sheet covered the shape of what was quite clearly a dead body.

The sheet was slowly rolled back to reveal the young woman's face. Doctor Samuels looked down with no change to his expression or any other obvious sign of emotion.

"Yes, that is my Julia," he eventually said and stepped back to allow the body to be covered once more.

"My sincere condolences, Doctor Samuels," Jake then said. "Perhaps we can return to my office as there are, unfortunately, one or two more questions that need to be asked in light of what we now know about your daughter. Of course, if you would prefer that we leave these questions until early next week then I would quite understand."

Samuels met the question with the same stoical indifference that he had shown to everything else. Jake just couldn't read this man at all. Was he actually as detached as he appeared to be or was he simply keeping his true emotions hidden from public view. Would those same emotions come tumbling out of him once he was back in the privacy of his own home? Judging from Samuels' next statement, Jake did not think that that would be the case.

"No, if you have any questions then let us deal with them here and now. The sooner you can solve this crime then the sooner I can bury my daughter."

They went back to Jake's office and he arranged for two cups of tea to be brought to them. He even broke one of his own rules by allowing Doctor Samuels to smoke in his office. Once they were both settled Jake steered the conversation in the direction of what Julia seemed to be doing on a Wednesday.

"When we first spoke, Doctor Samuels, you said that your daughter worked at the Sailor's Institute on a Tuesday, Wednesday and Thursday of each week?"

"That is correct," Samuels said immediately.

Jake continued. "We have since ascertained that Julia stopped working at the Institute on a Wednesday around a month ago. Did she ever intimate to you that her work circumstances had changed?"

Samuels looked genuinely confused. "I had no knowledge of her changing her working habits. A month ago you say?"

"Around then, we can't be specific at the moment."

Samuels seemed to be thinking over what had just been said and it was a few seconds before he finally said anything.

"She must have still been leaving the house on a Wednesday or my housekeeper would have told me."

"On the day that she was murdered she was visiting a woman called Jessie McGill in a flat in Marischal Street. Had you ever heard your daughter mention someone by the name of Jessie McGill?"

Samuels again took his time in answering the question.

"I believe she did mention the fact that she worked with someone of that name, but as I said before, Inspector, my daughter did not make friends easily and I really can't imagine why she would feel the need to visit someone that she only knew from work."

"At this moment in time, Doctor Samuels, we do not know why Julia was visiting Jessie McGill, nor do we know if this had become her normal Wednesday routine."

Samuels looked aghast. "Good heavens, man, my daughter would not routinely associate with someone living in Marischal Street."

The words Marischal Street were almost spat out with contempt.

"Whatever the reason, Doctor Samuels, your daughter was definitely there on the day that she was killed."

Samuels disappeared in to a sea of thought again for a few seconds. "But why would Julia lie to me about changing her working practise?"

"It is no more than a theory, Doctor Samuels, but if your daughter was there to meet a male friend whom she thought you would find inappropriate, then it would be perfectly logical for her to want to keep any knowledge of those meetings from you."

Samuels looked as if the air had been punched out of him. "Is there a man involved?"

"We don't know, I did say it was a theory but there is no evidence to back that up at the moment. However, your daughter was young and beautiful and she obviously felt a strong need to lie to you about the fact she was no longer working on a Wednesday. You have to admit that were she to have been seeing a male friend then that would certainly explain a lot."

"Not my Julia," Samuels announced emphatically.

Jake wasn't sure if he should say anything about the missing dress, but eventually decided that it might be a possibility that Doctor Samuels could actually provide a description of it.

"There was one piece of vital evidence missing from the scene of your daughter's death, Doctor Samuels and I was hoping that you might be able to help us with finding it."

Doctor Samuels looked confused but remained silent until Jake had explained himself a little further.

"When we found your daughter she was wearing a dress that actually belonged to Jessie McGill. Your daughter's dress, however, was nowhere to be found and we can only assume that her killer took it away with him. Now I know that you were not there to see what dress Julia was wearing that day but would it be possible for you to check her clothing at home and perhaps, by a process of elimination, draw a conclusion as to which dress we are seeking?"

"I am hardly an expert on ladies' attire, Inspector, but it is just possible that I might notice if one of her favourite dresses was to be missing. I will most certainly have a look when I get home and, should I find what you are looking for, I will let you know."

"Thank you, Doctor Samuels. I realise all this must be extremely painful for you but I would appreciate anything you can do that might help us solve this case," said Jake as finished his tea.

"May I ask one question, Inspector?" Samuels then said.

"You may ask, Doctor Samuels, but I may not be able to answer."

"Had my daughter been sexually interfered with in any way?"

Jake might not always have answered such a question but he felt a deep need to put this man's mind at rest regarding any other form of violence that might have befallen his daughter.

"The Doctor's report was very specific on that subject, Doctor Samuels, your daughter's virginity was still intact and there were no other signs to indicate that she had been sexually molested in any way."

"She was a virgin?" Samuels said. The words appeared to be out of his mouth before he realised he was saying them but it was the tone of disbelief that Jake picked up on immediately.

"You had reason to believe otherwise?" he asked.

Samuels now pulled himself together and returned to his more normal, bombastic self.

"No, of course not."

Jake felt that he had probably asked enough questions for one session and he made arrangements for Doctor Samuel to be taken home.

After Doctor Samuels had departed Jake remembered that he had never been round to the Douglas Hotel to confirm that the good Doctor had stayed there on Tuesday night as he had said he had done. Jake put his jacket on and took a walk round.

Jake spoke to a personable, young man at the reception desk who was able to check the register and confirm that Doctor Samuels had certainly booked a room for the Tuesday night and that there had indeed been a medical dinner that night that had been attended by around thirty doctors from all over Aberdeen.

There was nothing further that Jake needed to know so he returned to Lodge Walk where he cleared some more paperwork before deciding, just after lunchtime, that it might be the right time to pay a visit to the weasel-faced menace, Scroggins.

Jake knew that on most afternoons Scroggins could be found in The Ramparts public house, which was situated on the corner of the Castlegate. The Ramparts had been there for decades and had little done to it, by way of decoration, in that time. The frontage was dirty with paint peeling around the door and windows and as Jake approached that front door he could hear the usual rowdy noises coming from the regulars who had been imbibing for some time.

Jake walked through the door and spotted Scroggins, almost at once, standing over by the skittles. Jake marched across to him and took hold of his arm with some force.

"A word, Mr Scroggins, through here," Jake said as he pulled him through to the toilet at the back.

Once they were alone Jake spun Scroggins around and slammed his back against the wall with such a force that he was left with little breath in his lungs. Jake stood up close, to make his point, but found the experience all the more unbearable as Scroggins' breath was beyond repulsive.

"Listen carefully you odious piece of shit," Jake began, keeping his arm close to Scroggins' throat, "if you as much as walk down the same side of the street as Alice I will personally seek you out and rip your head off. I want you to leave her alone, completely alone; no contact whatsoever. If you don't leave her alone, Scroggins, then you will have me to answer to, do I make myself clear?"

As Jake spat the final words in to Scroggins' face he applied even more pressure to the man's throat so that he was once more gasping for breath. He was clearly shaken by the experience, however this did not stop him trying to argue about the potential effects it would have on his business were he to completely ignore Alice.

"She is one of my employees, Mr Fraser and if I were to carry out your instructions then that would obviously have an effect on my business."

Jake's anger rose in an instant and the pressure on Scroggins' throat nearly closed off his windpipe completely.

"Look, as of this moment, Alice is no longer an employee of yours or anyone else for that matter. You will leave her alone and you will make it known to your many contacts that she is no longer a woman who should be approached by scum such as yourself, who may have thoughts of a little sexual activity in mind. Now, am I continuing to make myself clear?"

Jake stopped short of actually killing Scroggins, who was now on his knees gasping for air and clutching his throat. It was a little while before a coughing fit had passed and Scroggins seemed able to speak again. He slowly got to his feet.

"I'm hearing you, Mr Fraser," he finally said. "I'll leave Alice alone, as you suggest, but I need to remind you that she is staying in one of my properties and at present I ask no rent from her...."

Jake snapped again and pushed Scroggins back against the wall once more. He stepped up close to him again and spoke directly in to his face.

"Alice has paid her rent through the work you've forced her to do. I'm guessing that she has paid you ten times more money than any rental agreement would have been so don't you try and tell me that she is due you anything by way of lost income."

Scroggins tried to defuse the situation a little.

"I wasn't going to suggest anything of the kind, Mr Fraser, I was merely pointing out that she is currently living in one of my properties."

Jake stepped back. "Okay, Scroggins, I agree that that little shit-hole in which Alice lives does come under your ownership and as such, I will arrange for her to move out so that you can put some other poor wretch in there to maintain your income. In return for that, however, you will do as I ask. Now repeat after me," Jake said and once more had Scroggins pinned to the wall. "I will never speak to Alice again and if I see her coming my way I will make a point of crossing the street. I will also inform my contacts of this agreement."

Having heard those words from Scroggins own lips Jake then turned and left. As he passed through the bar area he was aware of all eyes not only being on him but then quickly diverting to the toilet door. Jake felt sure that many of the regulars were convinced that he had just killed Scroggins.

Jake returned to work feeling satisfied with himself that he had definitely got his message across to Scroggins. Of course, he had said quite a lot to Scroggins in a fit of anger, but he hadn't actually thought through the consequences of those words. It was all very well taking Alice out of the property in which she currently lived, but he had no idea where he would put her after that.

He knew that there was only one place to which she could realistically move and that was downstairs to his place. The main problem with that arrangement was that she would still be in the same building and men might still come looking for paid favours. Jake felt sure that Scroggins would put the word out on Alice but it might take some time for that word to filter around town.

For Alice to be completely removed from her previous profession Jake knew that he would have to get her as far away from the Guestrow as was possible. Jake thought it best to get home and move Alice immediately so that she would no longer be bothered with unwanted callers.

It was mid-afternoon when he got back to the Guestrow and he found Alice still lying in bed. She looked so peaceful and it seemed that she had hardly moved since Jake had left all those hours earlier.

Jake gently woke Alice and got her out of bed. She put on a dress and he briefly explained what he had said to Scroggins.

"So you see," he concluded, "we need to get your things down here as quickly as possible. I'll find a more permanent solution as quickly as I can, but at least for the moment you can stay here and forget about the need to do anything for scum such as Scroggins."

"Oh Jake," Alice said and threw her arms around his neck," am I really free of that awful man?"

"Totally clear. Now let's get your stuff out of his property and that way he will have absolutely no claim over you whatsoever."

Alice seemed reluctant to let go of Jake. She eventually kissed him and stepped back. They went upstairs and Jake was appalled at the living conditions that Alice had had to suffer. The walls were marked with damp and there was an almost permanent cold chill in the air, even though the outside temperature was still quite reasonable.

Everything that truly belonged to Alice could be packed in to one suitcase and Jake found it sad to think that a girl of Alice's age could have such few belongings. The only positive aspect of it all was that it made it all the easier to move her. Satisfied that they had collected everything they went back downstairs where Jake opened a couple of bottles of beer and they celebrated the start of the next phase of Alice's life.

At that point in time there was no thought of where she might go next and no real plan as to how she might get there. For just now it was all about the joy of breaking away from the hold Scroggins had had over her and for Alice, the further joy that she had found a man who was more than willing to help her make something of her life. She went over to Jake and put her arms around his neck again.

She kissed him with a passion that almost overwhelmed him.

"I love you, Jake Fraser," she said and kissed him again. She then stood up and took hold of Jake's hand. She led him over to the bed and they made love for an hour, losing themselves in the feelings they had for each other and the burning desire to make each other happy.

It also continued to be the only way that Alice felt she could truly say thank you.

EIGHT   .

Sunday 16 September - lunchtime onwards

It was another glorious day. Jake had wakened with the sound of the church bells calling the faithful to worship. He was definitely not going to be one of them. He had seen too many terrible sights, in his working life, to feel that there was any place in his life for religion and in his opinion, the misguided belief that God was the answer to everything. He couldn't help thinking that if there was a God who cared for his people then why would he let someone like Scroggins ruin the lives of so many young girls.

Jake turned on to his back and looked across at Alice who was facing the wall and sleeping soundly. After their love-making session the previous afternoon they had spent the evening having a meal and talking about what the future might hold. Jake had gone in to the office, briefly and by the time he had got back home Alice had been fast asleep.

She seemed so settled, safe in the knowledge that she would no longer have to be groped at by strange men; no longer have to take money for sexual favours and then be expected to hand nearly all of that money over to Scroggins.

Jake pondered on what might happen next. He even had a passing thought about making this arrangement a permanent feature in his life. Maybe there was a possibility that Alice could live with him all the time.

Then he considered the practicality of it all. She would always be an ex-prostitute and no one in the City Police would be likely to accept the fact that a senior officer was living with such a woman. There was also the other little matter of how Alice would ever be able to make legitimate money for herself. He didn't think he would be able to go on supporting her in the future and she would then need to find work for herself.

Jake looked at the bedside clock and decided that it was time to get up. He was due at Mary's in a little over an hour so he made his way over to kettle and filled it from the tap. He then went out to the toilet on the landing to relieve himself. On his return he poured some water in to the bowl he always used and started to shave.

He had managed to do all that without Alice moving at all. However, as he started to splash some water on his face there was movement in the bed.

"Good morning," a sleepy voice announced.

"Good morning," said Jake, looking round at Alice, who had sat up in bed.

"What time are you due at Mrs Thomson's?" Alice then asked.

"Around noon."

Jake pulled on some clothes and then stopped halfway trying to fit the collar to his shirt. No matter how much he tried he couldn't get the stud in place.

"Let me help," Alice then said and jumped out of bed. She hurried across to him, her small breasts jigging and took the collar from him. Having a naked woman standing so close to him made it slightly more difficult for Jake to keep his mind on the matter of an ill-fitting collar but fortunately for him, Alice soon had the collar attached and he was then standing in front of the mirror, combing his hair.

Alice sat on the edge of the bed, completely unfazed by her nudity. Jake looked across at her and again he was overcome with an overwhelming desire to protect this young woman. He just wanted to throw his arms around her and stop the world from trying to harm her in any way.

Was that love? He let the thought pass and then made two cups of tea for them. He suggested that Alice might like to put something on and then told her to help herself to what little food he had in the flat. After he had drunk his tea, Jake kissed Alice and then left.

Outside the sun shone and the air was as warm as to have many of the men he passed out walking without a jacket. Some of the women carried parasols to protect them from the worst of the sun's heat and there was a general air of contentment on the streets of Aberdeen that morning.

Jake made his way round the Viaduct and then through Leadside Road to Esslemont Avenue. He then walked up the hill to Mary's flat. He entered the building and rang her bell. The door was opened almost at once and a smiling Mary stepped back to allow Jake to enter.

Jake was shown through to the back room this time. This was the room where Mary spent most of her time. There was an alcove in the back left hand corner, in which she had her bed, but this area was covered by a curtain, which was kept shut during the day.

Directly across from the alcove was the wall in which the back window was situated and immediately below the window was the double sink. To the left of the sinks was the cooker and between the sinks sat an impressive looking wringer.

There were three chairs placed around a small table, which was pretty much set in the centre of the room. Against the wall to the right of the sinks was another table that had been set for dinner. To the left of that table was a door, which Jake knew led to the larder, situated underneath the landing stair.

The smell of cooking filled the air and Jake could not wait to get seated and to start enjoying Mary's fine culinary skills. First, however, Mary poured a couple of glasses of sherry and they sat in more comfortable chairs to drink them.

"How are you doing?" Jake then asked.

"I think I'm doing quite well," Mary replied. "Sometimes I burst in to tears for no apparent reason, but most of the time I feel that I am slowly coming to terms with the loss of Tommy."

"Time is a great healer," Jake then said and Mary smiled.

"Yes, everyone wants to tell me that."

They finished drinking their sherry around further general conversation before Mary stood up and made her way over to the cooker. She began to ladle soup in to two plates and as she did so Jake found himself studying her. She really was a very attractive woman with a figure that would have made most women proud.

Strangely though, as he sat looking at Mary Thomson, Jake could not stop himself from thinking about Margaret Gifford. It was strange how Margaret's face kept appearing in his mind; strange that he had an overwhelming desire to see her again. Perhaps these thoughts were driven by some strange notion that there just might be a spark of interest being shown in him by Margaret. Perhaps there was a possible relationship forming there and one thing that Jake now knew for sure was that there could never be anything other than friendship between himself and Mary.

On the other hand there was still Alice. She was undoubtedly a problem needing solved and she was so much a part of his life at the moment that trying to have a relationship, of any kind, with another woman might prove a trifle awkward. Why was it always the forbidden fruit that seemed to taste the best?

Jake stopped staring at Mary and leapt to his feet. He crossed the room and offered to carry the soup plates over to the table. They were soon seated and enjoying what was a thick, hearty broth made from a ham shank. The soup was quite salty but tasty none the less.

"Have you thought about you might do in the future?" Jake eventually asked after they had eaten most of their soup in silence.

"I've been thinking of nothing else," Mary replied. "With Tommy gone there really isn't much of a future for me. I've never had to fend for myself up until now and it won't be easy starting at my age. To be honest I'm just not ready to start making plans just quite yet. Tommy's pension will help for the moment but I suppose, looking longer term, I'll have to either find myself a job or a new husband.

Jake knew that Mary was joking about the husband but the thought did cross his mind that she would always find it easy to attract men, should she ever wish to do so.

"Well, Mary, you could always be a cook because that soup was excellent," Jake quipped and they both laughed.

Mary rose from the table and took the dirty plates over to the sink. She then went over to the cooker and took the ham she had used for the soup out of a pan and laid it on a board for carving. After cutting the meat off the bone and placing it on two plates she then added potatoes and peas and brought them over to the table. They were fairly quiet again as they ate the main course and once they had finished, Mary suggested that they go through to the front room to have a cup of tea.

A few minutes later they were both seated through on the comfortable chairs with a cup of tea in hand.

"My sister has invited me down to Edinburgh to stay with her for a while," Mary suddenly announced.

"A change of scenery might do you some good," added Jake. "How long will you be away?"

"I really don't know, Agnes has suggested a month at least."

An idea popped in to Jake's head. "Would you be averse to someone else staying here while you are away?"

Mary smiled. "Are you thinking of moving in?"

Jake's face reddened with embarrassment. "I've just taken Alice away from Scroggins, which means that she is now, currently, homeless. I have her staying with me at the moment but I know that that arrangement cannot go on for much longer. I was wondering if she might stay here. It would only be while you were away and that would buy me a little time to come up with something a bit more permanent."

Mary thought for a moment. "I don't wish to be unkind, Jake, but would Alice not attract a certain type of gentleman to this area were they to learn of her new, all be it temporary, accommodation?"

"I understand your concerns, Mary, but I have Scroggins well warned that if anyone bothers Alice then I will personally hunt the little weasel down and separate his head from his shoulders. I also firmly believe that if I can get Alice to a better neighbourhood then it will take away the possibility of her simply bumping in to her previous clients."

"I'm not at all sure that a change of neighbourhood, within Aberdeen, would make enough difference to allow Alice to completely escape the life she is trying to leave behind," Mary insisted.

Jake gave it some thought. He knew she was correct, of course, but for the moment could not think of a better plan. Mary allowed a few more seconds to pass before speaking again.

"If I may make a suggestion, why don't you let me take Alice to Edinburgh with me?"

The suggestion hit Jake hard in the stomach as if someone had punched him. As an idea it was obviously a perfect solution to the situation, but the thought of Alice not being around was something that he had not contemplated. He wasn't at all sure he could agree to her leaving Aberdeen, even if it was only for a month.

"What would she do down there?" he asked while his mind continued to turn things over.

"My sister has a very big house and I'm sure she could appreciate an extra pair of helping hands. It would give Alice a chance to make some proper money and to be able to then spend that money on herself. If she likes it down there then we can arrange something more longer term for her, but if she really hates it then she can come back to Aberdeen when I do, even if that is a few weeks away."

Jake knew that this was the best plan for Alice. No one in Edinburgh would know who she was and it would give her a proper chance to start her life over again.

"And you don't mind helping her?" he then said.

"I know how much she means to you, Jake and I'd be delighted to give the girl a proper chance in life."

Jake pondered a few seconds longer. He now realised that any argument he may have made against Alice going to Edinburgh would have been purely selfish.

"In that case, let's do it," Jake finally said, though he was quickly adding, "One thing, however, Alice hasn't really got proper clothes to wear. If I give you some money would you arrange to buy a couple of dresses for her so that she doesn't feel too out of place in Edinburgh?"

"I leave for Edinburgh on the mid-morning train on Saturday. I'll get another ticket for the journey and I'll let my sister know that she'll have another member of staff, at least on a trial basis. If you bring Alice over to me on Thursday, she can sleep here for a couple of nights and it'll give us time to buy some clothes and get them packed. I have an extra case that she can use. She can provide me with some company on the journey down and to the people we meet down there she will just be one of my sister's maids, so no one should ever think of her as being anything different."

"I hope Alice sees this as being good for her," Jake then said.

"She may take it bad at first but I'm sure we can win her round," Mary added. "This will be the perfect chance for her to make something of herself and I'm sure she'll see the sense in getting out of Aberdeen if she wants to do that."

Jake took out his wallet and counted out some money. "I have no idea how much dresses are likely to cost so you'd better take this and I'll add a little more to cover the cost of the ticket."

Mary took the money, counted out some and gave him the rest back. "Clearly you have no idea about the price of anything if you think I'd need all that for a couple of dresses," Mary commented as they returned their attention briefly to their tea.

"Going back to this place," Jake then said looking around the room," I'll arrange for the constable on the beat to keep an eye as he passes. A house left empty for a while could well become a target for some of our house-breakers and I'd hate to see any of your possessions removed while you were away."

"Thank you, although there's nothing here that is likely to be of any interest to anyone."

"Unfortunately they don't know what might be here until they've broken in and that can do enough damage in itself," Jake explained. "If you keep me up to date by letter then I can make any necessary arrangements for you coming home, once you've decided when that will be."

Mary looked around the room and her eyes misted with tears. "I sometimes wonder if I ever want to come back here," she then said. "The memories are just too powerful and getting over Tommy's death may prove impossible if I were to go on staying here. On the other hand, the thought of moving somewhere else on a permanent basis scares me more than a little."

"Go to Edinburgh and enjoy the experience," Jake then said. "Let time heal your heart a little first and then you might feel strong enough to start making decisions on your future. There's no rush you know."

Mary smiled as she dabbed at her tears again. "Ah yes, time, the great healer."

Mary freshened their tea and they then sat back and enjoyed some general chat about happier times. It didn't last for very long, however, as Mary's thoughts were soon back to her dead husband.

"Jake, do you think that Tommy had turned bad by the time he was killed?"

Jake was slightly taken aback by the bluntness of the question. "I really don't know, Mary. We just don't have enough evidence on which to make a judgement."

"I've had a lot of time to think just lately, Jake and I've come to the conclusion that Tommy was a changed man in the last months of his life. With hindsight I know now that it was the little things that weren't the same. I didn't really notice at the time, but thinking back Tommy seemed to be more on edge, more likely to get annoyed. There was no doubt he was drinking more as well."

Jake tried to pass it off with a joke. "Now, Mary, you know that Tommy always liked a drink."

"But not every night," Mary replied without a sign that she could lighten on the subject. "It seemed as if there was something heavy weighing on his mind, Jake. There were times when he may have been in the room with me but his mind was miles away and any time I asked him if anything was wrong he passed it off with comments of work being busy or whatever. Then there's the matter of how he died," Mary continued, though now she was reaching for a handkerchief again as she was clearly upsetting herself just talking about Tommy.

Jake moved a little closer and put a comforting hand on Mary's shoulder. "Don't upset yourself," he said.

Mary wiped her eyes then looked up at Jake. "I need to face these things, Jake. I need to prepare myself for you and your colleagues possibly having to tell me things about Tommy that I don't particularly want to hear. However, if my husband had turned crooked in his last few months then we all need to know."

"Mary, there could be a variety of reasons for Tommy getting a bit moody in those months leading up to his death. That doesn't mean to say that he was hiding anything criminal from you."

"I used to think I knew everything there was to know about Tommy but now I'm just not so sure."

Jake sat down again. He didn't know what to say next so he let the silence hang in the air a bit longer and then tried to move the subject on to happier topics. Eventually he managed and they finished their time together laughing about memories gone by that had not involved Tommy. It was soon time for Jake to leave.

They finalised arrangements for Jake to bring Alice across on the Thursday and Mary also gave Jake a key for the property so that he could drop in now and again and check that all was well. With further thanks for the food and a last comforting embrace, Jake made his way out of the door and set off down Esslemont Avenue.

He made his way home and sat Alice down. He poured a couple of beers and then sat down beside her. He went through what Mary had suggested and at first he could see the look of disappointment and almost horror that crossed Alice's face. However, he continued to explain what they were suggesting and more importantly why they were suggesting it.

He eventually began to get through to Alice that this really was the best option for her if she wanted to escape her past life altogether.

"But I'll miss you," she then said and threw her arms around his neck. "You look after me like no one else has ever done."

"Mary will look after you in Edinburgh, even though you'll be there to work and make some money. If you really don't like it down there then you will come back to Aberdeen when Mary does. At least by being away for a few weeks it will give your past clients a chance to forget about you."

Even Alice could see that everything Jake had said had made sense. She didn't want to be away from Jake but the idea of being away from Aberdeen certainly wasn't a bad one. The further she was from Scroggins the better.

Alice eventually happily agreed with everything and by the time the beer was finished she was laughing and joking about becoming a lady in Edinburgh and how posh that all sounded. Jake laughed with her but in his heart he felt pain at the fact he wouldn't be able to see her or to hold her for some time to come.

As if trying to compensate for that he drew her too him and gave her the tightest embrace she had probably ever had. He didn't have to say anything, Alice knew from that embrace how much he was going to miss her.

As usual, the only thing that she could think about doing was to take Jake to bed and let him make love to her. On this occasion, however, Jake did not want to make love, he just wanted to hold her. He just wanted to feel her lovely, little naked body pressed against his own and he just wanted, for one last time, to enjoy that feeling of being this girl's protector.

Then they both fell asleep.

NINE

Monday 17 September - early to late afternoon

Detective Superintendent Samuel Harris was shown in to the Chief Constable's office at a little after one o'clock in the afternoon. Harris was a short, stocky looking character with a thick, cultured beard and sharp, piercing eyes. He removed his hat as he entered the room and shook hands with the Chief.

"So nice to meet you, Superintendent," Anderson said, "I hope you had a pleasant journey down from Balmoral?"

"Indeed I did, sir, the weather has been truly amazing and I have to say that the scenery on the way here was absolutely magnificent."

"The scenery is always magnificent, Superintendent," Anderson then said, "though as to the weather, unfortunately I cannot claim that that is exactly normal for the North East of Scotland. However, we take what we can when we can."

Harris smiled. "Well the King and Queen have certainly enjoyed a relaxing time at Balmoral and they are both sorry to have to return to London on the twenty-seventh."

"I'm sure they are," agreed Anderson, inviting Harris to sit down. He then offered the Superintendent a cup of tea, which he quickly accepted as he had not had time for any lunch that day and his stomach was already growling.

"Milk and sugar?" the Chief then asked.

"Milk and three sugars, please sir."

Anderson left the room for a moment while he found a constable to get the tea organised, then he returned to the office and sat down at his desk across from where Harris had now made himself comfortable.

"Is the main purpose of your visit to allow us to review the arrangements that have been put in place for the royal visit?" the Chief then asked.

"Not at all, Chief Constable," Harris replied, "the safety of the King and Queen, whilst they are in Aberdeen, is firmly in your hands and I am sure that you have everything covered with regard to that. I do not come to review your arrangements, sir, but I may be complicating them a little with what I have to tell you."

Anderson sat forward with concern etched on his face.

"Their Majesties are not changing their plans are they?"

"No, nothing like that," Harris replied with a wave of his hand. "My news concerns someone who may wish harm to the King and Queen and I felt it was in everyone's interest in Aberdeen to be aware of all the facts."

"In what way does this person wish to bring anarchy to what ought to be a day of great joy for this city?" Anderson then asked.

Harris now sat forward as if fearing there were ears close by to hear what he was about to say.

"As you will know the wedding day of the King and Queen of Spain last May was completely overshadowed by the fact that some lunatic threw a bomb at the royal coach moments after the wedding ceremony. As you will also be aware the Spanish royal couple were at Udny Castle last month for the grouse shooting. A pleasant time was had by all and the visit, I'm pleased to say, passed off without incident. However, we knew that they were followed to this area by a notorious Spanish anarchist by the name of Sergio Arconada. Arconada is a known acquaintance of Frederico Aguilafuenie who was arrested at the beginning of July whilst being a nuisance to the Spanish Royal Family in La Granja. We believe that Arconada also knew the man who threw the bomb in Madrid. Arconada was in lodgings at a farm in the Udny Castle area but, perhaps due to the fact he knew we were watching him, he did nothing of concern while he was there. After the King and Queen left the area we maintained our interest in Arconada but, unfortunately, he managed to slip away in the night and we no longer know where he is. We checked the railway station and also some of the local carriage companies but there has been no evidence of him definitely leaving this area. I fear that having failed to take any action against the Spanish royal couple that he will now plan something against our own royal couple, especially with the Spanish Queen being the niece of our own King."

"When did you last know where he was?" Anderson then asked, his mind already thinking of that chest that Mabel Lassiter had taken off the London train.

"He disappeared during the third week of August I'm afraid, so he has had some time to move here and set a plan in motion."

"Is he dangerous?" the Chief then said.

"Many of these anarchists are dangerous, sir, but to what extent Arconada would be prepared to go then that I couldn't say. We don't know that much about the gentleman apart from the fact he seems to follow the Spanish royalty around."

"So he could well still be doing just that?" Anderson added quickly.

"Indeed he could, we just don't know for certain and as such, I think it would be wiser if you prepared for the possibility of Arconada still being in the area," Harris said as the door opened and a young constable came in carrying a tray on which was placed two cups of tea and a plate of biscuits. He carried it over and laid it down on the Chief's desk.

"That is your one, sir," the constable said, rather nervously pointing to one of the cups.

"Thank you, Leask," Anderson said as the young constable turned and headed back towards the open door.

Anderson passed the other cup across to Harris who picked it up and then gratefully accepted the offer of a biscuit or two. Once they were both settled again Harris returned to where they were in the conversation.

"I took a drawing that we had made of Arconada," Harris began, laying his cup down again and fishing in his inside pocket for a piece of paper. "I believe it is quite a good likeness."

Anderson took the piece of paper from Harris and unfolded it. The drawing was of a handsome looking young man, possibly in his twenties, who had a thick head of wavy, black hair and close set eyes. Had anyone looked at the drawing, without any prior knowledge of the subject, they would have found it hard to believe that the person illustrated was in fact a wanted anarchist capable of murder.

"He looks a personable enough chap in the drawing," Anderson commented, "so what makes someone like that feel the need to rebel against common decency?"

"Anarchists are constantly making a political statement and quite frankly they rarely care how that statement gets made as long as it garners some publicity along the way. The more front page news they can drum up the happier they feel about getting their message, all be it a somewhat misguided message, across to the public at large. There is a sense, certainly down in London, that some of these women who are now shouting for the right to vote are heading down the same road. They take action to get noticed and care little for what others might think of them. I do not believe that these women will ever do anything particularly dramatic but the horrific incident in Madrid has already shown how far these anarchists are prepared to go in support of their twisted cause."

"Let us hope that that is not the case on the twenty-seventh of this month," Anderson added.

"I am sure there will be little opportunity for anyone to get that close to the King and Queen, Chief Constable."

"Unfortunately, as you well know Superintendent, a person does not have to get that close to fire a gun or throw a bomb. As you have already said these politically driven fanatics are resourceful in their approach to criminal activity. We, therefore, have to be equally resourceful to combat them."

"It would be unlikely that, unless he carries it with him, Arconada would have had the time to organise a bomb for later this month. It would also be unlikely, unless he has local connections, that he could have got his hands on a gun so I would assume, if he is in Aberdeen to do anything at all, that he will refrain from doing anything too dramatic. They sometimes settle for something as annoying as throwing a bag of flour. As I said, how they get their message across is not the point, it is the publicity that really matters."

"Am I to take it, Superintendent that you and your men will be travelling with the royal couple?"

"Myself and five men will be able to assist you on the day, Chief Constable. I will also have two men on horseback to ride just behind the royal carriage."

"Excellent. In that case I will double the number of men I had intended to post at the points where the royal couple are to disembark. I will also have one of my best men review the arrangements for the day, just to ensure nothing has been missed. It is often the case that the closer you are to something the more chance there is of you missing something."

"As I knew you would, Chief Constable, you have everything in hand and I feel confident that the day will go off without incident. In the meantime, if I hear any more about Arconada, I will contact you immediately."

Both men stood and shook hands. Harris then left the office and made his way downstairs and out of the building. He could just about remember how to find his way back to the Joint Station where he boarded the first train that could take him back to Ballater.

Anderson sat down and pondered on what had just been discussed. It was certainly another unwanted inconvenience having to now plan for the possibility that this Arconada was in Aberdeen. It would have been so much easier had they known that he was in the city and better still, exactly where he was.

Anderson rose from his desk and crossed to the door of his office. He opened the door and shouted for Constable Leask who came hurrying from another of the rooms along the corridor. Leask was despatched to find Jake and to bring him back to the Chief's office as soon as possible.

Leask hurried downstairs to Jake's office where he found him hunched over his desk reading through some paperwork that had just arrived.

"Excuse me, sir," Leask said, as he popped his head around the door, "but the Chief Constable would like to see you in his office."

"Very well, I'll be up in a moment," Jake replied and sat back in his chair, slightly annoyed at having his concentration interrupted but none the less having to accept it as it was the Chief who sought his company.

Jake arrived in the Chief's office and was invited to take a seat. The Chief then went over all that he had discussed with Harris and introduced the possibility that Mabel Lassiter may have brought Arconada in to Aberdeen. He concluded his mini report by asking Jake to review all the plans to date just in case something had been missed.

Jake already had a very busy schedule and the idea of now going over old ground regarding the royal visit did not fire him with much enthusiasm. He was not usually in the habit of questioning the Chief but on this occasion he had started to do so before he's even thought about it.

"Forgive me for saying so, sir, but surely your plans have already taken in to account any eventuality. Also, I really don't believe that there is any connection between this lost anarchist and Mabel Lassiter. It seems highly unlikely to me that I would come up with anything that you had missed."

"If Arconada wanted to slip back in to Aberdeen then it seems perfectly possible that he could have made his way to a station, on route from Dundee and had himself put on board in that chest. I mean, have you confirmed that the chest came all the way from London, it could have been put on at any stage of the journey?"

Jake had not actually confirmed that the chest had come all the way from London, but he was willing to bet his pension that it had. However, rather than upset the Chief any further he agreed to check out the full details of the chest.

"This Arconada has followed the King and Queen of Spain around Europe, Jake and surely he would not have done that had he not intended to do something at some point in time."

"Perhaps to the King and Queen of Spain, sir," Jake added, "but there is no evidence to even hint at him wishing to bring harm to our Royal Family."

"The Queen of Spain is our own dear King's niece, Jake; it's not as if the families are not directly connected. These anarchists are capable of anything if they feel that their actions, in some way, further their cause" the Chief then said as if he was an expert on all matters relating to anarchy." As long as they get the publicity for their actions they'll be happy. That being the case it is quite likely that, having not had a chance to do anything against the Spanish royal couple, this man may now turn his attention to our own King and Queen."

"I don't disagree, sir," Jake added, "but as I said there is no evidence whatsoever to say that he will be planning to do something here. I would suggest, sir that any action these anarchists take will most likely be in London where they can maximise that precious publicity and perhaps make a bigger statement at the same time."

"Perhaps, Jake," said the Chief, "or perhaps he might view he has a better chance of doing something in a backwater like Aberdeen. When the safety of our own Royal Family is at stake I do not think it is asking too much to ensure that we have covered everything."

Jake knew he would not move the Chief once he had made his mind up. "Very well," he eventually said, "but is there any chance that I might get a little bit more in the way of assistance. With two main enquiries already on the go and an active part to play in Tommy's case I'm not sure I have much more time to devote to reviewing royal plans."

The Chief thought for a moment.

"Obviously staffing remains tight until the twenty-seventh, but I am sure I can find a few men for you in the lead up to that date. The best option would probably be to allocate to you the other three men who are due to retire after the royal visit. That will give you another three along with Smith and Mathieson so hopefully that will suffice as there is no other resource available at the moment."

"Thank you, sir that will be a big help."

Jake left the office and made his way back down to his own office. Inside he was boiling with anger at the fact he seemed to be getting more and more work piled on to him while some of the other Inspectors were being left with very little to do.

Sandy Wilson, for example, only seemed to have Tommy's murder on which to spend his time while here was Jake with two murders, an input to Tommy's investigation and now he was expected to review security arrangements for the royal visit.

Ah well, at least it confirmed that the Chief had faith in him. That obviously wasn't the case for some of his colleagues.

When he got back to his desk Jake returned to the Doctor's report on Julia Samuels murder. Jake ran an eye across it again as if hoping that reading it afresh would bring forward some vital piece of information that he had missed the last time. There was nothing new; it was all still the same.

An attractive, young woman had had her life snuffed out for no apparent reason. She had died leaving far more questions than answers; in fact Jake was concerned that they would never get to the bottom of what had happened that morning in that Marischal Street flat.

Jake gave some thought to the two murder scenes again and tried to picture the type of man who might have committed the crimes. Julia Samuels had been murdered by someone who seemed to have shown signs of remorse at what he had done and yet the same man had murdered Jessie McGill without, it seemed, the same consideration as to how she would be found. He had dumped Jessie's body on the floor like a discarded rag.

There was also the mystery of the dress. The killer had stripped Jessie and yet left Julia fully clothed. However, it had been Julia's dress that he had taken away.

But above all, he had not touched either woman in a sexual manner. A man has two women at his mercy in an environment where no one could have interrupted him and yet he had no inclination to rape either of them.

Jake knew that rape was not always an active part in the murder of a woman. There were other reasons for killing a woman but the removal of clothing seemed to indicate sexual intent and yet nothing further happened.

Perhaps Julia Samuels had been there to meet a young man and perhaps, as Mathieson had suggested, she had rebuffed his advances. Had that been the case, however, it would have been Julia Samuels who would have been found naked. There seemed no logical reason for Jessie to be the one found naked.

On the other hand Mabel Lassiter had been a prime example of a crime driven purely by sexual lust. The man who murdered her didn't just want to kill her, he wanted to make her suffer. He took enjoyment from inflicting pain and death was just that last minute release from all the suffering he had brought upon her.

The more Jake thought about both cases, however, the more he came to the conclusion that one aspect of both crimes seemed to be the same. He felt sure that Mabel Lassiter had known her killer and he now felt equally sure that Julia Samuels knew her killer as well.

That could be the only explanation for Julia being treated the way she was; her killer knew her and had instant remorse for having killed her. By arranging her body on the bed and leaving her fully clothed it was his way of apologising for what he had done.

But who was he? That was the burning question that Jake was still nowhere near answering.

Prompted by the thoughts he had just had, Jake decided to go back to the Palace Hotel and see if he could uncover anything further in the Mabel Lassiter case.

On his way up Union Street he stopped at the Empress Cafe, which was just passed the top of Market Street, where he had a meat pie with gravy and washed it down with a mug of tea. It was quite rare for Jake to eat in the middle of the day but a fine drizzle had started to fall as he had walked up Union Street and it had provided him with the perfect excuse to seek shelter.

The cafe was busy, which was normal for a place that held weddings as well as provide tea and cakes to the, mainly ladies, of the city. Jake enjoyed his food and watching his fellow diners for half an hour. By the time he left the cafe the sun was hinting at putting in another appearance and the drizzle had ceased.

Jake continued up Union Street until he reached the Palace Hotel. He went inside and made his way over to the reception desk where a girl, who looked to be no older than eighteen or nineteen, was standing smiling at him as he approached. She was one of those plain looking, young women, who seemed to have an aversion to looking in the least bit attractive. She wore the clothes of an older woman with her hair tied up in a tight and unattractive bun.

"Can I help you?" she announced as Jake reached the desk.

Jake showed her his identification. "Is Mr Bainbridge in his office?"

"I believe he is......"the woman began.

Jake did not wait for further discussion but simply made his way to the door of Bainbridge's office, knocked once and went in. On this occasion he did not find the manager hurriedly pushing incriminating evidence in to a top drawer. No, on this occasion Bainbridge was actually reading through some financial information relevant to the business of the hotel.

He looked up with some annoyance as Jake walked in to the room. "I really wish you would let someone show you in to my office," Bainbridge said, waving away the young woman who was now standing behind Jake.

Jake closed the door and sat down. Bainbridge now sat quietly and awaited some new line of questioning to begin.

"Perhaps you would be so kind as to arrange for the desk register to be brought through here for a moment," Jake said.

Bainbridge considered saying something but decided against it. He left the room for a few moments but was soon back with the requested register, which he placed on the desk in front of Jake.

Jake took a note of the names of those people who had registered around the same time as Mabel Lassiter. He also took a note of the men who had registered the day before.

"I believe that when Mr Scott dealt with Martin Bagshaw there was some fuss made about the fact Miss Lassiter would be taking a large chest with her?"

"That is the case."

"Was the chest coming from London or being put on the train somewhere else?" Jake then asked.

"I always assumed it had come from London with Miss Lassiter but, to be honest, no one here would know where the chest went on board the train."

"I know roughly what was said between Mr Scott and this Martin Bagshaw but I'll still need an official statement sometime soon. I also have a statement from Mr Hardy regarding him finding the body. Apart from yourself, Mr Bainbridge, is there any other member of your staff whom you think might be helpful to this investigation?"

Bainbridge thought for a moment. "As far as I am aware there was no one else directly involved with Miss Lassiter."

"Very well. At least I now have some fresh names to check so we may yet come up with something useful."

Jake left the hotel and headed back to Lodge Walk where he found the box containing all the witness statements that had been taken from the staff and guests of the hotel on the day of the murder being discovered. Jake now sat down with the list of names he had just taken from the hotel and the pile of statements.

He began to work his way through the names in the register and checking them against the statements that had been taken. As he matched a name to a statement he then took time to read the statement they had made and only after he had done that did he place a tick against the name.

However, most statements amounted to nothing more than the person saying they didn't really know anything.

Most of the guests had claimed to be in their rooms, or down in the dining area, at the time of the murder. No one had seen or heard anything of significance and yet they nearly all expressed their horror at what had happened beneath the roof of what was perceived to be a better class of hotel.

Three people had checked out around the time that the body had been discovered and Jake made a note of their names and addresses so that he could ask the Force, local to each person, to clear them from the enquiry.

After he had completed his matching exercise Jake was left with three names that did not have a corresponding statement. Three people who had not given a statement to the police at the time of the murder. Jake immediately returned to the hotel.

The plain woman on the reception desk was still there and she agreed to help Jake check his short list of names. She was able to confirm that two of the names on his list had left that morning. The third name, that of Basil Statham, should still, certainly as far as hotel records were concerned, be in room thirty-five. Mr Jones, who was also on the desk at that time, agreed to take Jake up to the room.

Room thirty-five had a Do Not Disturb sign hanging on the handle of the door and Mr Jones seemed to find that a suitable barrier to prevent him doing anything more. He paused at the door, looking at Jake as if seeking permission of some kind.

Jake glanced at his watch. "I hardly think we'll be disturbing anyone at this hour of the day. Open it."

Mr Jones knocked on the door and waited a few seconds. There was no response so he eventually put the key in the lock and opened the door. They both went in.

The room was completely empty and had the look of a room that had not been occupied for some time. The bed was made and there were no signs of luggage, or any other personal belongings, lying around. It was quite clear that there was certainly no one occupying the room at that moment.

"This is all very puzzling," announced Mr Jones still looking around the room, as if someone would jump out of the wardrobe at any moment.

Jake walked around the room, checking surfaces for signs in the dust that had settled for anything that may have been laid down or touched. There was nothing. Jake then looked down at the details he held for the supposed occupant of that room.

Basil Statham. Travelling Salesman, 133 Upper Richmond Road, Putney, London.

Mr Statham had checked in to the hotel half an hour after Mabel Lassiter but he had never checked out again. However, it was now perfectly clear to both Jake and Mr Jones that this room may never actually have been occupied at all.

"But he can't have gone," Jones suddenly blurted out. "He still has to pay his bill."

"I think you can forget about Mr Statham paying his bill," Jake then said, "as I am willing to bet that there never was a Mr Statham."

"Oh but there was," Jones added. "I was on the desk when he registered."

"Can you describe him?"

Jones then went on to describe a man who was average in every respect apart from the immense amount of facial hair that seemed to cover most of his features. Again it was the description of a man who did not want to be identified and who had gone to great lengths to ensure that there would be no clues left behind that might allow the police to get a credible line on him. It seemed that every time his face was described by a witness it would be the face of someone in disguise.

Basically the descriptions they were gathering were useless.

"Was the gentleman foreign?" Jake then asked just in case there was a small chance this was all about the anarchists.

"He didn't say very much but from what little he did say I'm sure he was English," Jones replied.

"Could you put a specific dialect against how he spoke?"

"Not really. He was quite well spoken but definitely not Scottish, I'm sure of that."

"Are there any of the maids still on duty?" Jake then enquired.

Mr Jones checked his watch. "They should be just about finished but if they are still in the building then they'll be on the top floor."

"Can we please find the maid who would have been cleaning this room?"

"That should be Dora," Mr Jones said and set off towards the door. Jake followed him out of the room and over to the stairs. They went up to the top floor and Mr Jones led Jake to a room, which had the door to it slightly ajar.

They could hear voices and giggling coming from within and when Mr Jones pulled the door open they found three maids looking almost conspiratorial as they stood, close together, discussing something of immense interest to them.

Even after Mr Jones had explained who Jake was and why he was there the maids were still prone to giggling nervously and gave no indication that they actually recognised the seriousness of the situation.

Dora was identified and Jake asked her if she had been in room thirty-five. She explained that there had been a Do Not Disturb sign on the door the last twice she had visited the room and that it had been the day before the murder when she had last been in that room.

"So as long as that sign was on the door you would have left the room alone?" Jake asked, somewhat amazed at the effect one little sign could have.

Dora said that she would never enter a room if instructed not to do so. She was not to know what the guests might be doing in the privacy of their own rooms and no one would ever have suspected wrongdoing amongst the clientele of the Palace Hotel.

Jake and Mr Jones left the maids to their giggling and headed back to the staircase. As they started their descent Mr Jones spoke.

"You know, now that I think of it, I should have been suspicious of Statham right from the start. What kind of salesman travels without samples?"

Jake felt that it was a bit late for Mr Jones to now declare his suspicions but decided there would be little point in saying anything. Jake left Mr Jones at the reception desk and headed off back to Lodge Walk.

He had a mental list of things that were needing to be done, starting with contacting colleagues in London and asking them to check out that address in Upper Richmond Road. Jake did not think for one moment that the address would be anything other than fake but he needed to check it out anyway. Clearly this man 'Statham' did not want to be identified and would, therefore, have done all that was required to leave nothing but dead ends in his wake.

Once back at Lodge Walk Jake went up to see the Chief and to update him on the events that had just unfolded in the Palace Hotel.

"So we have a name and a description, but neither of them are of any use to us," the Chief summarised after Jake had talked him through the latest developments.

"We have that tenuous link to London through that address and we'll obviously check it out, though I doubt if it will lead us anywhere," conceded Jake. "At least I think we can safely say that this 'Statham' is our killer and we can also safely say that he is not our Spanish anarchist as this man was definitely described as being English."

The Chief pondered on what he had just been told for a few seconds. "It would seem logical to assume that 'Statham' and Mabel Lassiter met in London and came to Aberdeen to do more than dance."

"I'm also pretty certain that 'Statham' was the mysterious Martin Bagshaw as well, so that would confirm that this man has been coming to Aberdeen for some time and that means that whatever he is planning it has been in the planning stage for quite a few weeks."

"Which means it's something big," added the Chief.

"But not necessarily connected to the royal visit," suggested Jake.

"Perhaps not, but I still think there can be nothing more concerning than someone trying to bring harm to the King and Queen in some way."

"The problem, sir, is that even if this man and Mabel Lassiter were in Aberdeen to work together, the fact he has now killed Mabel proves that the plan has changed and she is no longer needed. He's on his own and we have no idea who we are looking for just at this moment."

"We need to find him, Jake and fast."

"I know, sir. I'll keep working at it and update you with anything new that I might uncover."

"Very good, Jake," concluded the Chief as Jake walked to the door and let himself out.

TEN

Monday 17 September - evening

Jake left the office earlier than would normally be the case. He had much on is mind. He felt like one of those illusionists with the spinning plates. Jake knew, that if he wasn't careful, one if not all of his plates would come crashing down all too soon.

The one plate that he had devoted little time to, mainly because he'd only been presented with it that day; was the security for the King's visit. Jake was still unsure of the part he was playing in keeping the King and Queen safe during their visit. A whole team of officers, led by the Chief himself, had been working on that particular task for months and Jake felt sure that they had everything covered. He actually felt uncomfortable being put in the position of possibly having to question the work of officers who carried the same rank as his own.

However, like it, or not, he would review everything that had been done to date paying close attention to the fact that there just might be an anarchist loose in the city hell bent on carrying out some random act of violence upon the King and Queen.

Instead of going home Jake booked a bicycle out from the store and made his way to the newly refurbished railway station on Holburn Street. They had already started building the stands that would hold the crowds who would gather to give the King and Queen a rousing welcome to the City of Aberdeen. Jake felt that it would be all too easy for someone to hide himself in the crowd but that there were likely to be far too many witnesses for any trained assassin to think it wise to do anything there.

A chill passed through Jake's body at the thought that this miscreant may not be concerned with being caught. If that were to be the case then no amount of planning would prevent the inevitable. Jake remembered that the anarchist who threw the bomb in Madrid had shot himself immediately afterwards rather than be arrested. Clearly they were not averse to dying for their cause.

Jake checked the station area and decided it was unlikely anyone would try anything there due to the high number of police and military. He continued on his way, following the route that the King and Queen were to take.

The entire journey was mainly flanked by housing and it seemed to Jake that anyone could occupy any one of those houses and harbour thoughts of harming the King and Queen as they passed. On the day, the route would be fenced off so that no one would be able to get that close to Their Majesties. However, were the plan to throw something or to fire a gun then there would be no need to get that close.

Jake followed the route to Union Terrace. He stopped beside the Wallace Statue and looked around. The entire length of Union Terrace had been high buildings one of which was The Grand Hotel. Again someone could be at one of the hotel's windows and have a clear view of the carriage passing below.

Jake knew that the public would be kept away from the Union Terrace Gardens side of the street but whether that would afford total protection remained to be seen. Jake turned to face the buildings that Wallace appeared to be pointing at. The Central Library, St Mark's Church and the soon to be finished theatre were all being decorated for the big day.

St Mark's Church already had a banner hanging over the main entrance. *Fear God – Honour The King.* Jake smiled; he wasn't sure that in not fearing God perhaps he should not, therefore, honour the King. Jake got back on his bicycle and made his way to Marischal College.

At no point of his journey had he felt the King and Queen were totally safe from potential attack. It was going to be very difficult, if not impossible, to guarantee the safety of Their Majesties, especially when taking in to account the sheer volume of people who were likely to be lining the route.

There were simply too many opportunities for some hot-headed assassin intent on committing an atrocity of the greatest magnitude.

The last thing anyone wanted was for Aberdeen to find a place in history as the city in which the King and Queen were attacked and God forbid, received serious injuries or worse.

Unlike the rest of Aberdeen, Jake was not looking forward to Thursday, the twenty-seventh of September one little bit.

ELEVEN

Wednesday 19 September - mid morning

Tuesday had passed, for Jake, in a bit of a blur. He had, for the first time, been able to pull his entire team together and give them their duties in the lead up to the King's visit. It had been a day when a plan of how to tackle all the jobs requiring his attention had been drawn up and then been totally undermined by the intrusions of the day to day running of a police station.

Jake rarely got five minutes peace to do anything and Tuesday had been a day of taking statements and generally being interrupted. He had been very late in leaving the office and by the time he got home Alice had already fallen asleep. Jake had undressed and joined her in bed forgotting completely that he hadn't eaten all day and that there had been a particularly nice piece of meat in the larder.

Wednesday morning had arrived with the usual blue sky overhead and Jake had arrived back at the office at a little after seven. There was a feeling of having never left the place as he took his jacket off and hung it over the back of his chair. His desk was strewn with papers and he firstly put them all in to some kind of order before he started to read through them. He had the reports from the Police Doctor and all the statements taken from the staff at the Palace Hotel.

He sat back in his chair and found his thoughts drifting back to Julia Samuels. The seemingly motiveless murder of such a young and attractive woman had hit Jake hard. He had seen everything in his time as a police officer but this was a case that had really got under his skin. He so wanted to solve this case and yet he had little to work on.

It was often the case that murder was committed by someone known to the victim. If her father was to be believed then Julia Samuels had few friends, thus perhaps there would be few suspects. On the other hand, as Detective Smith had said, daughters don't always tell their fathers everything.

Jake wondered if the connection was no more than the Sailors' Institute. Maybe someone had seen her there and had believed there was a relationship forming between them when, in fact, there hadn't been. It was a possibility but Jake was not convinced by any of it.

Even if there had been some connection at the Institute how would anyone else know about Marischal Street unless they were there at Julia's bidding; which brought Jake back to the idea of it being a budding relationship gone wrong.

He was still pondering on that thought when the door opened and Sergeant Turnbull came in to the room.

"There's a young gentleman in the interview room who is asking to speak to the officer investigating the death of Julia Samuels. I thought you would want to see him."

"Indeed I would," added Jake eagerly as he rose from his desk and followed Turnbull back along the corridor towards the interview room.

Jake took out his notebook and pencil and then entered the room. He walked to the table and placed the items in front of him before sitting down. Across from him sat a young man who looked to be no older than seventeen. He was quite handsome though his face was etched with a roughness that comes from being brought up in hard times. He looked slightly undernourished and his hair hung long and lank. He was nervously tapping his fingers on the table and his icy blue eyes looked straight through Jake with an intensity that was slightly off-putting.

"I'm Inspector Fraser," Jake said. "I believe you may have some information regarding Julia Samuels?"

"What's happened to her, you have to tell me?" the young man then blurted out, tears forming in his eyes.

"We can come to that," Jake then said, "but, firstly, let me get a few details written down first."

"I just need to know what has happened to Julia. People are telling me things and I don't know what to believe."

"I may be able to answer some of your questions but, as I said, I need to get your details recorded first. Now who might you be, sir?"

"My name is Billy Sim and I work on the *Mary G*, which has just returned to harbour after being away for a few days."

"And how did you come to know Miss Samuels?"

"We were friends."

Jake studied the young man's attire for a moment and also detected a faint smell of fish in the air.

"You don't look the sort of man who would be-friend a girl like Julia Samuels."

The young man took instant offence. "I don't care how I look to you, Inspector, but to Julia I looked good enough to become what I would like to think was a close friend."

"I'm guessing you met her at the Sailors' Institute?" Jake added.

"That was where we first met but as our friendship grew we began meeting at Jessie McGill's place on Marischal Street."

"When did you meet there?"

"A Wednesday morning."

"Why did you meet there?"

"To get peace and quiet and have a proper chance to talk."

Jake knew that Julia had still been a virgin when she had died so he doubted that there had been any sexual intent in their meetings. It still seemed strange to him, however, that a girl brought up to recognise her Class should befriend someone so much further down the social ladder.

"You just wanted to talk?" Jake added with a tone of disbelief evident in how he had said it.

Billy got angrier and the tears started to roll down his cheeks. "I knew no one would believe me that's why I've never said a word to anyone. Julia and I were friends. We met and we talked. We just liked being in each other's company and we'd laugh a lot and the whole time I was with her I was just so happy. I loved that girl so much from the very first time I saw her but I knew that we could never be together properly. Her tyrant father would never have accepted his precious daughter marrying a fisherman."

Just as a Chief Constable was hardly likely to agree to one of his Inspectors marrying a prostitute, thought Jake fleetingly. Social rules were the hardest rules to break as they were only set in the minds of the individual.

"How long had you been meeting at Marischal Street?"

"About six weeks. Julia used to work at the Institute on a Wednesday but she told them some story about getting a job elsewhere and would come to meet me at Jessie's instead. Jessie saw no harm in letting us have time together but there was never anything dirty in what we did, it was just a friendship."

"So you never tried to force yourself on Miss Samuels and she rejected you?" Jake then asked.

Billy's tear filled eyes widened in horror. "We were friends, how many more times must I tell you that? I loved Julia and would never have harmed her in any way. Our time together was precious and I would never have spoiled one moment of it by doing anything dirty."

"Sexual contact doesn't always have to be dirty," Jake said.

"A Doctor's daughter and a fisherman? Had we been doing anything, Inspector, other people would have made it sound dirty. Julia deserved better, which is why I would never have touched her like that."

"So you never as much as kissed Miss Samuels?"

Billy looked down in a slightly sheepish gesture. "Yes, Inspector, we had kissed each other. Julia wanted to be kissed; she wanted to know how it felt. Neither of us were what you might call experienced in life and it was just a bit of fun, nothing more."

Jake made a last note in his book and then looked up again.

"So what happened to you last Wednesday?"

"That's just the thing," Billy then said, sitting forward and getting his emotions in better order," we were supposed to meet that day as usual but on the Tuesday and with no warning, the skipper decided we were going to sea. I had no way of getting a message to either Julia or Jessie. I knew Julia would be there and worrying about me but I never imagined she would actually go looking for me."

Jake now sat up with interest.

"What do you mean she went looking for you?"

"That's the main reason I'm here," Billy continued. "We got back in to harbour last night and I was having a few beers in the pub when Lenny Bassett rolls up and starts telling me he'd seen Julia down at the harbour the day after our boat had sailed. He'd had his suspicions that I might be seeing Julia and he wondered if she might have been looking for me. I tried to ignore the bastard but then he started talking about Julia being down at the harbour dressed like a whore. I just lost it for a moment and hit him as hard as I could. I didn't mean to lose my temper like that but no one calls my Julia a whore and gets away with it."

"Did he say when he saw her?"

"He just said the morning after I'd gone."

"And did he say anything else?"

"Oh yes, the bastard started to taunt me and I ended up hitting him again."

"Taunt you? In what way?"

"He said he'd done something with Julia that he bet I hadn't and then he went on to say that he'd made a grab for one of her breasts because he thought they were so big and inviting. I lost it again and hit him a few more times until he shut up. Just as he walked out the door he turned and said that the fact she looked like a whore made him want to treat her like one. I'm telling you, Inspector, if I had caught the little shit at that moment then I'd be in here for murder, make no mistake. I was then told by the landlord to drink up and go home to cool down, which I did. This morning I went to Jessie's in the hope that she could tell me more about what happened that Wednesday morning but when I got there I was met by a neighbour who told me all about the police being there and bodies being found. I came straight here. That is all I can tell you so now you have to tell me what happened to Julia?"

"We'll get to that, Mr Sim, but first you need to tell me more about this Lenny Bassett?"

"There's nothing to tell. He's a loud-mouthed shit and that's about it. The only difference today is that he'll be a loud-mouthed shit with a sore nose."

"Do you know where he lives?"

"Somewhere in Torry. I'm surprised you don't know him already as he's been in trouble with the law more times that I've had a beer. That big mouth of his just keeps getting him in bother."

"We did find the bodies of two women in that property last week," Jake then said and Billy began to weep openly again.

"Oh Jesus, why, can someone tell me why?"

"Unfortunately, at this precise moment, I can't give you a why, Mr Sim. Is there anything else that you can tell me?"

Billy thought for a moment as he wiped his face with a handkerchief that looked as if it hadn't been washed in weeks.

"I can't think of anything apart, perhaps, that if a dim-wit like Lenny Bassett could see that there was something between me and Julia then maybe someone else at the Institute was beginning to think the same way. If they knew about our meetings and also about me being away then maybe they went there thinking that, in some way, they could take my place?"

"It's a possibility I'll grant you that, but if you didn't tell anyone about your Wednesday meetings then how would anyone else know to go there?"

"We didn't tell anyone but it might just have been that someone saw us going in to the building and put two and two together."

"You said something about her father being a tyrant, Mr Sim. I've met Doctor Samuels and whilst I would certainly put him down as a strict father I find the word tyrant rather strong."

"To be honest," Billy responded," it's a word that Julia used about him. I don't even know what it means but it didn't sound like she was being nice when she said it."

"Miss Samuels described her father as a tyrant?"

"That was the word she used and if you ask me she was terrified of the man. She often spoke of what he might do were he ever to find out about our meetings. She seemed scared for me as well as herself."

Jake thought for a moment then spoke again.

"What did you talk about?"

Billy Sim seemed somewhat confused by the question. "Sorry?"

"You said you talked with Miss Samuels when you met on a Wednesday, so what was it you talked about?"

Billy seemed to lose himself in thought for a few seconds. He suddenly had the clearest of images in his head of Julia sitting across from him, her eyes wide with excitement as she talked about all that life might bring her. She had been looking forward to making a great life for herself and yet here she was dead. He started to weep again and Jake gave him a moment to compose himself before asking the question again.

"Our hopes and dreams mainly," Billy replied this time. "Julia spoke about being a nurse one day and I spoke about owning my own boat, Julia so much wanted to help others; that was the kind of girl she was, Inspector."

"And beyond someone perhaps putting two and two together you are sure that no one else knew about your meetings?"

"Not as far as I know."

"Very well, Mr Sim," concluded Jake, "I think that's all I need for just now. If I could just have an address in case I need to contact you again?"

"Aboard the *Mary G*, Inspector, is where you'll find me."

It was a broken man who left Lodge Walk a few moments later. Billy Sim felt as if someone had ripped his entire world apart and he wondered how life could ever be the same now that Julia was no longer a part of it.

Jake went to see Sergeant Turnbull and ask if he, or anyone else, might know Lenny Bassett.

"Bassett is a nasty piece of work, Jake," Turnbull had said. "To be honest I'm amazed you've not heard of him; you must be the only one here who hasn't arrested him at some time in our working lives."

"Do we have an address for him?" Jake enquired.

"He was in here a few weeks ago," Turnbull said, "so we're bound to have a recent address for him."

Turnbull went over to the row of filing cabinets at the back of the work area.

"What was he arrested for the last time?" Jake asked.

"As I recall he ripped the front of a young lady's dress in a drunken attempt to grope her breasts," Turnbull replied. "Bassett has a lot of trouble keeping his hands off the ladies, especially when he's had a drink in."

"So he has a history of violence against women?"

"He does and if you're thinking he might be a suspect for one of your murders then it would have to be Mabel Lassiter. Lenny Bassett could do violence but he could never do compassion."

"Once you find his address bring it through to me," Jake concluded and turned to leave.

"Will do," Turnbull said, though it was highly likely that Jake hadn't even heard him.

Once back at his desk Jake gave some thought to the information he had just received. In Lenny Bassett he had a good suspect for Julia Samuels' murder and yet, with his previous, he was actually more suited to the Mabel Lassiter murder.

The only problem was that there was nothing connecting Bassett to Mabel but there was, if Billy Sim was to be believed, a clear connection with Julia Samuels. The more he thought about things the more Jake felt he had to agree with Turnbull. A man who found it difficult to keep his hands off women would never have left Julia Samuels unmolested. If Julia had been the reason for him going to Marischal Street in the first place then he would most definitely have done something to her once he'd got there, especially if he intended killing her anyway.

Lenny Bassett might have information about Julia Samuels and he might have messed with her in the street, but Jake felt sure that he was not her killer. Moments later Turnbull came in to the room with Bassett's address and Jake decided to pay him a visit later that day.

TWELVE

Wednesday 19 September - early afternoon

Just after lunchtime Jake met up with Sergeant Mathieson and they took two bicycles from the store before setting off towards Torry. It was not a long journey and yet it proved to be surprisingly dangerous as they manoeuvred around trams, carts, horses and the general public who seemed to cross the road oblivious to the fact that the vehicles they were narrowly missing were all capable of killing them.

People rarely checked for vehicles before stepping off the pavement and there was a general disregard for their own safety as they crossed and re-crossed the cobbled streets. Expectation amongst the pedestrians seemed to be that the vehicle should stop for them and not the other way around.

Jake and Mathieson made their way down Market Street, passing the Post Office at the corner of Regent Quay before continuing their journey along South Market Street, passed the harbour on their left and the railway yards on their right. Here the traffic was even more congested as now there were trains running back and forth between the ships unloading at the harbour and the goods' trains loading in the railway yard.

They reached the Victoria Bridge, which had finally opened up a clear route from the city centre in to Torry and beyond. It had been decided that a bridge was essential after the loss of life in the Torry Ferry disaster of 1876. Eleven years later the bridge had opened and brought a new life to the Torry area.

Victoria Road was immediately on the other side of the bridge and Jake and Mathieson stopped outside the block in which they had been told they would find Lenny Bassett. They chained their bicycles against a lamp-post and entered the building. They made their way up to the third floor and banged on the door to their right.

It took a few moments before the door was opened by an apparition whom, they assumed, was Lenny Bassett. He was dressed in long johns and a vest, both of which may have been white at the time of purchase but were now a faded yellow. His hair was long and straggly and his face, which had probably never been what could be described as handsome, was bruised and scratched, no doubt as a result of Billy Sim's fists.

"Lenny Bassett?" Jake said.

"Yeah," came the reply through a stifled yawn.

"Inspector Fraser and Sergeant Mathieson of Aberdeen City Police; we'd like a word."

Bassett made no attempt to stop them entering his property and he casually closed the door behind them. Once they were all in what passed for a living room, Lenny Bassett immediately went on the defensive.

"Look, whatever you may have heard about me and that lady-friend of Billy's I'm willing to bet it won't be true. I admit I have a problem with keeping me hands off the ladies and I did make a grab for her tits. That was it though, nothing else happened and I certainly had nothing to do with her death."

Lenny was looking really rough from the effects of yesterday's drinking. In the better light of the living room Jake could now clearly see the bruising around Bassett's left eye.

"Who are you talking about?" Jake then asked.

"That Julia. The one seeing Billy Sim and thinking no one knows about it."

"Are we talking about Julia Samuels?" Jake then suggested.

"If that's the girl who works at the Institute and knows Billy Sim then, yeah, I'm talking about Julia Samuels."

"And you're admitting to molesting her?" Jake then said by way of clarification.

Bassett realised that he now needed to be very careful in what he said, after all he may already have said too much. His brain was still foggy from the hangover and just the sheer effort of thinking was proving to be quite painful.

"Look, Inspector, I may have overstayed my welcome but all I did was make a grab for her."

"What exactly happened?"

Bassett took a cigarette from a packet lying on the table and lit it. He dragged on the end and held the smoke in his system for what seemed like a lifetime before eventually exhaling a cloud of smoke that floated towards the ceiling.

"You'd better sit down," he then said and they all sat down before he continued with his account of the previous Wednesday morning.

"Last Wednesday, around half past nine in the morning, I was making my way home along Regent Quay. I had been playing cards on one of the boats and having a few beers with the men and hadn't noticed that night had turned to morning. Anyway, I was a bit boozy and I saw this young woman coming in the opposite direction. She looked like a whore so I thought I might be lucky, if you get my meaning. I was just sorting out my money when I noticed that this woman was the one who worked at the Institute. I couldn't understand why a woman of her class would be dressed like a whore but the fact that she was sort of got me going. She started to ask me about Billy but all I could see was a pretty woman and I made a grab for her. I know I touched her where I shouldn't have but she pushed me away and I fell over. By the time I pulled myself to my feet she had turned and fled."

"Did you tell her anything about Billy?"

"I think I said something about him being at sea and then I may have asked if I might do instead."

"So you were aroused, were you?" Jake then asked.

Bassett puffed on his cigarette. "I found her attractive, yes and I know I was in the wrong to make a grab for her, but that was the end of it. I got up and went home, so if anyone has told you otherwise they are lying."

"You're telling us that you didn't follow Julia Samuels so that you could finish what you had started?" Jake enquired.

"No," Lenny Bassett replied quickly, his eyes widening with horror and the pain from his eye obviously causing him some discomfort. "I knew I was in the wrong for what I'd done so I got myself home as quickly as possible. I just knew that you coppers would pay me a visit at some point."

"Why did you know that, Lenny?"

"Because I guessed that someone may have seen me and with my record it wouldn't be long before you'd come hammering on my door."

"Or maybe the truth is that you wanted to stop Miss Samuels from reporting your actions to the police so you followed her and ultimately killed her?" Jake then suggested.

The blood drained from Lenny's face and he drew hard on his cigarette once more. "I've already said that I had nothing to do with her death," he then said.

"Yes, Lenny, I heard what you said about not having anything to do with her death. However, you have admitted molesting her and you have admitted being aroused by her so it is not a major leap from those confessions to you attacking her in the Marischal Street flat, is it? Now, are you still claiming to have gone straight home?"

"Oh, wait a minute, "Lenny now said with growing horror in his tone, "you really think that I killed her, don't you?"

"It has to be a strong possibility," Jake suggested.

"Jesus, I might be a bit free with me hands when I've had a drink but I'm no murderer."

Jake had watched Bassett very closely during their verbal interchange. He had gone there in the firm belief that Bassett was not his killer and now, having been able to study the man's face as they had spoken, he felt even more certain that this was not his man. Lenny had looked totally shocked to be accused of killing Julia Samuels and Jake did not credit this man with acting skills that were good enough to hide guilt that well.

For the moment, therefore, Jake was prepared to believe the account that Lenny had just given him. There seemed little point in arresting him for molesting Julia Samuels and anyway, Billy Sim had already dished out a punishment for that particular misdemeanour.

"I'm prepared to believe you, Lenny," Jake then said and Bassett visibly crumpled in his seat with relief. "Did you happen to notice anyone else hanging around Regent Quay at the time you met Julia?"

Lenny finished his cigarette and gave Jake's question some thought.

"Like I said, Inspector, I was a bit boozy and beyond seeing what I thought was a whore appear in front of me I don't remember much else."

Jake stood up and crossed over to where Lenny was sitting. He leaned forward until his mouth was down at the level of Lenny's ear.

"A word of advice, Lenny, boozy or otherwise you'd better learn to keep your filthy little hands to yourself because if I hear of you being arrested one more time for molesting a woman then I will make sure that you get the maximum penalty for the crime and that any time that you do spend in prison will be pure hell for you. Do I make myself clear?"

"You do," said Lenny not even looking up.

"Good. Now we'll be on our way and you can continue to sleep off last night's hangover."

Jake and Mathieson went back downstairs and were somewhat relieved to find that no one had nicked the lamp-post along with their bikes. They unlocked the bicycles and set off back across the bridge towards the city centre. The journey back proved a little less hazardous and a good deal quicker. They put the bikes back in the store and then went to Jake's office.

"Well at least that explains why Julia Samuels was dressed the way she was," Jake said as he sat down. "However, it still doesn't explain why the killer would take her proper dress away with him."

"It all points to the killer knowing Julia but not knowing Jessie, doesn't it?" suggested Mathieson.

"Or maybe the killer just had second thoughts over what he had done to Julia but not Jessie," added Jake. "All the compassion was shown towards Julia so perhaps it was the fact she was so young that made the difference. It does open up our suspect list a little further though. I mean if an ape like Lenny Bassett could work out that there was something going on between Billy and Julia then it is perfectly possible that someone else did as well."

"Only we're nowhere nearer knowing who that someone might be," added Mathieson.

"We have to presume that it was no one that close to Julia, given that her father maintains she had few close acquaintances."

"Just remember, sir, that her father didn't seem to know about Billy Sim, so maybe Julia had more friends and acquaintances than he seems to think?"

"Billy said that Julia described her father as a tyrant and that she worried about what he might do were he ever to find out about their Wednesday meetings. It begs the question; did he find out?"

Mathieson looked horrified at the implication. "Even if he did, surely a father could never murder his own daughter and then carry on as if everything was normal?"

"Maybe he went there that day to confront her on why she wasn't at work and then, seeing her dressed the way she was, jumped to all the wrong conclusions?" Jake then said.

"You mean he thought his daughter was selling her body for money?" Mathieson asked, his eyes ever wider in a look of complete horror.

"If that was what he thought then flying in to a rage would not be too farfetched a theory and once in that rage he might be capable of anything."

"The theory makes sense," admitted Mathieson," but I just find it hard to believe that a father could do such a thing."

"As do I, for just now," agreed Jake. "We need evidence that might connect the good Doctor to Marischal Street. If we can at least prove that he knew about his daughter's meetings then we would be some way towards breaking down his account of what happened. Leave this with me just now while you concentrate on the possibility that we may have a mad anarchist loose in the city."

"Very good," concluded Mathieson as he left the room.

Jake sifted through the papers on his desk until he came to the statement provided by Doctor Samuels. Jake's intention was to work his way through that statement questioning everything that the Doctor said. If there was anything in there that might point to his possible guilt then Jake was intent on finding it.

THIRTEEN

Friday 21 September - morning

Alice was standing at the front window of the Esslemont Avenue property. Mary was sitting on the settee finishing off an adjustment that was needed to one of the dresses bought for Alice. Alice was hiding behind the curtain as she was dressed only in her underclothes as she awaited the adjustment to be completed so that she could, once more, try on the new purchase to ensure that it would now fit properly.

Alice had arrived the previous morning and they had spent all afternoon shopping. They had been in a number of stores and Alice had noticed, quite early in their travels, that there was a man apparently following them.

Mary Thomson seemed oblivious to the fact that the same man had been in practically every store and that he never seemed to be buying anything. Perhaps Alice was just that little bit more aware of her surroundings and certainly more aware of men and their ways. She had felt sure they were being followed but said nothing.

She may have had her suspicions yesterday but today she was certain. The same man was now standing across the road smoking a cigarette. It might have been coincidence but Alice had never believed in such things. But why was this man watching the house and why had he followed them yesterday?

"Come away from the window, Alice, someone might see you," Mary said from the settee and as she did so she snapped off the thread she had been using and held the dress up for inspection. "There, that should do."

Alice hurried across and took the dress from Mary. She quickly pulled it on and then spun to look at herself in the mirror. The dress was beautiful and it made Alice feel beautiful. If only Jake had been there to appreciate how she looked and how happy she was.

"When will we be leaving tomorrow?" Alice then asked.

"Around ten o'clock in the morning."

"Would it be in order for me to visit Jake and say goodbye?" Alice then asked.

Mary sounded surprised as she replied. "But you said goodbye yesterday and I'm sure Jake is busy enough as it is without finding time to say goodbye again."

"I'll be quick," Alice insisted with a pleading tone to her voice.

Mary checked her watch and although she felt sure that Jake would not be able to see Alice, agreed to her going down to Lodge Walk anyway.

Alice changed out of her good dress and put on her coat. She then picked up her bag and after saying that she wouldn't be away long, closed the door behind her and left the building. The man across the road paid little attention to Alice as she left the building and certainly showed no sign of wanting to follow her. That confirmed to Alice that it was Mary who was of interest to him.

Alice had a fleeting moment of panic as she wondered if something might happen to Mary now that she had been left on her own. Alice looked back but the man had not moved and she felt a little more certain now that this man was there purely to observe.

Alice made her way down to Lodge Walk and was greeted by Sergeant Turnbull as she walked through the door and up to the counter.

"Would Jake be able to spare a moment?" she asked.

"For you, Alice, I'm sure Jake could spare a little more than that," Turnbull replied with a grin. He then showed Alice through to the interview room before heading off along the corridor to let Jake know that she was there.

As soon as Jake knew that Alice was in the building he jumped up from his desk and hurried along the corridor, all manner of thoughts racing through his mind. His first thought was of Scroggins and if that man had come back, in any way, in to Alice's life then he was going to regret it. Jake reached the door of the interview room and stopped for a moment to gather his thoughts and try to look a little less uptight as he entered the room.

Inside he found Alice sitting at the table. She stood up as Jake entered the room and he embraced her tightly.

"What's the matter?" he said with some urgency, his eyes checking every visible inch of Alice for any signs of violence.

Alice smiled and sat down again. "Nothing is the matter, at least as far as I'm concerned."

Jake sat down opposite. "Has something happened to Mary?" he then asked.

"Not yet, but I wanted you to know, before we leave for Edinburgh, that someone has been following Mary and watching the house."

Jake's look of concern returned.

"Are you sure?"

"Positive," Alice replied. "We were out shopping yesterday and I noticed the same man in nearly all the shops we attended. I then saw him standing across the road from the house today. He's not very good at blending in. He also showed no interest in me as I left just now so I have to assume that it is Mary he has been watching."

"In which case it is even more imperative that you both go down to Edinburgh and stay there for a little while. When is it you go tomorrow?"

"Around ten."

"Good. Thanks for telling me this. I'll get the beat Constable to check the property on his rounds and I'll go in passed myself at every chance I get."

"I take it you have a key?" Alice then asked.

"Yes, Mary gave me one on Sunday. Don't say anything to Mary about this it will only upset her more than she is already."

"I wasn't going to say anything; that was why I came to you."

"Good girl. Would you be able to describe this man to the Police Artist?" Jake then enquired.

Alice thought for a moment. "I should think so, I'm pretty good at remembering faces. It used to be a talent that proved useful in my old profession."

Jake left the room and went through to ask Turnbull to arrange for Paddy Flanagan to nip through to the interview room and draw up a quick sketch of the man whom Alice would describe. Turnbull was on the case immediately and Jake went back in to the interview room where he said goodbye to Alice, one more time and gave her a final embrace. They refrained from kissing seeing as they were on official premises.

Alice then sat down to await Paddy Flanagan and Jake went back to his office.

He sat down and pondered on the information he had just received from Alice. Why was someone so interested in Mary Thomson? Obviously because of something her dearly departed husband had been up to as there could be no reason why Mary, in herself, would be of any interest to anyone. Jake decided to go through to the muster room and have a word with the Constables who patrolled Esslemont Avenue.

Of the four Constables who included Esslemont Avenue as part of their beat only Constable Abbot was on duty and in the muster room when Jake went through. Abbot was happy to make sure that the others knew what was expected of them when it came to the Thomsons' home. Jake was about to leave the muster room when another young Constable stood in his way. Jake knew the young man to be Constable Angus Troughton who had one of the city centre beats.

"Yes, Gus?" Jake said with a bright smile, which he hoped might put the young man at ease as he was looking extremely nervous.

"Sorry to trouble you, sir, but might I have a word?"

"Follow me through to my office."

Once in Jake's office the door was closed and the young officer accepted the offer of a seat. Jake said nothing more, waiting for the officer to say whatever had to be said in his own good time.

"There is word in the building, sir, that there may be an anarchist loose in the city," Troughton began. Jake said nothing so Troughton assumed the word was right and continued. "I fear I may have had a chance to apprehend the man a few weeks ago and failed, sir."

Jake now sat forward with immediate interest. "You think you've met our anarchist?" he said.

"I really don't know for sure, sir, but the man I met was foreign and very, very shifty. He also became very agitated when I stopped him."

"Tell me exactly what happened?" Jake then said.

Troughton took out his notebook and flipped through some pages until he came to the one he had been looking for.

"On the evening of Wednesday, the Eighth of August I was patrolling in the Castlegate when I saw two men fighting beside the entrance to the toilets. I went across and separated them. One of them immediately ran away but I got a good hold of the other. He was talking to me in a foreign language and I couldn't make any sense of what he was saying. I was in the process of trying to apprehend him and get my notebook out when three men appeared from nowhere and pushed me to the ground. All but one of the men then ran off. The one man who stayed behind then picked me off the ground and hit me to the face three times. I fell down again and he ran away. I had a black eye for a few days after but it was mainly my pride that was hurt. I filed my report and thought no more about it until I heard that there just might be an anarchist on the loose. I mean, those four men were together, I'm sure of that."

"What language was the foreign man speaking?" Jake then asked.

"I have no idea, sir. All I know is that it he wasn't speaking English."

"Which direction did the foreign man run off in when he left you?"

The Constable thought for a moment. "He ran off down King Street, sir."

"And the others?"

"I'm not so sure about what the others were doing as I was being hit in the face at the time."

Jake stopped himself from smiling. The incident had been very serious but there was something mildly amusing about the way in which the young Constable was describing it.

"Have you any idea what the men might have been fighting about?" Jake then asked.

"No sir. There was no obvious reason; I just put it down to them having both been drinking."

"So they were drunk?" Jake added by way of clarification.

"Well now you ask me like that, sir, I'd have to say no. The foreign gentleman certainly spoke with a clarity that belied someone with an excessive amount of alcohol inside him and the others seemed in complete control of their actions when they attacked me and then ran off."

"Are you saying the whole thing may have been staged in some way?" Jake then asked, looking a little confused in the process.

"I don't think I'm saying that, sir. The men were definitely fighting and there is no doubt that the punches thrown at me were real enough. I also thought the panic that gripped the foreign gentleman was real enough. He thought he was being arrested and that seemed to scare him."

"As if he already knew what the inside of a prison was like?" Jake suggested.

"Yes, sir, that pretty much explains it. He had the look of a man who did want to go back to prison."

"So he'll have a record," Jake said, more to himself than anything else. Jake then opened a drawer on his desk and took out the drawing of Arconada that had been supplied by Superintendent Harris. "Have a look at this, Gus and let me know if it resembles the man you grappled with in the Castlegate?"

The Constable looked at the drawing. He could not be sure but there certainly was a likeness.

"The man I saw was definitely dark haired but his face was covered with a rather bushy beard the likes of which I haven't seen outside of the theatre," the Constable eventually said.

"So he was disguised?" added Jake.

"I would say so, yes."

This was not what Jake wanted to hear. This sounded like the same man who had murdered Mabel Lassiter, only he was supposed to be English. Nothing added up.

Was it possible that the murderer and the anarchist could be different men and both with a liking for theatrical disguises?

Whoever it was this was someone who would stop at nothing to prevent his true identity being known. It was definitely someone who was well organised and probably working to a specific plan. That meant he was many steps ahead of the police, which worried Jake immensely, especially if there were two of them.

Even Jake was coming around to the thought that whatever was being planned had to be happening on the twenty-seventh of September and it almost certainly had to involve the King and Queen. Anything else would surely be pure coincidence.

If there was an anarchist group in Aberdeen then they had been there for some time and they had been planning for some time. The chances of something happening during the King's visit had just increased a hundred times over. Jake thanked the Constable for the information and allowed him to go. Jake then referred to some notes he had taken at the time of Superintendent Harris's visit.

Harris had spoken about Arconada being in the Udny area at the time of the visit of the Spanish royal couple and that had been the middle of August. It seemed perfectly possible that Arconada could have been in Aberdeen on the 8th, with no guarantee that that would have been his first visit Jake noted that the incident in La Granja had been at the beginning of July.

Perhaps, he thought, having had their actions against the Spanish royal couple foiled they had now turned their attention to Britain. Perhaps the opportunity of getting close to the British royal couple, by way of the celebrations in Aberdeen, had been too good a chance for them to miss?

A chill ran through Jake's body and he wondered if he should pass this information on to the Chief Constable. He decided to hold on to it for a little while longer. He would go to the Chief when he had proper evidence that might support the fact that Arconada and his gang were in Aberdeen.

Until then he would keep his thoughts firmly to himself.

FOURTEEN

Saturday 22 September into Sunday 23 September

Constable Stanley Flett turned in to Esslemont Avenue and walked alongside the wall of the Grammar School. He stopped occasionally and shone his torch through the railings, checking for any obvious intruders. There was no sign of life, which was no surprise to the Constable as it was just passed eleven o'clock at night. Darkness had fallen and the air was a lot cooler now than it had been earlier. The sky overhead was inky black with a wondrous array of stars, which the Constable stopped and admired as he reached the end of the railings separating him from the school.

He crossed the road and started to walk up the slight gradient of Esslemont Avenue that would take him up to Rosemount Place. On either side of him were tenement buildings, all occupied by people who were likely to be a lot better off than Constable Flett would ever be. He found himself pondering on what it would be like to live there and then he began to wonder how Tommy had managed it. Maybe the stories about him were true. Maybe he did have a second income coming in from another source; one that no one wanted to talk about in the muster room.

There was an occasional light visible through the drawn curtains as he made his way up the hill but in the main there was nothing more than a feeling that most people were already in their bed getting a good night's sleep ahead of the Sabbath. He was still pondering on the lives of others when he noticed, some way ahead, a man come out of one of the buildings and start to run away up the hill and round in to Rosemount Place. In itself an act that shouldn't have drawn attention but Constable Flett was pretty sure that the man had just come out of the building in which Tommy had lived.

Flett hurried up the hill and entered the building where Mary Thomson was now living. He'd been asked to check out the premises anyway but now that he had seen that man running away there seemed even more need to give the place the once over. Flett did not have to go far.

He shone his torch in to the hallway and then on to the front door. There were marks around the lock of the door which indicated that someone had been attacking it with a metal bar, or some other item, intent on getting the door open. Flett tried the handle and to his horror the door did open.

"Police; I'm coming in!" he shouted with forced bravado and then he entered, shining his torch in all directions as he did so.

There was no one there but all around there were signs that someone had been there and that that someone had turned over practically everything in an attempt, presumably, to find something. Flett hurried to the front door and ignoring the fact he was about to waken half the street, put his whistle to his lips and blew three times sending a shrill sound through the night air.

Constable Hill arrived almost at once. He had been round in Rosemount Place and had seen the running man go down Watson Street. Flett told Hill to go to Inspector Fraser's flat and to tell him what had happened. Flett said that he would stay and keep an eye on the property until the Inspector arrived.

***

Jake was in a deep sleep. He was having a wonderful dream where he was sitting by a river enjoying a picnic with Margaret Gifford. She was looking beautiful and he was feeling good to be in her company. He was just in the process of opening a bottle of Champagne when there was a terrible knocking, which at first he couldn't place, but which finally reached his conscious mind and told him that there had to be someone knocking on his door.

His eyes opened and he jumped out of bed, almost falling over in the process as he really wasn't properly awake. He got to the door and opened it. Constable Hill quickly told him what had happened and Jake told him to come in for a moment. He put Hill in the front room and then went through to the back room to throw on some clothes. Within five minutes both men were hurrying back up the hill in to Rosemount.

By the time they got to Mary's property Constable Flett had the lights on and the mess that the intruder had left was even more evident. Drawers had been pulled out and the contents emptied on the floor. Cupboards had had their contents pulled out and strewn on the carpet and the bed had been all but pulled apart.

"What could they have been looking for, sir?" Flett said as he and Jake surveyed the mess.

"Perhaps the more important question might be, did they find it?" Jake added.

"He certainly took off in a hurry and it couldn't have been because he saw me as I doubt if he did."

"And you said that Hill saw the running man go down Watson Street?"

"Yes, sir."

"Is Hill still here?" Jake then asked.

"Yes, sir, he's at the front door. We've sent word to Sergeant Mathieson and we're just waiting for him to arrive."

Jake went outside and spoke briefly with Constable Hill. The Constable reiterated the fact that he had seen the running man but at some distance and never had the chance to see the man's face. He could, however, say with some certainty that the man looked quite small and from the speed that he was running the Constable was willing to hazard a guess that it had been a young man.

Neither description fitted the man that Alice had seen watching the property, which meant they were either unrelated or there was more than one person involved in finding something relevant to Tommy's past.

Jake went back inside and within a few minutes Sergeant Mathieson arrived. Jake dismissed the Constables, asking one of them to arrange for a joiner to be sent up to mend the door. He then reminded them both to write up their reports before they went off duty. Jake and Mathieson then sat in the back room and surveyed the mess around them.

"Someone was thorough," Mathieson commented.

"Indeed they were," agreed Jake. "What the hell was Tommy up to?"

Mathieson knew that the question did not require an answer for neither of them knew what that answer was. However, they also both knew that until that particular question *was* answered then there seemed little chance that Sandy Wilson, or anyone else, would solve Tommy's murder.

"What do we do now?" Mathieson then said.

"We check the premises just to make sure the man didn't leave any useful clues and then you go home again and I wait for the joiner. I think I'll move in here for a few days just in case someone feels the need to come back."

Mathieson looked around again. "I doubt they'll need to come back."

"They will if they didn't find what they were looking for," Jake added. "On the other hand," he then continued," if what they were looking for is still here then maybe I'll have better luck."

The two men took a room each and began clearing up whilst at the same time checking for anything that the mystery man may have left behind. They found nothing that would help but did manage to tidy the rooms enough so as not to be too upsetting were Mary to return quickly. Mathieson then left and Jake sat down to await the joiner who eventually arrived at a little after one in the morning.

The door was temporarily repaired and the joiner said that he would come back during the day when making a noise might not be quite so intrusive. With the door once more secure Jake headed home to collect some things before returning to Esslemont Avenue and setting up camp for a few days.

FIFTEEN

Sunday 23 September - afternoon

The joiner had returned at lunchtime and repaired the door properly much to the annoyance of the immediate neighbours intent on having a quiet Sunday. Jake made himself a light lunch and then after he had eaten he set about checking the house for anything that the mystery man may have missed.

He started in the front room where there were more drawers and potential hiding areas. Having no idea what he was looking for or, indeed, if there was even anything there at all, did not help Jake in his search. He assumed he was looking for papers, perhaps items left by Tommy to be found in the event of his death; items that might point the finger at those people behind his murder.

Jake spent a long time checking the front room, taking his time so that he felt sure he hadn't missed anything. He found nothing of any consequence, though he did find a box containing papers and photographs that were personal to Tommy and Mary. Jake wondered if there had been something in there that the man may have taken away with him. He had a quick scan through the contents of the box and decided that it was unlikely that Tommy would have kept anything related to his illegal operations with his legitimate paperwork. He would never have put anything where Mary just might have come across it.

No, whatever he was looking for, it had to be better hidden than that.

Jake then went through to the back room. He stood and looked around, deciding there were very few places in which anything could be hidden. He decided that before he did anything else he would make himself a cup of tea and eat some of the biscuits he had taken with him from the flat.

He put the kettle on and then went in to the larder under the stairs to get the packet of tea that he knew was there. As he reached across to take the packet off the shelf his foot gave way slightly beneath him as a floorboard appeared to dip under the downward pressure that he was applying.

Normally he wouldn't have thought anything of such a slight movement but today was not a day for normal thinking. Today was a day for searching everywhere until he found something or, failing that, was totally convinced that there was nothing to find.

Jake dropped to his knees and checked the piece of linoleum that covered the floor. It wasn't fastened down in anyway so he found it rather easy to remove it and get a better look at the floorboards underneath. One of the boards was most certainly loose and Jake tried to lift it with his fingers but found that he couldn't get a good enough grip on anything to achieve his objective.

He quickly hurried to the cutlery drawer and took out a knife. He then hurried back to the loose floorboard and with the help of the knife managed to lift it and set it to one side. Jake then looked in to the space below and at first could see nothing other than dust and dirt. He put his hand in to the hole and searched around a little. Eventually he found a box that had been pushed well under the boards. He took it out and with a sense of triumph carried it over to the table.

The box was very dusty and Jake laid a newspaper on the table first before he placed the box down. He then prised the lid off of the box and placed it to one side. The box was filled with papers. Jake started to remove the papers, reading each piece as he unfolded it. He couldn't believe the half of what he was seeing.

The paperwork was all in the name of Tom Anderson.

Jake studied all the items very carefully. There were statements from the bank showing an account, in the name of Tom Anderson, with hundreds of pounds sitting in it. Whoever Tom Anderson was he was a very rich man indeed.

There were other bank papers, all relevant to the same account and all showing regular deposits of large sums of money the last of which was less than a week before Tommy's death.

There were also papers relevant to Esslemont Avenue, which showed that the property had been bought in the name of Tom Anderson. If these papers actually belonged to Tommy then it was clear that he had been living some kind of double life for quite a while. The bank statements went back eighteen months.

Jake took his notebook from his jacket pocket and jotted down some details of the bank account and a few other, relevant matters concerning Tom Anderson. He then put all the items back in the box and closed the lid. He put his jacket on and put the box in a paper bag that he found in the larder. He then put the floorboard back and replaced the linoleum so that everything looked as it had done before.

Jake then left the house and made his way down the hill towards the city centre. It was another lovely day with warm sunshine and he passed a multitude of people out enjoying the air. How many of them were living double lives, thought Jake? How could it possibly be that a friend as close as Tommy had been to him, managed to hide something as dramatic as a second identity?

What had Tommy been involved in that allowed him to amass so much money? Clearly whatever it had been it had not been legal. Someone had wanted to pay him a lot of money for something. Presumably that same someone had then decided to get rid of him once they decided there was no further use for him.

Jake had intended taking the box back to the office but he changed his mind halfway down Leadside Road. He decided, instead, to take the box to his own flat and to hide it there. He would tell others about his find in good time but just for the moment he would keep this to himself, at least until he had had a chance to visit the bank and try to make some sense of it all himself.

Tommy had been his friend and there had to be an explanation for all this that perhaps did not paint him so completely in the black. The fact that he did not appear to be spending any of his ill-gotten gain, apart from buying the flat, hopefully meant that his conscience continued to tell him that what he was doing was wrong.

Maybe he had done no more than infiltrate a criminal group and all the time he had been building a case to unmask them all? Were that to have been the case then perhaps someone had got wind of what he was doing and had ordered him killed? That would have at least provided a motive for the murder but it would also have put Tommy in a better light once everything became public knowledge.

When Jake opened the door to his flat he found a handwritten note lying on the mat. The spelling was terrible and half the words were wrong but somehow it still managed to convey a message to him. It was clearly from a man Jake knew only as Stinky, for obvious reasons to anyone who had met him. Stinky provided Jake with little items of gossip now and again, which often went a long way to him solving crimes.

The note told Jake that if he wanted to know why Stinky had called then he'd find him in the Tea and Toast any time that afternoon, at least up until five. Jake checked his watch; he had half an hour. The Tea and Toast, referred to in the note, was situated on the corner of the Guestrow and Upperkirkgate. It was a cafe providing basic food to those in the community who were less fortunate. It was also a cafe that was often frequented by men willing to impart a little information to a police officer for a few pennies.

Jake knew that he would have to see Stinky but first he hid the box at the back of his wardrobe covered it with various items of clothing. Jake then went back outside and found himself checking to see if he had been followed. He hadn't stopped to think that someone may still be watching the Esslemont Avenue property and that that someone had been right behind him as he walked down the hill. Had that been the case then they would have noticed that he went in to his own flat with a bag but did not have it when he came out again.

He looked up and down the Guestrow but saw no one, certainly no one who didn't look as if they belonged there. Jake sighed with relief and then cut through on to Broad Street before walking round on to Upperkirkgate and down to the cafe. All the time he kept checking for the possibility that he was being followed but, again, he convinced himself that all was well.

Jake got the Tea and Toast, opened the door and went in. Inside the place was packed with an assortment of men and women dressed in anything but their Sunday best. Jake felt a little overdressed as he walked in and all eyes looked in his direction. He was about to scan for Stinky when he noticed him stand up in the far corner. Jake went to the counter and ordered a cup of tea. The man behind the counter looked every bit as dirty as his customers and the general mess that lay around the place was anything but inviting.

Stinky may have felt at home in a place like this but Jake had no intention of staying any longer than he had to. In fact he had no intention of drinking the tea he had just bought; that was for Stinky.

Jake made his way over to the spare seat beside where Stinky had been wiling away his afternoon reading the paper. He now folded that and placed it on the table. He thanked Jake for the tea and then leaned forward to speak in tones that were unlikely to find their way to prying ears. Jake fought the desire to sit back as the aroma rising from Stinky was almost unbearable.

"Okay, what have you got for me?" Jake said, taking out his handkerchief and holding it over his nose as if it were needing blowing.

Stinky slurped at his tea, looked around to make sure no one was listening and then began to speak.

"Information about the Marischal Street murders, Mr Fraser, that's what I have for you."

Jake forgot momentarily about the smell and moved a little closer. "What kind of information?"

"I've heard that there was a man hanging around Marischal Street about the time those women were murdered."

"I'm sure there were lots of men hanging around Marischal Street, Stinky, it's a very busy street," said Jake in a rather dismissive manner.

"Maybe so, Mr Fraser, but this man looked a little out of place.....so I heard."

"What do you mean out of place?" Jake asked, his interest aroused again.

"A friend of mine, who shall remain nameless, saw a man walking up and down Marischal Street as if he was trying to make his mind up about something. My friend said this man seemed lost in thought."

"And could your friend describe this man?"

"He said he was a bit of a toff, Mr Fraser. He was well dressed for Marischal Street. He walked in a very upright, military style. He was clearly a man who has seen military service at some time in his life; my friend was sure about that. The gentleman also carried a cane."

Jake sat back a little. "Most Gentlemen do."

"This was a very ornate cane. I'm sure my friend would know it if he saw it again."

Jake thought for a moment. "Did your friend get a clear view of this man's face?"

"Not a clear view, no. The man's face was quite heavily whiskered, but they were well trimmed in keeping with his overall appearance."

"And he was hanging around Jessie McGill's property?" Jake then asked by way of clarification.

"My friend said he saw this man in Marischal Street, he didn't actually say he was outside the place where the crime was done."

Jake took a moment to think things through. This man could easily have been Doctor Samuels and if that were the case then it proved that the Doctor knew far more about the Wednesday morning meetings than he had implied so far. If he did know about Julia meeting with someone then maybe he had gone to confront them and things had got out of hand?

Jake took some change from his pocket and passed it across the table to Stinky.

"Thank you, Mr Fraser," Stinky said, scooping up the money and pushing it in to his jacket pocket.

"Before I go," Jake then said, "there's something else that I'd like you to do for me but I need it done quickly."

"Anything for you, Mr Fraser, you know that."

"What I am about to say is strictly between you and I, Stinky, this is not to be repeated anywhere else, do you understand?"

"Cross my heart, Mr Fraser."

"There is a slight possibility that there is a group of foreign gentlemen in Aberdeen at the moment planning some kind of attack on the King and Queen when they visit on Thursday."

"That's terrible, Mr Fraser," Stinky added, drinking some more of the tea.

"I want you to ask around and find out if anyone knows anything about this gang. I need to know, one way or another, by Tuesday; can you do that for me?"

"I've not heard anything about foreigners, Mr Fraser, but I'll put the word out and get back to you on Tuesday evening. Where can I find you?"

"I'll meet you in the Ythan around eight."

"Very well, I'll see you then."

The Ythan was the Banks of Ythan public house, which was situated on the corner of Queen Street and Lodge Walk. Jake said farewell and made his way out of the cafe and onwards up to Esslemont Avenue.

This had certainly been a day for gathering information. Jake wasn't sure exactly what he might do with his information but he at least felt that he was moving forward again on two out of the three cases he was currently involved with.

He let himself in to the property and then settled down for the evening. He opened a bottle of beer and allowed himself to sit for a while without having to think about murders and the people who may have committed them.

SIXTEEN

Monday 24 September - morning

Jake got to work early as he knew it was going to be a long, though hopefully productive day. He tidied up the items left lying on his desk and then made his way down to Mearns Street for another visit to the Sailors' Institute and perhaps more importantly, another chance to see Margaret Gifford. Even though Jake had been really busy at work he had never completely forgotten about Margaret Gifford and he was really looking forward to speaking to her again.

As it turned out Margaret Gifford seemed rather pleased to be speaking again to Jake. She greeted him with a warm smile and a handshake that seemed to linger a few seconds longer than was absolutely necessary.

"I thought you were to be visiting my home were you to have any further questions for me?" Margaret asked with a teasing tone to her voice.

Jake knew that he was blushing again.

"Time is of the essence, Margaret and it was easier to find you here."

"Very well, let us go through to my office this time."

They had then gone to a small office after Margaret had arranged for some tea to be brought through to them. The office was small but comfortably furnished and definitely with a woman's touch.

"What may I do for you this time, Jake?" she said, using his name with ease as if she had known him for a while.

"The last time we spoke you said that you had met Doctor Samuels on a few occasions. You further said that the man did not leave a good impression on you and that you were rather glad he wasn't your doctor."

"Goodness me, did I say all that?" Margaret added with a smile.

There was a knock at the door and a young girl came in with a tray on which lay a pot of tea, two cups and some biscuits. She placed the tray on Margaret's desk and left the room without as much as smile breaking across her slightly sullen face. Margaret poured the tea and handed a cup across to Jake. She then offered him a biscuit which he readily accepted.

"Anyway," Jake continued," I wondered how many times you had met the Doctor?"

Margaret thought for a moment. "A handful of times. He did come to the Institute occasionally and I also met him socially at one or two events around the city."

"Did he attend the social events with Julia?"

"Nearly always."

"So he liked to keep an eye on her?" Jake prompted.

"He is a father, Jake, aren't they all protective of their daughters?"

"Would I be wrong to think that he might have been over protective?"

Margaret thought again. "He certainly kept her on a tight rein. Why all this interest in Julia's father, if you don't mind me asking?"

"Just routine enquiries," Jake lied," we gather information on anyone connected to a murder victim, you never know what might turn up."

"Like us meeting?" Margaret suggested and Jake sensed she was teasing him again.

There was no doubt that this highly attractive woman seemed interested in him and as he finished off the last few questions concerning Doctor Samuels he was beginning to play with the notion of asking her to dinner. He had an ever growing feeling that she might just accept his invitation and it would be such a wonderful distraction from all the work-related activities in his life at the present.

"What can you tell me about Billy Sim?" Jake then said, deciding that quicker he changed the subject the better.

Margaret looked surprised by the question. "My goodness, why ever would you be asking about Billy?"

"Just routine, as I said," Jake replied though he knew that Margaret Gifford was never going to believe that.

"Billy's a nice lad. He has great plans for himself. I'm not at all sure that any of them will ever come to fruition, but you have to admire him for his optimism."

"Were you ever aware of a relationship forming between Billy and Julia?"

Margaret's eyes opened even further in surprise. "I was never aware of Julia starting to form a relationship with anyone. The men liked her because she was young and pretty and there was some light-hearted joking went on but never anything that indicated she may have been any closer to one other than the other. Do you have a particular reason for thinking there was something between Billy and Julia?"

"They were seeing each other," Jake replied, knowing that Margaret would not say a word of this to anyone else. "Julia did not start work somewhere else on a Wednesday morning, she simply wanted to create time to meet Billy."

"And they met at Jessie's?"

"Yes."

"Was it a sexual liaison, or maybe you can't say?"

"There was never anything sexual about the relationship beyond the odd kiss perhaps. They were just two, young people who had found a pleasure in each other's company," Jake replied. "They liked to meet and they liked to talk. Billy tells me that they spoke of their future and what they hoped that future might bring."

"Poor Julia has now been denied that future," Margaret added.

"I believe Billy would have liked Julia to have been part of his future but he was honest enough to realise that he would never have been in a position to offer Julia the life her father would have wanted for her."

Margaret's face filled with horror again. "Surely Billy didn't kill her?"

"Billy was at sea at the time of the crime so he can have nothing to do with what happened. Billy knew nothing about what had happened until a nasty piece of work called Lenny Bassett took some pleasure in telling him."

"Lenny's a lovely man," Margaret added with heavy sarcasm. "I had to throw him out of the Institute's restaurant one day when he tried, unsuccessfully, to grab one of the girls working as a waitress that day."

"Lenny appears to have a problem with his hands," Jake then said, "but I've recently had a word with him on that subject so, hopefully, from now on he'll think twice before touching anyone."

Margaret smiled. "Very much the knight in shining armour aren't you, Jake?"

"I'm just doing my job," responded Jake, feeling the flush return to his face.

"Do you have any idea who might have killed poor Julia?" Margaret then asked finishing her tea and then pouring fresh cups.

"I may have, but obviously I can't comment on that at the moment."

"Of course not, but I sincerely hope that you get this person and you get him quickly."

Jake spent a little while longer talking to Margaret, though this time about more general matters. Once he had finished his tea he stood up and thanked Margaret for her help. He then, rather tentatively, asked her if she might allow him to escort her to watch the Students' Torchlight Procession that was due to pass through the centre of the city the following night.

Margaret thought that to be a delightful idea so Jake very quickly floated the suggestion that they might have dinner first.

"I have an arrangement with the Athenaeum, if you would be happy to go there?" Jake had added.

"An arrangement?" mocked Margaret. "That sounds all very mysterious."

Jake smiled. "I happen to know the Head Waiter that is all."

Margaret accepted the invitation and said how much she was looking forward to going to such a prestigious restaurant. Jake felt a surge of joy pass through him as they arranged for him to collect Margaret at half past six the following evening

Jake then left the Sailors' Institute with an even stronger spring in his step and made his way to The Douglas Hotel on Market Street where he asked for confirmation of Doctor Samuels' booking on the night of the medical dinner. One of the Assistant Managers was able to confirm that Doctor Samuels checked in at five o'clock on the Tuesday afternoon and checked out again at noon on the Wednesday.

He was also able to confirm that, at least according to the hotel records, Doctor Samuels had arrived in the dining room for breakfast at eight o'clock on the Wednesday morning.

Jake thanked the young man for his help and made his way out on to Market Street. So Doctor Samuels had breakfast at eight but did not check-out until noon. Plenty time to go round to Marischal Street and the come back before going through the checking-out process.

***

Jake quickly made his way to this property in the Guestrow and took some papers from the tin box he had found in Esslemont Avenue. He also put a photograph that he had of Tommy in his pocket and made his way back down to the street.

Jake now made his way round to the North of Scotland Bank on the corner of King Street and Union Street. Flags and bunting were stretched from the bank across to the Mercat Cross in the centre of the Castlegate. Red material hung down across the entrance to the bank parting in the middle to allow customers to enter.

Jake carried out one final check to ensure that he had all that he needed with him before entering the building and walking the length of the public hall.

Above him there was nothing but ornate woodwork and the doors, that were visible to his right, were finished in the finest wood that had been polished to within an inch of its life. The building positively screamed affluence at its customers as they waited to be seen by a member of staff.

At the far end of the room from the entrance doorway were the cashier points; a row of faces hiding behind grilles. Jake was delighted to find the bank very quiet and he was able to walk up to one of the cashier points without having to wait any time at all. The cashier was a very serious looking gentleman with round spectacles perched towards the end of a rather long nose.

Jake showed the man his identification and asked to see the manager. The man did not seem very keen on bothering the manager and tried to persuade Jake to speak to someone else. Jake insisted that the matter was far too serious for it not to be brought to the attention of the manager and said, once again, that it was police business and were they not to help him with his inquiries then there could be serious repercussions. The man's face paled visibly and he asked Jake to take a seat before hurrying off to see someone about Jake's enquiry.

Jake was left sitting for twenty minutes, which did little for his mood. In that time he had watched a number of clearly wealthy people come and go. Eventually a man appeared from a door to the right of the cashiers. He was dressed in a very formal looking suit and he too had a very serious expression on his face. Jake was rapidly coming to the opinion that no one was allowed to smile in this place if they were employed to work there.

"Inspector Fraser," the man said," my name is Royston McIntosh and I am the Chief Clerk of this branch. I am afraid that Mr Muir is with someone else at this moment and he has asked me to deal with your inquiry."

"Mr McIntosh, I am sure that you have a great deal of authority within this branch but I can assure you that only the manager will be able to deal with my inquiry and as I said to your cashier, if the manager fails to help me with my enquiries then there may be repercussions that would not be favourable to the reputation of this branch."

In reality Jake knew that there would be no repercussions but it always sounded an effective threat and it had never failed to work in the past. It did not fail to work in the present either as McIntosh's face went the same pale colour as the cashiers as he suggested that Jake follow him.

They went back through the door from which McIntosh had come in the first place and Jake found himself in a small hallway, off of which came a variety of doors. McIntosh led the way through one of the doors to their left and this in turn led them to what looked like a back door to the building.

They passed that door and turned left, coming out in another hall area, which had a staircase rise from it. They climbed the stair and then followed a short corridor before coming out on another staircase. To Jake this was one rabbit warren of a building and he was pleased to have a guide with him as he felt sure, that left to his own devices, he would have got lost.

At the top of this last, short staircase they turned right and McIntosh led Jake along yet another corridor to a door on their left. McIntosh knocked on the door, opened it and led the way in. The room that Jake now found himself in was that of perhaps a secretary, or more likely the personal assistant to the bank manager.

It was quite a large room with a row of chairs along the wall to the right and two windows allowing a view of Union Street set into the wall facing. To the left was a door through to the next room and a large desk behind which sat a very pretty young woman with smiling eyes.

"If you would like to have a seat, Inspector Fraser," McIntosh then said and knocked on the door behind the young woman. He did not wait for an invitation but opened the door and went in. It seemed quite clear to Jake that the manager was not with a customer at all but perhaps he had some other reason for not wanting to see him.

It was only a brief wait before McIntosh came out again, leaving the door behind him open. Seconds later a small, rather round gentleman in an ill-fitting suit and highly polished shoes appeared and held out his hand.

"Inspector Fraser, my name is Bertram Muir, the manager of this branch. My apologies for the fact you had difficulty in seeing me but I had made it known that I was not wanting to be disturbed while I looked over the monthly accounts. Of course that instruction was never meant to include police inquiries."

Muir gave McIntosh a withering look and then stepped back to allow Jake to enter his office. The room was palatial in its design with a large fireplace almost filling one wall and three windows allowing light to flood in. It was a room that put the Chief Constable's office to shame.

Muir invited Jake to sit down and then returned to his own chair which was on the opposite side of the desk. As Muir sat down Jake looked around the room again, paying particular attention to that ornate fireplace. Jake had a vision of some lowly bank clerk having the rather dubious honour of lighting the fire on a cold and wintry morning so that by the time Mr Muir arrived for work his office would be up to his preferred temperature.

Looking at Mr Muir, with his stern expression and sharp tone, Jake imagined that were that room not up to the preferred temperature then that poor clerk would get hell from his manager.

Muir had a round face to match his round body with extra chins appearing where he may have preferred them not to. Mr Muir obviously lived a good life and enjoyed his food. Perhaps to try and hide the extra chins he had attempted to grow facial whiskers but this had failed rather badly with only a sporadic outbreak of bristles in certain parts of his face. All in all the whiskers made him look rather comical and not at all as masculine as he probably hoped.

Jake took the papers from his pocket.

"We are currently investigating the murder of a police officer, Mr Muir and I believe that you may be able to help us with that enquiry."

Muir looked puzzled. "I seem to remember reading about that particular murder, Inspector. A terrible business but I can't imagine that this branch has anything to do with such a horrendous crime."

"This branch is directly connected to the crime, Mr Muir, through the fact that the victim had papers relating to an account here."

Muir looked even more puzzled. "As I said, Inspector, I remember reading about the case in the paper but I have no recollection of the victim being a customer here. I assume we are talking about the same case?"

"The victim was Constable Alexander Thomson and I don't recall that I said he was a customer here."

Muir looked annoyed at being scolded like a small child.

"Perhaps, in that case Inspector, you would care to explain what the connection between the dead man and my bank might be?"

"As I said, Mr Muir, the connection is in the form of paperwork."

Jake took a couple of the papers and slid them across the desk top to Muir. The manager picked them up and cast an eye across them.

"These papers are in the name of Tom Anderson."

"Quite so, Mr Muir and I am trying to find out what the connection might be between Tom Anderson and my dead colleague."

Muir now looked very worried.

"You're not suggesting it might be a fake account?"

"I don't know, that is what I am hoping to find out here today," Jake added.

Muir then began to bluster that, fake or otherwise, it was unlikely that he would be able to give Jake much information due to their strict rules of confidentiality. After all, it was still perfectly possible that Tom Anderson did exist and that Alexander Thomson simply had the paperwork for some other reason.

Jake reminded Muir that this was a murder enquiry and that it was also perfectly possible that the account holder and the murder victim could be one and the same person. Muir had looked like he might continue to protest but he finally took a sheet of paper from the drawer to his right and sat with pen poised.

"Very well."

Muir wrote down the details of the Tom Anderson account. Jake also asked if Muir could arrange for a member of staff, who might be able to identify Tom Anderson, to come up and see him. Muir walked over to the adjoining door and Jake overheard him ask the young woman to bring him the file on Tom Anderson and also to ask Miss Scott to come up to his office.

Muir then returned to his desk. A matter of moments later there was a knock on the door and the young woman came in clutching a file to her chest. She crossed the floor and placed the file on Muir's desk.

"Thank you, Miss Lindsay," Muir said.

"Miss Scott is just finishing with a customer and then she will come to your office as requested, Mr Muir."

"Very good. That will be all just now, Miss Lindsay."

Jake almost expected Miss Lindsay to curtsey before she left. There was no doubting that Mr Muir looked the type to expect nothing less from his staff.

Muir started to look through the file and read one or two of the sheets of paper before there was another knock only this time at the main door to the office rather than the adjoining door through the Miss Lindsay.

"Come in," Muir shouted.

The door opened and an older woman walked in. She was dressed all in black and had that same stern expression that seemed essential for all the staff. This, Jake assumed, was Miss Scott and she looked far less likely to be intimidated by Mr Muir. In fact, Jake was of the opinion that it was far more likely to be the other way around.

Miss Scott was introduced to Jake and then asked to take a seat beside him. Jake briefly explained why he was there and then, without actually mentioning the name Tom Anderson or tying that name to Tommy in anyway, he let Miss Scott see the photograph he had of Tommy.

"That's Mr Anderson," she said immediately, "he's a very nice man."

Jake took the photograph back. "You are quite sure that the man in this photograph is the man you know as Tom Anderson?"

It was Miss Scott's turn to look puzzled and ever so slightly nervous as the words the man you know as Tom Anderson.

"But this is Mr Anderson," Miss Scott insisted. "I was the one who opened the account for him and also dealt with most of his visits when he came to pay in cash to the account."

"The man in this photograph is actually Constable Alexander Thomson," Jake then said. "Did he produce any evidence that he was Tom Anderson when he opened his account?"

Muir looked back at the file on his desk. "He had details pertinent to the house he had just bought in Esslemont Avenue."

Miss Scott was still looking puzzled. "Mr Anderson did not come in very often, but when he did it was always to pay in a large sum of money. The last visit would have been at the end of last month and I remember joking with him that business must have been good. He was always laughing and joking when he was here. I never thought for one moment that he had any connection to the police."

"Mr Anderson wasn't connected to the police; that was Alexander Thomson."

"But they were one and the same person," Miss Scott added.

"So it would seem. Miss Scott I have to ask you to keep this information to yourself for moment and that goes for you as well, Mr Muir."

Muir looked suitably offended. "Inspector Fraser the staff of this branch work to the highest levels of confidentiality and are not in the habit of spreading official business around town."

Miss Scott left the room at that point.

"As Mr Thomson is no longer in a position to play the part of Tom Anderson might it be possible for me to have a look at that file?" Jake then said, his eyes looking down on the file lying in front of Muir.

There was a momentary pause whilst Muir still considered the possibility of claiming client confidentiality but eventually he again decided that he might as well co-operate with the police and be as helpful as possible. He slid the file across the desk and sat back again. Jake spun the file round and started to look through the contents.

Much of the information was actually still about Tommy though there were a few fictional additions to pad out the character of Tom Anderson. The one element that clearly separated Tom Anderson from Alexander Thomson was the amounts that had been paid in. The balance of the account was currently sitting at two thousand pounds; a sum of money that lay beyond the wildest dreams of almost everyone.

Payments in to the account had been made roughly quarterly. The account had been opened for eighteen months and on each occasion the money that had been paid in had been in cash. It was patently obvious to anyone who knew Tommy that this money had not come from his police work.

It was also obvious that Tommy had not been involved in any other form of legitimate employment as all police officers were required to get permission before taking second jobs. By the size of the account it was further obvious that Tommy could not have made that kind of money by simply taking a second job. There had to be a more sinister side to this money but neither Jake, nor anyone else at Lodge Walk, currently had the slightest idea what that might be.

Jake finished looking through the file but learned nothing as to why Tommy should be running a second account under an alias. The occupation of Tom Anderson was given as self-employed; unfortunately he did not say what form that self-employment took.

It seemed incredible to Jake that Tommy had managed to amass this amount of money without any suspicion being cast on him. He had managed to buy Esslemont Avenue without Mary knowing anything. Jake knew that Mary was under the impression that she was renting the property and he also knew that she made payments each month towards that rent.

That meant that Tommy had been paying rent to himself; but where was that account? This was developing in to one of the most puzzling cases that Jake had ever been involved in. Nothing made any sense and even when clues did come along they failed to move the case in any positive direction.

Jake took a few notes then closed the file and slid it back to Muir. He thanked Muir for his time and stood up to leave. Muir went through and asked the young woman in the other room to take Jake downstairs.

"Miss Lindsay will see you out," Muir said, shaking Jake's hand once more.

Miss Lindsay then led the way to the staircase though this time they took a different route out of the building. On the way down Jake asked Miss Lindsay what she thought of Mr Muir as a boss. She looked very wary about answering the question and it was quite clear from her nervous disposition that Mr Muir ruled with a rod of iron that seemed to keep his staff in a constant state of fear.

Jake thanked Miss Lindsay as she opened a door and let him out. He found himself back at the front door, though at a different exit point. He watched as Miss Lindsay closed the door and then set off for Lodge Walk, all the time thinking about Mr Muir and his managerial style. Just as he reached the archway that led in to Lodge Walk Jake walked in to Alan MacBride, who was coming the other way.

"Ah, Inspector Fraser, fancy meeting you on such a lovely day."

"It was a lovely day until you came along," Jake commented and MacBride looked suitably hurt.

"I've heard that you might have a lead in the Julia Samuels' murder?"

"You really must stop believing everything you read in the papers," Jake quipped. "I've told you before, when I have something that might be of interest to the Press then you will be the first person I contact. Prior to that, however, I will not be drawn in to conjecture and half-truths."

"So you don't have a lead?" MacBride pressed.

"You don't give up do you?" was all that Jake said as he brushed passed and continued on his way.

MacBride called after him. "What about PC Thomson then, is that investigation going anywhere?"

"Not my case," Jake called back and quickened his step to cover the short distance to the front door of the police office.

MacBride made no attempt to follow Jake. He casually lit a cigarette and set off along Union Street.

SEVENTEEN

Monday 24 September - late afternoon in to evening

It was late in the afternoon before Jake got a chance to speak to Sandy Wilson. He took time to update him on the bank visit and the information he now had about Tom Anderson. Sandy sat in silence and growing disbelief as Jake spoke. Here was a major breakthrough in the case and yet all it did was add even more mystery rather than provide a means for solving it.

At least it appeared to prove, without any doubt, that Tommy had indeed been involved in illegal activities prior to his death though they felt no closer to knowing what those activities may have been.

"So, was someone paying Tommy to look the other way?" Sandy then said once Jake had fully brought him up to date.

"Who knows, Sandy," replied Jake. "These are large sums of money so whatever he was into, it was big."

"And yet the fact he was reported as being on such a short fuse might indicate some form of inner turmoil," Sandy added. "Maybe the Tommy we all knew was still fighting in some way, still trying to find a way out of the mess he had got into?"

"He certainly hadn't spent any of the money, apart from at the very beginning when he bought the flat," Jake said," so maybe you're right, maybe he was being forced to take the money, though that wouldn't make much sense either."

"But Tommy didn't usually lose his temper that easily," insisted Sandy as if that had some major part to play in the solving of the case.

"Apart from at the football," joked Jake. "You know that Tommy always believed that any team with Aberdeen in its name should never lose."

Sandy laughed and they both fell silent for a moment as they remembered Tommy's face get redder than ever when he went off on one of his famous Pittodrie rants.

"Tommy was paying in large amounts of cash to the Anderson account," Sandy then said, "so how did he get the money in the first place?"

Jake shrugged his shoulders. "They maybe met him on his beat or Mary did say that Tommy had been going to the pub more so perhaps that was where they met."

Sandy thought for a few seconds and then announced that he was going to take a walk round Tommy's old beat just in case he found inspiration in something.

Jake, on the other hand, went in search of Mathieson. On route, however, he was met by the Chief, who was on his way home.

"I've just heard back from London regarding your query about Statham and the London address you got from the Palace Hotel."

"They've taken their time; I'm assuming it's another dead end, sir?" Jake said somewhat pessimistically.

"The address is a guest house and there was no obvious connection to anyone called Statham."

"Considering Statham doesn't even exist that comes as no surprise, sir."

"Our colleagues in London did say, however, that they will mail us a list of those names they took from the guest house register, just in case any of the names are of any help to us."

"I can't imagine they will be, but it was good of London to think it might."

The Chief went on his way and Jake continued his search for Mathieson.

Jake had decided that they would pay Doctor Samuels a visit that evening and see if at least that case could now be brought to a conclusion.

***

Janet Lindsay had been worried from the moment she had closed the door after seeing the police Inspector out of the building. She had been fairly confident that the police officer's visit was only to do with the Anderson account and was in no way connected with what her boyfriend was planning for Thursday. However, the mere fact that there had been a police officer in the branch that close to Thursday had unnerved her slightly.

Thankfully she was due to see Reynolds that evening and now she couldn't wait for the time to come around.

It had been just after six when she arrived at the first floor property in a rather scruffy looking block in Park Street. She hated going there. Park Street was full of undesirables and she also had to pass the Saltoun Arms, which usually had drunk and uncouth men pouring out through its doors at all times of an evening.

It was also still fresh in Janet's mind that only five years ago there had been a murder in the Saltoun Arms when a man named Harrow had murdered two of his butcher friends. Harrow had been quite insane, of course, but the fact that an act of such brutality could take place in a public house chilled Janet to the bone.

She knocked on the Park Street door and waited. Time passed and it seemed that no one was coming to open the door. A man came up the stairs and gave her a rather lustful look as he passed. Janet was just about to knock again when the door opened.

Reynolds smiled at the fact it was Janet and after he had allowed her to pass and enter the property he then checked the staircase as if satisfying himself that she had not been followed. He knew that it was highly unlikely that anyone would be paying any attention to Janet, but he was a careful man who left nothing to chance. Satisfied that she was alone he stepped back inside and shut the door, turning the locks in the process.

Janet Lindsay had gone straight through to the bedroom. She had the excited look of a child being given a new toy as she undid the buttons on her jacket. She then threw herself in to Reynold's arms and they kissed passionately.

Nothing more was said as clothing was removed and they tumbled in to bed where they found sexual satisfaction in each other's embrace. Janet had let out a low moan of pleasure as he had entered her and together they worked themselves to a climax that was accompanied by further groans of pleasure.

Janet Lindsay had never been with a man sexually before she met Reynolds. Apart from her father no man had ever really played a major part in her life although she had been kissed once by way of an experiment with the boy next door when she had been fifteen. However, the day her brother had introduced her to this man called Reynolds had been the day that she had found herself engulfed in a sexual magnetism that took her breath away at times.

She had never thought that she would ever have given herself to a man who was not her husband. She had been brought up to believe that there was no place in an unmarried woman's life for sex. She sometimes felt that she had been destined to have no sexual pleasure of any kind in her life and yet here she was brazenly going to bed with a man whom she had only known for four months.

Prior to meeting Reynolds she had known nothing about sex, now she couldn't stop thinking about it; couldn't stop yearning for his touch and the feel of his hard body lying against her own. She also knew that whatever this man asked her do she would do and she would do it without question. She loved him and that was all that mattered.

Once their climax subsided Reynolds rolled off of Janet and reached for a packet of cigarettes that was lying on the bedside table. He sat up and lit one of the cigarettes, taking a lungful of smoke in to his system before exhaling it towards the ceiling. Janet pushed the blankets down a little so that her small breasts were visible as they lay flat against her chest.

"There was a police officer at the bank today," she said.

Reynolds took another drag on his cigarette. "It can't be anything to do with us, no one knows we're even here let alone know what we're planning."

"He was asking about a specific account."

"There you go, told you it had nothing to do with us."

"It just seemed bad timing having a copper visit this close to Thursday," Janet then said as she sat up beside him.

Reynolds turned to face her. "Look, the coppers can sniff around as much as they like because it won't change our plans in any way whatsoever. And talking of plans," he then said looking at the clock, "the gang will be here soon so we'd best get some clothes on."

***

At the moment Reynolds was getting out of bed Jake and Mathieson were climbing aboard a tram that would take them up to Fountainhall Road. From there they walked the short distance along Hamilton Place until they came to the Doctor's property. Jake rang the bell and waited for someone to open the door. Surprisingly it was Doctor Samuels himself who opened the door and bade the two police officers to enter.

Samuels led the way in to the sitting room and they all sat down before anything of any importance was actually said. As Jake began to speak Doctor Samuels picked up a pipe and started to fill it with tobacco from a pouch lying beside it.

"I have a few more questions to ask regarding the day that your daughter died."

Samuels showed little change in his facial expression as he listened to what Jake was saying, but he continued to pack his pipe as casually as if he were listening to a variety show singer rather than to a police officer talking about his daughter's murder.

Jake continued.

"We have now been made aware that Julia had recently stopped working at the Institute on a Wednesday morning. Had she discussed a possible change with you, Doctor Samuels?"

The Doctor fired up his pipe and briefly disappeared in a cloud of thick smoke. He puffed a couple of times on the stem to satisfy himself that he was fully lit then settled back in his chair to enjoy his smoke. He took a little while longer before answering the question.

"No, my daughter did not discuss that with me."

"But you did know that Julia had stopped working at the Sailors' Institute on a Wednesday morning, didn't you?"

Jake was fishing a little. He didn't know for certain that the man seen in Marischal Street was Doctor Samuels but his policeman's stomach was complaining and that usually meant he was getting closer to the truth. Doctor Samuels sucked on his pipe and seemed to be considering the answer that he would give. Jake was happy to let the silence hang in the room and await a response, however long that might take.

"On the night of the medical dinner I was talking to an old friend who has a property in Marischal Street. He is currently decorating that property with a view to leasing it once he has finished and he happened to mention that he had seen Julia, on three consecutive Wednesdays, entering a building across the road. That was the first I knew that she probably wasn't going to the Sailors' Institute every day as she claimed to be."

"Why didn't you mention this before?"

"I didn't think it was relevant, Inspector. After all, I didn't kill Julia so what difference would it have made?"

"The fact you knew more than you were saying is very relevant, Doctor Samuels. It leads to the question of what else you might be hiding from us."

Samuels took his pipe from his mouth and looked across at Jake with his temper rising.

"Are you saying that I am a liar?" he snapped.

"Keeping information from the police is a form of lying, Doctor, you surely wouldn't disagree with that?"

Samuels remained silent again for a little while. Jake let him calm down again before saying anything further. Eventually he felt the time was right to continue.

"We have a witness who saw someone hanging around Marischal Street on the morning during which your daughter was killed. The description given of that person matches yourself, Doctor Samuels. We also know that you had breakfast at around eight that morning but did not check-out from the hotel until noon. What were you doing for the intervening four hours?"

"I sat in my room and read a book. It was nice to have some peace and quiet."

"So you weren't in Marischal Street that morning?"

Doctor Samuels paused again. His eyes had been looking across at Jake but he now looked away before answering. "No, I wasn't."

That movement of his eyes was enough for Jake. He had seen a procession of liars throughout his career and he had come to look for certain tell-tale signs that someone was no longer telling him the whole truth. Not making eye contact was high up on the list of things to look for. A person finds telling lies a lot easier if they are not looking at anyone. Eye contact can say so much more than words sometimes.

"In that case," Jake continued," just so that we can conclude this particular line of enquiry, I would like you to attend the police station tomorrow evening so that we can place you in an identity parade and have our witness confirm that you are not the man he saw that morning in Marischal Street."

Samuels put his pipe back in his mouth and puffed thoughtfully. Jake wasn't even sure that he could find the witness let alone be sure that he would then remember exactly what the man in Marischal Street looked like. However, he was hoping that the Doctor would not want to put his request to the test.

"Very well, Inspector," Samuels eventually said and Jake knew immediately that he was finally breaking through that facade of a heartbroken father. Mathieson took his notebook from his pocket and sat expectantly awaiting some form of confession. "I was in Marischal Street that morning."

"And you were outraged at being taken for a liar," Jake said with a shake of his head. "So far, Doctor Samuels, you have chosen to tell me nothing of importance until I have pulled it out of you as if I were removing teeth. Isn't it about time that you started telling me the truth?"

There was another silent pause. Doctor Samuels' pipe had gone out and he now took time to relight it. Once he was again puffing contentedly on the stem he began to speak.

"I had had a sleepless night pondering on what I had been told about Julia. I eventually came to the conclusion that I would go round to Marischal Street in the morning and watch for her, just to see where she went or what she did."

"Were you annoyed that she had kept this from you?"

The Doctor's eyes flashed anger. "Too damned right I was annoyed. I did not bring up my daughter to lie to me."

"Of course, Doctor Samuels, just as you would never dream of lying yourself," Jake added with heavy sarcasm in his tone.

The Doctor's eyes flashed anger again and Jake could see that just under the surface of this man's demeanour was a temper that could well be capable of anything.

"Anyway," Samuels eventually continued," I had breakfast and then made my way out of the hotel whilst everyone at reception was too busy to notice me passing. I went round to Marischal Street and walked up and down for a little while. Obviously I had no idea if Julia would even turn up but I decided to give it a little time just in case."

"And Julia did turn up, didn't she?" prompted Jake.

The Doctor's expression changed from one of anger to one of deep sorrow.

"Yes she did."

"Where did she come from when you first saw her?"

"She came up Marischal Street, Inspector and then went in to the house almost opposite where I was standing. She didn't see me as her head was down and she looked upset, as if something had just happened and she was in a hurry to get away from it."

"How was Julia dressed, Doctor Samuels?" was Jake's next question.

Fleetingly the sorrow left the Doctor's eyes and anger returned.

"She had just come from the harbour area, Inspector and she was dressed like a common prostitute."

The words were almost spat at Jake.

"You thought your daughter was a ....," Jake began.

Samuels cut him short. "I thought she was acting in a very unladylike manner."

"What happened next?" Jake prompted once more.

"I followed her in to the building and saw which property she went in to. I checked the name that was on the door and when I saw it was J McGill I knew at once that it had to be Jessie, who also worked at the Sailors' Institute."

Jake felt he was nearly there in terms of extracting the full story from Doctor Samuels. "I presume you knew that Jessie used to be a prostitute?"

"Used to be?" Samuels added with some surprise. "Do women like that ever change?"

Jake felt his own anger rising and fought to control it. "Women like that, as you rather crudely put it Doctor, change all the time. Jessie McGill was making something of her life and I'm sure that your daughter would have gained much from knowing someone like Jessie who had shown what you can make of life with a bit of hard work. Did you honestly think that Jessie would do anything to change Julia, especially lead her in to prostitution?"

"It was seeing her in that dress and the fact that she came from the harbour area. What else was I to think?" Samuels said, almost pleading for an answer.

"That's why you expressed surprise when I said that Julia was a virgin?" Jake then said. "My God, man, you really thought that your daughter had taken to selling her body at the harbour?"

"It was that damned dress!" yelled Samuels. "Why else would she be wearing a dress like that?"

"Doctor Samuels, your daughter went to Marischal Street every Wednesday to meet a young man. His name was Billy Sim and he was a fisherman."

Samuels looked horrified but he said nothing. Jake continued.

"Both Julia and Billy knew that you would not approve of them meeting so they said nothing to anyone. They met simply to talk, Doctor Samuels and Jessie provided the place for them to meet. There was nothing sinister, nor was there anything sexual in their relationship. They were simply good friends."

"But what about that dress?" insisted Samuels.

"That particular morning Billy had gone to sea without being able to tell either Julia or Jessie. Julia simply went looking for Billy and probably chose to wear one of Jessie's dresses as it would have looked a little less noticeable down around the harbour than one of her own. She was only at the harbour for a very short time as she would have quickly noticed that Billy's boat had gone."

"Oh my God," Samuels now said and tears started to roll down his cheeks. "What have I done?"

"Perhaps this might be the time to tell us exactly what happened that morning?"

Doctor Samuels put his pipe down and stood up. He crossed to a chest of drawers, which lay against the main wall. There were three decanters lying on a tray and he proceeded to pour himself a drink, which he downed in one. He then poured himself a second drink and returned to his seat.

"I knocked on the door. I wanted to confront Julia. I wanted to know what she was doing in a place like that and dressed in that manner. I was angry with her and I wanted answers. Can you imagine my increased horror when the door opened and I saw a woman I assumed was Jessie McGill, standing there wearing my daughter's dress? It was an outrage that a dress of that quality should be worn by a woman who sold her body for money."

"Used to sell her body for money," interrupted Jake.

Samuels looked across at him and what Jake now saw was a broken man. "I was not to know that, Inspector. The anger in me rose. I pushed her back in to the room and before I was even aware that I was doing anything my hands were around her throat and I was squeezing as hard as I could. I wasn't thinking at all, you understand, it was as if I had been taken over by some evil spirit intent on squeezing the life out of this woman. My hands were still around her throat when Julia came in to the room. I took my hands away and Jessie fell at my feet; she was quite dead. Julia became hysterical. She was saying all manner of cruel things about me and threatening to go to the police. Well, of course, I could never have allowed her to do that. I am a well-respected man around Aberdeen and I could never allow anyone, not even my own daughter, to do anything that might have an impact on my position in society."

"So you killed her?"

The outrage in Jake's tone was there for all to hear. The thought that the Doctor had murdered his own daughter simply to protect his position in society was almost beyond his comprehension. Julia's only crime was that she had been intent on doing the right thing and reporting her father to the police. She had basically died due to her father's total misreading of the circumstance that had been presented to him.

"The anger just rose in me again. It was like a mist descending and when it had cleared again my beautiful daughter lay dead at my feet. I picked her up and carried her through to the bed. I went back to Jessie and took my daughter's dress off her. My intention was to swap the dresses so both women would be found as they should be but something made me change my mind. Instead I decided to take Julia's dress away with me. I put it in a bag and carried it under my arm. Before I left the flat I wrote a note and once outside I asked a young boy to take the note to the police office. I didn't want my Julia lying there any longer than she needed to."

"You do now realise, Doctor, that neither Julia, nor Jessie, needed to die that day. Everything was perfectly innocent and only your sick reading of the circumstances made it any different. You believed something of your daughter that, quite frankly, sickens me. You never even gave her a chance to explain the true circumstances of her visits to Marischal Street and now you must live with the knowledge that you committed double murder for no reason at all. You can think on that for the rest of your days, Doctor, assuming you are spared the rope at your trial."

Samuels was now weeping openly as the magnitude of what he had done sank in. He had indeed misjudged Julia and had acted upon his own misguided ideas rather than ever taking the time to seek the truth. It was too late for regrets. He had committed a terrible crime and for that he must now face the consequences.

"It was never meant to happen the way it did," the Doctor eventually muttered through his tears.

Jake did not want to hear anymore. "Charge him, please, Sergeant Mathieson and I'll go and arrange transport to take him down to the cells. If he wants to speak to his solicitor once you get there then arrange that as well."

"Very good," said Mathieson as Jake walked out of the room and then out of the house.

Jake walked to the end of Hamilton Place and continued down Craigie Loanings He turned left at the bottom and walked along to the sub-station at Leadside Road where he arranged for a young Constable to go to Lodge Walk and organise transport for Mathieson.

Jake carried out this work with a sense of satisfaction that at least one of his cases had been solved. However, it was with some regret that the first case solved had not been that of Mabel Lassiter. The violence with which that poor woman had died led Jake to fear that her killer might strike again. He had never felt that the murderer of Julia Samuels and Jessie McGill was ever likely to kill again.

Satisfied that everything concerning Doctor Samuels had now been dealt with, Jake strolled down through Rosemount Viaduct and along Union Terrace. As he arrived at Union Street he was immediately struck by the intense illumination being created by the coloured, electric lights that had been strung the length of the City's main street. Jake had heard that there was around three thousand lights on Union Street and a further three thousand around the Town House.

Large numbers of people had already started to gather as the natural light faded to enjoy the effect of electricity. Jake stood for a moment, with the statue of Prince Albert behind him and looked the length of Union Street. There was little doubt that the City was making every effort to create the right atmosphere for the visit of the King and Queen.

Eventually he continued on his way down Union Street and then right in to Broad Street where he entered the offices of the Aberdeen Daily Journal. There was a small reception area at the door manned by a small, balding gentleman who looked bored beyond words to still be at work.

Jake checked if Alan MacBride was still in the building and when it was confirmed that he was he wrote a quick message and passed it to the bored looking gentleman.

"See that Mr MacBride gets this," Jake then said and left the building.

Jake crossed the road and cut through in to the Guestrow where he continued up in to his flat. He then sat and waited. A few moments passed before there was knock at his door. Jake opened it and there was Alan MacBride standing in the hallway.

"I believe you wanted to see me," MacBride said with an element of disbelief in his tone.

"I did indeed, come in."

MacBride followed Jake in to the back room and accepted his offer of a beer. Jake opened two bottles and poured the contents in to two glasses, one of which he now offered to MacBride. The journalist accepted the drink with thanks and then sat down. Jake sat down opposite and sipped at his beer.

"I told you that if I had anything to tell the Press that you would be the first to hear what I had to say," Jake began. MacBride sat up with interest. "What I am about to tell you will be made available to everyone as of mid-morning tomorrow so you won't be able to print anything until after then. However, by telling you now I imagine you'll be able to publish the news in your lunchtime edition when everyone else will need to wait until much later. I believe that is what you would call a scoop."

MacBride grinned. "Indeed it would be," he agreed, gulping down some of the beer.

"This evening we arrested and charged Doctor Nathaniel Samuels with the murder of his daughter. He had found out, quite by chance, that Julia was going to Marischal Street on a Wednesday morning rather than to her work. He had gone to investigate what she might be doing and one thing unfortunately led to another. He has pretty much confessed to the crime but until he has spoken to his solicitor I would not take that as a given conclusion to this case. We have enough evidence against him, however, to be confident of a conviction once we get him to court whether, or not, he ever officially confesses to the crime."

MacBride now had his notebook out and was jotting down some of the things that Jake had been saying. MacBride had always thought the father might be a strong candidate but, even then, he too found it a horrifying thought that any father could murder his own daughter.

MacBride asked some questions and where possible, Jake answered them. At the end of their conversation (and the beer) they agreed that MacBride now owed Jake a morsel of information, were he to uncover anything that might be of help, to any of Jake's investigations.

They shook hands and MacBride left. Jake tidied up the flat and then left. He was heading along the Guestrow and beginning to think about the meal he was to be having with Margaret, the following evening, when it suddenly struck him that he had arranged to meet Stinky that evening as well.

Clearly, on Tuesday evening, there was only one person whom Jake really wanted to see. However, he also needed to know if Stinky had learned anything of value. Jake doubled back and made his way to the Banks of Ythan pub in the hope that Stinky would be there.

As Jake walked through the front door all eyes turned to look his way. It was not particularly well lit inside the pub and Jake took a little while before he focused on the faces around him.

Stinky was in the corner. He was quite drunk and nursing an empty glass. Jake sat down and it was a second or two before Stinky realised who it was sitting opposite him. His stubbled face lit up with a smile.

"Mr Fraser. Was it tonight we were meant to be meeting?"

"No, it was supposed to be tomorrow, but I have something else I need to attend to tomorrow."

"Might I borrow enough money from you, Mr Fraser, to allow me to buy another pint of ale?"

Jake took some money from his pocket. "Here, you can go to the bar and I'll have a half."

Stinky staggered to the bar, purchased a large and small beer, then staggered back again. He almost fell in to his chair and had to regain his balance before drinking his latest purchase.

"Have you anything for me?" Jake then said as he sipped at his half pint. The pub wasn't that nice but the ale was good.

"I put the word out, Mr Fraser, but no one seems to know anything about a gang of foreign gentlemen being in town."

"Nothing at all?"

"Nothing at all. I'm sure had there been such a gang someone would have been aware of it."

"In that case, thank you," Jake concluded as he drank his beer rather quicker than he might have preferred. He put a few more coins in front of Stinky. "Don't drink it all tonight."

Jake stood up and left the pub. He made his way up the hill towards Esslemont Avenue feeling happier, within himself, that anarchists were unlikely to cause any problems for anyone come Thursday.

However, that still did not explain what the Englishman was doing in Aberdeen and why he had felt the need to murder Mabel Lassiter.

EIGHTEEN

Monday 24 September - late evening

The Park Street flat was quiet again. An hour ago there had been four people in various parts of the flat but now Reynolds was all alone, just the way he liked it. The evening had been the last chance for anyone who may still be unsure about exactly what was going to happen on Thursday to ask questions and have their concerns aired and discussed.

Reynolds felt satisfied that there was nothing wrong with his plan and there seemed little chance of it failing. He knew, with certainty, that come late morning on Thursday he would be sitting aboard the London train with a sense of satisfaction that everything had gone like clockwork.

He felt a little bit sorry for Janet as he thought things over after everyone had gone. He had poured himself a drink and sat down, as darkness descended, to contemplate what he would do with the money that would be coming his way as a result of Thursday.

Janet had played an important part in the plan by providing him with all the inside knowledge that he felt he needed. They had a plan of the building, details of the security arrangements and knowledge of the safe in the manager's room and the vaults in the banking hall that would allow Fred Butterworth to do the rest with regard to getting them open.

The plan had begun some four months ago when Reynolds had met Janet's brother, Mike, in a Club in London. By the time they had met Mike had been in London for a year and had been involved in some small time crime prior to finally getting a proper job. Mike had known, therefore, that Reynolds did not always walk on the lawful side of life, therefore when Janet told him about the high level of cash that would be in the vaults during the public holiday of the twenty-seventh of September, Mike knew exactly where to go and who to talk to.

Reynolds did not usually get personally involved in the jobs he planned. He always felt it was much safer to get others to take the real risks and then he simply reaped the rewards at the end. However, in this case he had decided to be a little more hands on. He had gone to Aberdeen with Mike and been introduced to Janet.

She had initially been no more than a pawn in his plan, someone to provide information whether it be wittingly or not. However, once he had been introduced to Janet and found her to not only be a very attractive young woman but also a young woman who was openly attracted to him.

He decided to seduce the innocent Janet and create a situation where she could not help but fall in love with him. The more she loved him the more she would do for him. That part of the plan was simple and Janet fell for him with a passion that he found quite terrifying at times. He had acquired the Park Street property in the name of Lee Reynolds and also a room, elsewhere in the city, under the name of Lucas Spratt. He had also created one or two other personas in case they were needed, such as Martin Bagshaw of the equally non-existent Fritton Agency.

It had been during one of those earlier visits to Aberdeen that he had picked up on the story of an anarchist pestering the King and Queen of Spain. He remembered the incident in Madrid and was aware of the Queen of Spain's relationship to King Edward the Seventh. It seemed yet another perfect distraction that would keep the police busy and well away from both him and his plan.

As long as the local police were looking in entirely the wrong direction then how much easier would it be for Reynolds and his gang to break in to the bank and remove as much money as they chose? His plan was all about illusion; all about making the police believe something that simply wasn't true. What with them already involved in the royal visit, adding anything else to their workload would stretch them even further

It had always been Reynolds intention to add as much to the police workload as was possible. The double murder in Marischal Street had been an unexpected bonus.

The main stroke of genius, however, had been the incident with the policeman in the Castlegate. He felt sure that that would be remembered and reported and would surely go a long way towards convincing the police that there just might be an anarchist on the loose in Aberdeen intent on bringing harm to the King.

The other part of the plan which was also guaranteed to keep the police busy was the murder of Mabel Lassiter. Poor Mabel, she had never realised for one moment that her part in the plan was always as nothing more than a decoy. Her death was simply to tie up police time, nothing more.

Reynolds smiled to himself as he thought about the chest. That had been another idea designed to keep the police guessing. There never had been any use for the chest but the police were not to know that. In fact Mabel had never known that, she had died believing she was playing some essential part in the plan. It had been essential, just not the way she thought.

Yes, his plan was working perfectly. There seemed no way that any police officer even knew the gang was in Aberdeen let alone had some notion of what they might be about to do. Reynolds was happy with the gang he had put together.

Mike Lindsay was there purely for muscle and the fact it had been he who had brought the idea to Reynolds in the first place. Mike was the weak link in the chain but Reynolds hoped that he would be all right on the day. Mike had more to lose were they to be caught in the sense that it would get his sister in to serious trouble as well and he would do anything to prevent that from happening.

Although Reynolds had no proof he was also fairly certain that Mike had bedded Mabel on at least one occasion. Mike had been with Reynolds on one of the nights that they had gone to see Mabel dancing. There had been a spark there from the very beginning and Reynolds would have been surprised if they had not consummated their relationship at the first opportunity.

Mike had certainly taken the news of Mabel's death harder than the others. Reynolds had certainly noticed that.

Fred Butterworth was the best, at least in Reynolds' estimation. Fred could crack any safe and do it with speed. He had been involved in some of Reynolds previous work and could always be relied on to complete his part of any plan without rocking the boat by asking unnecessary questions.

The last member of the gang was Joshua Manyon, known to everyone as Josh. He could pick any lock presented to him and Reynolds knew they would have no difficulty getting in to the building with Josh in the team.

During the evening they had run through the plan just to make sure that they had everything that they needed. Fred was confident that the information provided by Janet had allowed him to ensure he had all the right tools to open both the safe in the manager's office and the vaults downstairs. Although they would have the keys to the vaults they also knew that Fred would have to identify the correct combination before finally getting them open.

Janet had told them that the combination changed every week and that only three people ever knew what it was. Reynolds felt sure that a man of Fred's ability would not take long to crack their code.

Josh had a note of all the doors that might potentially be locked as well as the types of locks fitted to those doors. Again he was totally confident that he could open any of those doors with comparative ease.

Mike Lindsay had purchased a supply of chloroform in London along with a hand gun, which he hoped he would not have to use. The plan was to knock out the guards with the chloroform and be long gone by the time they came round again. The gun was just insurance should anything go wrong. Reynolds did not like the gun being there but knew it made sense to go prepared as it seemed inevitable that the security men, within the bank, may have been armed as well.

After the plan had been discussed and everyone seemed happy that they had covered everything Reynolds had gone through to another room and returned with three suitcases. He gave one to each of the gang and they agreed that they would only take from the vault what was needed to fill the cases. They would then, separately, go to the railway station. They would travel as individuals, there was to be no indication that they might know each other.

Once they got to London they would take their case and disappear forever, at least as far as the Aberdeen police were concerned. They were never to contact each other again and they were never to say anything to anyone about the raid. Were they to be caught by the police, for some other misdemeanour, then it went without saying that they would never grass on their fellow bank raiders.

Agreeing not to see each other again until Thursday, the gang members then left one at a time. Once they had gone Janet had come through to the room where Reynolds was sitting. She was wearing nothing more than a dressing gown and the material parted in more places than seemed necessary. The sight of her naked body beneath the dressing gown had had a suitable effect on Reynolds and they had gone back to bed to make love one more time.

"Remind me again," Janet had then said as she lay in his arms, a warm glow still spreading throughout her body from her orgasm, "when can I join you in London?"

Reynolds had almost forgotten that he had told Janet they would be together again in London once the dust had settled after the raid. Of course he had never had any intention of seeing the silly woman ever again. He moved in circles that were well outside anything that Janet Lindsay would have known.

She may have been young and pretty but she was no lady; at least in the opinion of Reynolds. Janet had provided him with a little pleasure while in Aberdeen, but it could never have been allowed to become more than that.

There was no way she could ever be a part of his future. He had even considered killing Janet in the same way that he had killed Mabel. The idea of the police still hunting for some madman on the loose who seemed intent on raping and murdering young women, appealed to Reynolds. However, he just couldn't bring himself to murder Janet when there was little to be gained.

The main reason for allowing her to live was that she didn't know anything about him that would help the police if they came asking. The man she knew as Reynolds did not actually exist so whatever she told the police would have to be of no use to them whatsoever.

"You'll need to allow some time to pass," he'd eventually said. "The police will be buzzing around your branch for quite a while and they are bound to suspect there might have been inside assistance so you'll all be under the microscope. You, therefore, need to play things calmly for as long as you can until the police activity drops off and you'll be able to arrange a trip to London without attracting undue attention."

Janet had sat up. "But how long will that take?"

"I really don't know, we'll just have to see, but don't worry my love," he'd quickly added as his hand casually caressed her breast," when we are together again it will be forever and just think how rich we will be and what a life we can have."

"I love you so much," Janet had then said and they had made love one more time before she decided she had better go home.

Reynolds had walked Janet along to King Street where they hailed a cab to take her home. He had then gone home to that drink and his contemplations. Yes, everything seemed to be in place and now he couldn't wait for the day to come around and for Reynolds to finally disappear forever.

NINETEEN

Tuesday 25 September - late morning and early evening

The Chief Constable had called a meeting to go over all the issues that were currently taking up police time. Jake and Sandy Wilson were both summoned to his office and they were both surprised, when they arrived, to find Superintendent Harris sitting there already.

"Sandy, Jake, in you come. Superintendent Harris is just paying one last visit to make sure we're all ready for Thursday. Please, sit down."

Sandy sat next to Harris and Jake sat next to Sandy. The Chief sat back in his chair and surveyed the three of them. Eventually he asked Jake for an update on where he was with the cases he had been investigating. Jake was able to say he'd arrested Doctor Samuels for the murder of his daughter and both Harris and the Chief expressed horror at the fact any father could do such a thing.

Jake admitted that there was still a small chance that there was an anarchist cell active in Aberdeen, especially after the incident with the Police Constable in the Castlegate. He quickly added, however, that his sources had no knowledge of such a group and that he took heart from that.

"My professional opinion is that we have a gang in Aberdeen but that they are not anarchists."

"But might they still wish harm on the King and Queen?" Harris asked with interest.

"I believe the incident in the Castlegate with one of our Constables was intended to create the illusion that we had anarchists in our midst. I no longer accept that as a possibility, but in deciding we do not have anarchists I, in no way, provide an explanation for what we do have. It is, therefore, possible that this gang does mean to harm the King. On the other hand they may be here for some other purpose altogether" Jake answered.

"Why didn't you tell me about the incident in the Castlegate sooner?" the Chief then said.

"I was hoping to get some more evidence first, sir, but nothing more has come to light."

"Just in case anything untoward happens, I will add some more men to the number who travel through from Balmoral," Harris said.

"And we will strengthen the cavalry numbers around the King as well," added the Chief.

"Might I suggest we have extra men at the entrance to the Town House, sir," Jake then said. "The King and Queen will be standing still for a little while when they meet the Lord Provost at that point and it may just make them a slightly easier target."

"Agreed," said the Chief. "Are we any closer to finding the killer of Mabel Lassiter?"

"Nothing so far, sir," said Jake. "To be honest I have my doubts that we will ever find this man. It is quite possible that he came in on the London train and then went back the same way. I have no reason to think he is still in Aberdeen but if he is then I have no idea where he might be. Heaven forbid, but unless he commits another crime it seems unlikely that we will ever know who he is."

"And Sandy, what about Constable Thomson's murder?" the Chief then asked

Sandy talked them through the Tom Anderson account and how much money was in it. The Chief was horrified to think that one of his best officers could have turned bad but the evidence certainly seemed to point to that. It was agreed that Tommy's case and that of Mabel Lassiter could well run for some time. It was further agreed that preparations for Thursday were as good as they could ever be and that nothing more would be discussed prior to the day arriving. Jake and Sandy were dismissed and Harris went on his way soon after.

The Chief Constable of Aberdeen had then sat on his own for a few moments and said a silent prayer that all would go well on Thursday. The last thing he needed on his watch was for some group of political maniacs to try and make a statement by attacking the King or Queen.

Nothing much happened during the day to move Jake's working world any further forward. He left the office at a little after half past five and made his way up to Esslemont Avenue, stopping off briefly in the Guestrow to collect a few more personal items as well as his best suit. Jake then went in to a flower shop in Rosemount and bought some flowers, which he would present to Margaret when he called for her.

He got back to Esslemont Avenue and put on his good suit after giving himself a good clean. Apart from Alice, which hadn't exactly been the same, Jake had had no reason to court a lady in years. He felt rather nervous at the prospect of maintaining a conversation with a woman. He had never been that good with casual chit-chat.

He liked Margaret and he wanted to impress her. He was pretty sure that she had liked him from the start and that she was likely to make the evening as easy for him as possible. After all, it wasn't like she was some nervous little girl who did not know how to conduct herself when in male company.

Picking up his flowers and checking, in the mirror, that he looked all right, Jake then left the house and started to make his way down Esslemont Avenue. He was intent on enjoying himself tonight as this had been the first chance to have a little rest and relaxation in quite a well. The evening light was already starting to fade as he made his way round the Viaduct until he reached Margaret's address.

He went in through the door and started to climb. It may have been a different building but the similarity was still strong enough to remind Jake of Tommy's murder. The image of his friend's body lying on that landing would remain with him for the rest of his life. Jake shook the memory from his mind and kept climbing

Margaret was on the third floor and Jake was breathing quite heavily by the time he got to her door. Maybe he wasn't in such good shape as he had thought?

He knocked on the door and it opened almost at once. Margaret had a huge smile on her face and was already dressed for being outside.

"Right on time," she said. "I like a man who is punctual."

"These are for you," Jake then said holding out the flowers.

"Thank you," Margaret replied and took the flowers from him. "I'll leave these in water and sort them properly later."

Margaret quickly went through to the kitchen and poured water in to a basin. She placed the end of the flowers in the water and hurried back to the door where Jake was still waiting. She locked her door and they started the long descent back to street level. Once out on the street, Margaret hooked her arm through Jake's and they set off along Union Terrace.

The centre of Aberdeen was fully prepared for the royal visit. The area around the Wallace Statue was abundantly festooned with bunting, lights and small shields with crossed swords attached to the back of them. Union Terrace itself had bunting and flags strewn along the Union Terrace Gardens side and at the Union Street end of the street Prince Albert sat on his statued throne surrounded by even more bunting, flags and banners.

The bunting then continued across the Union Bridge and by the time they reached the entrance of the St Nicholas Church the gates and columns were barely visible due to the amount of paraphernalia that had been placed upon them. A banner proclaiming God Bless Our King and Queen was also visible.

The Athenaeum Hotel and Restaurant was situated at the very end of Union Street just before it became the Castlegate. Still classified as being part of Union Buildings rather than Union Street the building had begun life as a reading room but had now been converted in to a restaurant. Due to the fact it had originally been designed for people reading in it, the windows were huge and light could now stream in to an extremely well appointed restaurant rather than a library.

Jake led the way upstairs and they were met at the door by a young man in a smart uniform who took them to their table. As it was a table of arrangement rather than one for a wealthy guest, it was not so well positioned but Margaret did not seem to mind as she looked around her with awe in her eyes. With its high ceiling and chandeliers the dining room had the look of a palace and Margaret had never eaten in a place like it.

The young man took Margaret's cloak from her and Jake could now fully see the dress that lay below. The bodice had a scooped neck which showed off the beginning of her cleavage. The dress was nipped at the waist and then flared out as it fell to her feet. The dress was of the deepest blue and Margaret looked absolutely lovely as she sat down and started to look at the menu, which had been offered to her by the young man.

Jake felt very honoured to be in the company of such an attractive woman and it made him even more convinced that he was firstly going to enjoy the evening and secondly he was not going to embarrass Margaret in any way.

Jake's friend, Charlie Mearns, had been Head Waiter at the restaurant since the turn of the century and he now came over to shake Jake's hand and also to be introduced to the lovely lady sitting beside him. Margaret had made quite an impression on everyone as she had arrived and Charlie was eager to know what his friend was doing in the company of such a lovely looking woman.

"Special occasion?" Charlie eventually said after all the introductions were over.

"Just having dinner," Jake replied in a tone that clearly suggested to Charlie that be back off. Margaret found it all rather amusing.

Jake managed to divert one or two further questions from Charlie before they were left alone to decide on what they might like to eat. While they were perusing the menu Charlie came back with two cream Sherries and placed them on the table.

"House compliments," he said with a grin and then went away again.

"It's absolutely amazing in here," Margaret said, her eyes still bright with wonderment as she took in all the finery that lay around her.

"Cheers. Here's to a lovely evening," Jake then said holding up his glass.

"And the start of a beautiful friendship," Margaret added as they clinked glasses and sipped at the liquid within.

They sat studying the menu for a few moments though Margaret's attention kept being drawn to another aspect of the architecture or to the next person walking through the door. It was early and therefore still quite quiet. There were only four other couples seated at tables and Margaret didn't recognise any of them.

After much deliberation they both decided they would have soup for their first course. Although winter had not quite arrived yet, the start of the darker nights turned the thoughts towards a hearty plate of soup. Margaret chose the consommé and Jake the broth.

The main course proved a much harder decision with so many options to choose from and every one of them appealing to their tastes. Eventually they both decided to have the salmon cutlets along with potatoes and vegetables. A note on the menu informed the diners that all the salmon served in the restaurant had been freshly caught in the River Dee.

The waiter was beckoned to the table and Jake provided him with their order. He also added two glasses of wine seeing as this, at least for Jake, was a very special occasion.

Jake and Margaret then began a period of general conversation. Margaret spoke a little about her upbringing, which had been with an aunt after her parents had died, within three months of each other, with tuberculosis.

Margaret had been twelve at the time and she reckoned that the loss of her parents made her stronger as she grew up and tackled what life had to throw at her. Jake felt his upbringing had been considerably less traumatic and spent more time talking about his work and the effect that that had had on his life.

During the early stages of their conversation they had their soup brought to the table. A silence descended over their table as they had sipped at their soup although Jake did notice Margaret's attention being drawn to the new arrivals coming in to the restaurant.

There was a nice interval between courses, which allowed Jake and Margaret to return to their conversation whilst tasting the wine. Neither of them had the first idea about wine. Jake preferred his beer and Margaret rarely drank alcohol. However, they both found the contents of their glasses very agreeable.

The main course arrived in front of them and Margaret was very impressed by the way in which the food had been arranged on the plate. Any time that she cooked a meal there was never any thought given to presentation. It was simply a matter of putting it on a plate and eating it; nothing more complicated than that.

By the time the last of the salmon was being swallowed they were discussing the Royal visit. Margaret confessed to being quite excited at being given the chance to see the King and Queen at such close quarters. Jake agreed that the visit was good for the city and obviously good for the University, but it was a security nightmare and from that point of view he could have happily done without it.

The waiter returned with the menu so that they could decide what they might have for dessert. Jake decided on Peach Melba but Margaret felt some ice cream would be sufficient after such a lovely meal.

It was after they had eaten their sweet and were sitting back, along with a cup of coffee, to allow what had been a delicious but extremely filling dinner a chance to digest, that Margaret asked Jake why he had never settled down to marriage.

"It's the job," he had replied, "few women would want to put up with the hours I have to work, especially when I can't even say what I've been doing, half the time, when I get home."

"But other police officers get married," Margaret added.

"Maybe they are just lucky in finding the right woman."

"Or maybe you just haven't tried very hard," teased Margaret.

Jake laughed. "Perhaps you are right. But what about you, has marriage never been a possibility?"

"Not really. I have met men who might have made good husbands but they obviously never saw me as being a good wife. I realise that common belief nowadays is that no woman should ever go through life unwed but I can point to quite a few women, whom I know, whose married life is a sham. They have a husband who neither loves them nor, for that matter, cares for them but as long as they have the evening meal on the table when the man of the house gets home from work then all is well. Oh yes, there's also the little matter of producing an endless supply of children. I sometimes think I'm better off just being on my own."

"Although there are times when being on your own is not exactly the best situation to be in."

"Agreed. This, for example, has been very pleasant indeed and we must do it again some time."

"Indeed we must," agreed Jake.

Jake arranged to get the bill and he paid it as Margaret went to the ladies' room. On her return she put on her cloak, with a little help from Jake and after thanking Charlie one more time they set off down the stairs to street level.

It was a little before half past eight and the Torchlight Procession would, by now, be well through its route. Jake knew that they had planned to leave Marischal College at eight o'clock.

Margaret hooked her arm through Jake's as they made their way up Union Street to Belmont Street. They turned right and walked along to the other end of the street where they encountered a healthy crowd gathered outside Robert Gordon's College. This is where the procession would end and where the torches would be burned.

There was a growing excitement as the darkness started to descend and eventually the procession was seen to be approaching from the area of the Wallace Statue. It was a long and colourful procession with all the students in fancy dress. Everyone was having fun and there was a great deal of laughter in the crowd at the sights which were being placed before them.

A huge cheer went up as the first of the torches were lit.

Once all the torches were ablaze the crowd began to disperse and Jake walked Margaret back to her property in Rosemount Viaduct. Jake walked Margaret right to her door where they stood facing each other, yet saying nothing. Jake wanted to kiss this woman but did not want to appear too forward on their first night out together.

"Thank you for a lovely evening," Margaret then said.

"I noticed that they are showing the film of the King and Queen's visit at the Music Hall on Saturday," Jake then said, "would you be interested in accompanying me to such an event?"

"That sounds very interesting," Margaret said," I've never had the opportunity to see these moving pictures before."

"Wonderful. I believe the presentation begins at a quarter to eight, so would it be acceptable if I called for you at a little before seven?"

"I'm already looking forward to it," Margaret said and she took a step closer until there was little space left between them. "Now, would you please kiss me as I have no intention of opening this door until you do."

Jake was grateful for Margaret being so forward. He did not need a second invitation as he put his arms around her and they pressed their lips together. It was a long, warm and passionate embrace that it seemed neither of them wanted to end.

Eventually Jake stepped back and Margaret turned to unlock her front door. Once the door was opened she thanked Jake once more, said she was already looking forward to Saturday and then stepped inside. With one last smile she closed the door.

Jake almost floated down the stairs. He had never felt this happy in years and he too was already looking forward to the weekend.

TWENTY

Wednesday 26 September - late morning

The Business Club occupied a building in Bon Accord Square that was not far from the house once occupied by the architect of both the Square and half of the rest of Aberdeen. Archibald Simpson had liked the Square enough to not only have his own home there but to also build one for his brother.

What had once been a large and imposing house owned by a local merchant by the name of Russell Considine was now occupied by The Business Club, which was basically a meeting place for gentlemen with money. The Club was owned by Joe Tredwall and his brother, Cecil. The brothers had inherited a large amount of money when their father had died and decided to put it all in to a new business.

Neither Joe nor his brother had made any attempt to change the design of the building when they changed it from family home to money-making concern. The house had been designed on three levels so the Club operated on three levels.

The entrance hallway had two large rooms coming off of it to the left and to the right. To the left was now the bar and to the right the smoking room. At the back of the ground floor was the kitchen, which still functioned to provide the room in the middle of the property to operate as a restaurant. The top floor had three odd rooms, which had once been bedrooms and these were now used by paying gentlemen.

Basically as long as one of the Members paid the going rate for the room he could use that room for whatever purpose his heart desired. Some of the Members used the rooms to entertain lady friends whilst others used the rooms as somewhere to sleep if they were caught in town and couldn't get back home for any reason. There was also the occasional party held in one of the rooms and the less that was known about what went on at those events the better.

Joe had felt there was a need for somewhere in Aberdeen that could allow gentlemen to enjoy life and not be bothered by anyone asking stupid questions in the aftermath of whatever it was they had done.

Joe had had fun at Oxford University and it was almost an extension of the freedom he had felt there that he now wanted to create back in Aberdeen. The Club was basically an environment in which the Members could drink as much as they liked and wench as much as they liked and not have to explain themselves to anyone.

The only rule of the Club was not to do anything truly illegal. No one wanted to run the risk of having the place closed down through their own personal actions. Having said that many of them had sailed pretty close to the wind during the two years of the Club's existence.

Although it was a men-only Club there were no restrictions on females being there as long as they were guests of one of the Members. Membership involved an annual subscription and the cost ensured that only the wealthy were ever likely to be able to walk through the doors of the building and not be thrown straight back out again. The only room that was strictly male-only was the smoking room and it was here that many a business deal was completed over a cigar and brandy.

It was just before eleven thirty when a black carriage pulled up outside The Business Club. The carriage driver jumped down and opened the door. A young man stepped out. He looked resplendent in a black cloak, with maroon lining, worn over a black suit, white shirt and maroon cravat. He now placed a top hat on his head, to complete the image and then strode to the front door of the Club.

Waiting for all the Members as they arrived was a uniformed doorman whose job it was to open the door and keep it open until the Members and their guests had entered. He was then to inform newcomers to the premises of where everything was before returning to his post at the door.

Anyone wishing to leave hats, coats, cloaks or canes could do so at the cloakroom, which sat at the back of the building beside the kitchen. This was also manned by a uniformed member of staff every minute that the Club was open.

In return for these services the occasional Member would slip the doorman, or cloakroom attendant, a few pence, which came as a welcome supplement to the meagre wage that the Club paid to both of them.

The young man stood in the hallway and took off his cloak and hat. He handed both to the doorman and then made his way through to the bar. He was early for the meeting that he had arranged and felt there was time for a quick drink first. Being a private Club the premises were not affected by the same time constraints that were usually placed upon licensed premises.

The young man went in to the bar area and found a seat by the window. He had hardly had time to sit down when another uniformed gentleman appeared beside him and asked what he would like to drink.

"Whisky and water," the young man said.

The uniformed gentleman went away to the bar and the young man made himself comfortable. Once his drink had been brought to him he settled back in his chair and allowed the next half hour to pass in contemplative silence.

At just after noon the doorman came through and informed the young man that his guest had arrived. He thanked the doorman and said he would be through in a moment. He then asked the doorman to arrange for the guest to be shown to their table in the restaurant.

The young man drained the last of his whisky and then made his way out of the bar and up the stairs to the restaurant on the floor above. The Head Waiter showed him to his table where another young man was already sitting.

The second man had a healthy growth of beard and moustache though it all looked a little unkempt and showed that he was, perhaps, not the sort that the Club would normally allow through the doors. This young man's jacket and trousers also looked a little threadbare as if he were trying to portray the image of someone that he wasn't.

The poor relation went by the name of George Cathcart. The Member used no name at all.

The two men ordered their lunch and a drink to go with it. As they waited for their soup to arrive the Member invited George to update him on a matter that was of great interest to him.

George did not need to be reminded of what that matter might be.

"My man Yule called on the Thomson residence and pretty much took it apart. He didn't find anything."

"Shit," the Member said softly. "I suppose it was expecting too much for Thomson to keep anything in the house. What about his wife?"

"Gone to Edinburgh. The neighbours don't seem to think she'll be coming back."

"Which will mean new occupants, so your man Yule had better be right when he says there's nothing there."

"I trust him," Cathcart added.

The waiter came across with two plates of soup and the conversation was allowed to drop away while the plates were placed in front of them and the waiter went away again.

Cathcart was particularly hungry and as he very seldom had the opportunity to eat in such splendid surroundings he picked up his spoon and launched himself in to the plate of soup with some relish. The other man took his time; firstly picking up his napkin and shaking it out before placing it on his lap. He was about to pick up his spoon when he paused and spoke first.

"You said that Yule took the house apart, but what about the outhouse?"

Cathcart paused in mid-mouthful. "I didn't know there was one, it wasn't mentioned to me when we got the job."

"Of course there's a bloody outhouse. It's certainly where I would keep anything I did not want my wife to know about. Send Yule back to check any other parts of the property, which may have been owned by Constable Thomson."

"Very good. I'll get in touch with him tonight and he can pay a call there tomorrow when the city is tied up in all this royal visit excitement."

"Excellent," the Member said and finally began supping his soup. After three spoonfuls his hand dropped again and he leaned slightly further across the table. "And what news do you have of the business?"

Cathcart finished another mouthful of soup, which he was finding very tasty indeed and looked around as if checking for anyone who might be overhearing what was being said. The Member saw this brief movement and was deeply insulted by such a gesture as no one in the Business Club would listen in to someone else's conversation. This was a Gentleman's Club and as such all Members acted as Gentlemen.

"Each month brings us more customers and more money in the bank. We've replaced Thomson within the police so we still have eyes and ears on the inside. If they start investigating us in any way then we'll know about it and can deal with it accordingly."

"Excellent," the Member said again.

"There is one slight problem," Cathcart then continued and the Member looked worried.

"And what might that be?"

"Not many of the girls want to do more than the one film. Some of them are happy to do anything for the money but there are others who seem to have more of a moral conscience. It means we are constantly having to find new girls."

The Member had some more soup and thought for a moment. Cathcart took the chance to finish his soup while the silence hung over the table. The Member eventually spoke again.

"This is a business that cannot function without the girls. Use whatever tactic is necessary to keep these girls happy and willing to make many films with us but make sure we don't pay them anymore than we need to."

"I'll see what I can do," Cathcart added.

The rest of the meal passed without much more being said. Cathcart knew that he had now overstayed his welcome so he ate up his main course as quickly as he could and bade his host farewell.

Cathcart was no sooner out of the door when another young man, who had been sitting in the corner at another table, wiped the corner of his mouth with his napkin, placed it on the table and then stood up. He crossed the floor to where the Member was sitting and without invitation pulled out a chair and sat down.

"What did Cathcart have to say?" he asked.

"Nothing was found at Thomson's house but they forgot to check the outhouse. Yule is going back tomorrow."

"Good."

The Member stopped short of saying anything about the girls not being as cooperative as might be expected. He did not want to upset his partner quite yet as he felt confident that that particular problem could be solved relatively easily.

The two men then ordered two more drinks and once they had been delivered to the table they clinked glasses.

"To business," they said in unison and started to drink.

***

At roughly the time that Cathcart was leaving the Business Club Sergeant Turnbull was knocking on Jake's door and entering with a note that had just been handed in by a passing stranger. Jake took the note and thanked Turnbull. He then opened it and read the contents. It was from Alan MacBride; he was having some lunch in the Empress Cafe and he wondered if Jake might like to join him.

Jake put on his jacket and made his way round to the cafe on Union Street. As he walked through the door he was once more struck by how busy the place was. Ladies in their finery and wearing some of the most splendid hats that Jake had ever seen seemed to be sitting everywhere and it took a moment for him to finally pick out the table at which MacBride was sitting. Jake made his way through and sat down.

"Glad you could make it," MacBride said with a smile.

"How could I resist an invitation to lunch from the Press?" Jake replied.

A pretty, young waitress came over and Jake ordered a pot of tea and a meat pie with potatoes and gravy. Jake rarely ordered anything different on the few occasions he went to the Empress Cafe. MacBride had already ordered his food prior to Jake's arrival and was already enjoying the first few mouthfuls of his meal as Jake made himself comfortable. MacBride finished chewing and sat forward.

"When you provided me with my little scoop on Doctor Samuels you asked if I would keep you abreast of anything that I might hear with regard to current police activities. Well I'm sure you'll be as surprised as I was to get some information connected with Constable Thomson's murder."

Jake was immediately interested. "What have you heard?"

"I bumped in to one of my more reliable contacts this morning and he was telling me that someone apparently broke in to Constable Thomson's home and ransacked the place. Would that be true?"

"I thought you'd asked me here to tell me something, not just ask more questions?"

MacBride put his hands up in mock surrender. "So sorry, Inspector, but it really is very difficult for a journalist not to ask questions."

"Try," Jake added rather drily.

MacBride smiled and conceded defeat.

"Very well. Anyway, this man who may or may not have ransacked Constable Thomson's house did not apparently find what he had been looking for."

"And what had he been looking for?"

"My source believes that it may have been photographs."

"Of what?" Jake prompted.

"More likely to have been of whom, but my source didn't know much more than that."

"Had there been a ransacking of Constable Thomson's house," Jake began, "was your source aware of who would have ordered such an act?"

MacBride smiled; this was Jake's way of confirming the story was true.

"I'm sorry, Inspector, but if my contact knew that then he certainly wasn't telling me."

It was at that moment that the waitress came back with Jake's order. She placed it on the table in front of him with a sweet smile. Once she had left them alone again MacBride continued with what he had been saying.

"However, my contact did go on to tell me something else, which may or may not be connected, I can't be sure."

Jake poured some tea in to his cup. "Go on."

"Apparently there may a budding new partnership in town, keen to be the new crime lords of the north east."

Jake looked surprised. "Someone trying to muscle in on Willie Ifield's patch; surely not?"

"They may not want to exactly take Willie on in illegal combat but they do seem to be creating a few ripples with what they've done so far."

"Which is?" Jake added, cutting in to the pie.

"The newcomers seem to have found a niche in the market that Willie missed," MacBride said with a grin.

"Stop toying with me and tell me what this niche is?" Jake then said with growing anger.

"Pornography."

"Dirty pictures?" Jake said, almost laughing as he did so. "I'm pretty sure that Willie is in to dirty pictures already so good luck to the new lads if they think they can have any real effect on who gets the money in Aberdeen and its surroundings."

"These aren't just dirty pictures, Inspector, these are dirty *moving* pictures," MacBride then said with a note of triumph in his voice.

Jake put his fork and knife down and looked at MacBride with an expression of disbelief.

"These newcomers are making moving pictures of naked women?"

"Naked women with naked men I should imagine," MacBride added.

A woman at the table next to them gave them both a very funny and totally disapproving look. MacBride leaned closer to Jake and spoke a little more quietly.

"The cinematograph industry is becoming big business as you will already know, Inspector. Every time a film is shown in either the Music Hall or the Union Hall a large audience gathers and cheer their way through to the end. It seems obvious, therefore, that there is money to be made from the showing of moving pictures. It can hardly be a surprise to you that someone would then choose to combine the making of these pictures with the already lucrative market of pornography."

"Frankly it does surprise me," Jake then said. MacBride smiled and continued.

"You'll know yourself that there will be moving pictures taken tomorrow of the King and Queen, which will then be shown in halls around the north east of Scotland. Hundreds of people will flock to those halls. At a top price of two shillings for a seat at one of the presentations in the Music Hall alone, you do the arithmetic on how much money can potentially be made on one night. Now just imagine how many men would flock to rooms where there were moving pictures of young ladies involved in all manner of sexual activity. More importantly these men would surely be prepared to pay a lot more than two shillings for the privilege."

"I can understand great numbers wanting to see the King and Queen but surely there would be a limited interest in dirty pictures. The cost alone would prohibit most men from taking part."

MacBride laughed. "Cost apart, Inspector, men throughout history have gathered together to look at naked women. This is no different apart from the fact the naked women are images on the wall rather than actual people in the room with you."

Jake was at a loss for words. He immediately thought of Bainbridge and his top drawer picture collection. There was little doubt that Mr Bainbridge would certainly part with some of his hard-earned cash to look at moving pictures of naked women. Perhaps the market was there after all. Perhaps if men wanted to view these images they would find the money from somewhere.

Whilst Jake maintained a silence MacBride took the opportunity to finish his lunch. It was a few moments before Jake spoke again.

"But your contact did not know who any of these men were?"

"No. I'm guessing these are men of means and they will know how to keep a low profile. They are unlikely to play any part in the process that is even remotely public and there will be no obvious audit trail back to them were anyone to find a lead in this."

Jake knew that what MacBride was saying was true.

"Someone starting up in the business of moving pictures would obviously require a high initial investment. They would need to acquire all the equipment and presumably arrange to make their own pictures, unless they simply buy them in from another source, which would, of course, add to their costs."

MacBride nodded. "I've done a little bit of homework, Inspector and can tell you that there is a market for moving pictures with a sexual element in France apparently, though I have no doubt every country will have a budding pornography trade. Basically, if it makes money then you know there will be a market created for it, whether that market be legal or not."

"But where would they show these pictures?" Jake then said. The question was more by way of him thinking aloud and he was not really expecting an answer. However, he got one anyway.

"In private. At any gathering of gentlemen where money was no object. In someone's house, perhaps. Quite frankly, Inspector, anywhere where there is a wall and a power supply."

"You seem well educated in the world of moving pictures," Jake commented.

"As I said, I've done my homework and anyway, I'll always have an interest in new technology. We are living in a rapidly changing world, Inspector where much of what we take for granted is about to change. Moving pictures are just a small part of that change."

"Perhaps you're right. Maybe I'm just too old for thought of change."

MacBride laughed. "Good God, Inspector, you're not old. Embrace change and enjoy the bold new future that lies ahead of us."

"Minus the dirty pictures of course," Jake quipped and they both laughed.

They finished the last of their meal and after MacBride said that he would clear the bill, Jake thanked him and left. Outside it was still a pleasant day and Jake took a short stroll before returning to the office.

He had much to think about. It made sense that this could well be the business into which Tommy had fallen. There was clearly the potential for a lot of money to be made. Jake felt sure that Willie Ifield, though perhaps not directly involved, would know something about what might be going on with regard to these newcomers.

Jake eventually arrived back at Lodge Walk and he immediately went to find Sandy Wilson. He updated him on what MacBride had just said and both men agreed that they would go together when the time was right to speak to Willie Ifield.

TWENTY-ONE

Wednesday 26 September – late afternoon

There was an abnormal excitement growing in the city of Aberdeen. It was rare indeed that the King and Queen visited Aberdeen other for a few moments whilst they changed trains on their way back to London from Balmoral. This would be a proper occasion, providing an opportunity for the people of Aberdeen to truly show their affection for the Monarch.

There was no doubting that in the course of the morning large crowds would gather along the route, which the King and Queen would follow. The Chief Constable and his team of police officers were well aware that they had to be ready to deal with anything that might occur on the day.

With less than twenty-four hours to go before the King and Queen would step down from their train at Holburn Street Station the Chief Constable was running one last eye over the security plans and also discussing, with his senior officers, the part they would all play in those plans.

It was a little after four in the afternoon and the muster room had been cleared to allow the Superintendents, Chief Inspectors and Inspectors to gather together for what would be their last briefing on the subject of the royal visit.

There would be hundreds of extra police officers in Aberdeen on the day and they would have to be managed to military precision. These men, who did not naturally know the city of Aberdeen, would need to be given very explicit instructions regarding where they would be positioned for the day. They would also need to know what was expected of them should anything untoward happen and of course, there was the little matter of how they would be fed.

In their midst were a couple of officers who had been sent down from Balmoral. These men were usually employed in London and Aberdeen seemed a terrible backwater in comparison to the rough and tumble of that major city. Once everyone had gathered in the room the Chief Constable stood up and the general chit-chat that had been going on dwindled away to silence.

"Gentlemen, tomorrow will be the most important day that Aberdeen will have seen since I became Chief Constable. Tomorrow is to be a day of celebration and I do not want anything to get in the way of that, especially anything that has to be done in the name of security. Firstly, the King and Queen must feel safe at all times and they also must feel that they can interact with the crowds without concern for anything happening. The people of Aberdeen, in turn, must be free to wave and cheer at their monarch as he passes without police officers getting unduly in the way. We must not be a barrier between the King and his subjects but we must be vigilant to any sign of wrong-doing. As you will know by now, there is still a small possibility that a group of anarchists may try to spoil our day in some way. Unfortunately we have still not been able to gather any more information about whether this gang exists or not so we will continue to assume that something could well happen. Gentlemen, we must be professional in how we approach tomorrow and if we all do our duty to the best of our abilities then I feel sure the day will pass without any major incidents."

"May I ask a question, sir?" asked one of the Inspectors.

"Of course," came the reply from the Chief.

"Should we perhaps have asked for more help from the other Forces?"

"We have over seven hundred men coming in to Aberdeen from outside Forces," the Chief replied. "I'm not sure if there would be enough space in the centre of the city for any more."

There was a ripple of laughter around the room. The Chief continued.

"It is no longer a matter of how many men we have but what we choose to do with them. I have strengthened the number of officers on duty at the Town House as that is where we feel the King may be static longer than anywhere else and if someone wants to harm the King in some way he would certainly want as much time in which to carry out the deed as was possible. There will also be two more police officers on horseback riding with the military behind the King's carriage. Jake is going to travel ahead of the King, along with his small team of officers and they will have eyes only for the windows and vantage points that are above head height. The officers positioned along the route will be the eyes on the people."

"May I say something, sir?" Jake then said.

"Certainly."

Jake stepped forward so that everyone could see him. "The main problem about tomorrow is that we won't know for certain that someone is planning to harm the King until they actually make a move to do so. We don't know if there is an anarchist gang or not and we will only know that for certain a split second before they do something. That is why it is imperative that you ensure that all the officers under your command are aware of the threat and remain vigilant at all times."

"Could I also add," said one of the officers down from Balmoral," that we still have no confirmation as to whether, or not, the anarchist who was at Udny at the same time as the Spanish Royal Family has left the area. We lost contact with him and quite frankly, he could be anywhere."

"So there you have it gentlemen," the Chief then continued," we need to brief all the men tomorrow thoroughly and make sure that no one slacks on duty. Every man needs to remain sharp and alert at all times as it may well be that split-second sighting that alerts us to an attack. Now, I give the floor over to Inspector Forbes who will give out the specific instructions for you and the men under your command."

Gordon Forbes stepped forward. He gave the gathered masses a brief account of how the day would be organised from the early morning when they all started to gather through to the moment that they would be allowed to go off duty. It was highly unlikely that anyone would be off duty much before midnight.

The main issue for the officers was to ensure that their men got a break at some point of the day so that they could be fed. Once everyone had received their instructions they went away to hold meetings with their Sergeants and anyone else who was available. The Balmoral officers left to catch a train back to Ballater and Jake left to head back up to Esslemont Avenue and make sure that all was still well there.

Jake had some food and a beer then went to bed early as he had a long and difficult day ahead of him.

TWENTY-TWO

Thursday 27 September – early to mid-morning

Considering how many people were intent on pouring in to the city centre on the day of the royal visit the streets were remarkably quiet as a man, carrying a well-travelled and slightly worn suitcase, walked along Union Street and turned in to Lodge Walk. On Lodge Walk he could see, coming in the opposite direction, another man who was also carrying a suitcase, though his was considerably newer.

The men with the suitcases were Fred Butterworth and Josh Manyon.

As they grew closer to each other they continued to scan the area, making sure that there was no one around who might later act as witness to their actions.

There was also the fact that the main police office was a matter of yards away and that the largest number of police officers ever seen in the city had already started to gather.

Satisfied that no one was nearby the two men ducked in to what was one of the back entrances to the North of Scotland Bank. Both men knew that this was where postmen went to deliver special packages.

The gang had done their research into the building and its security arrangements. Within the building there would be eight guards. There would be one guard permanently posted at the back door, with others located at the front door and near the Manager's office.

Two guards would be almost constantly on the move and could turn up anywhere at any time. They did not work to timetables, they simply went for a walk round the building when the fancy took them. The remaining three guards would be in the main hall protecting the three, huge vaults that lay behind where the bank tellers would normally stand.

The main weakness about the bank's security plan was that, apart from the three guards in the main hall, all the other guards were on their own most of the time, which would make it easier for the gang to pick them off one by one.

Josh opened his suitcase and took from it a small package and a postman's hat. He then battered on the back door. A viewing hatch opened towards the top of the door and a pair of eyes peered out.

"Special delivery," Josh announced, keeping only his head in vision.

"You're not one of the usual posties?" the voice behind the door said accusingly.

"Some of the lads got the day off to see the King," Josh said with quiet confidence, "so they drafted the likes of me in to cover the special deliveries."

There was a moment's silence while the eyes continued to watch him, as if some difficult decision were being contemplated behind the closed door.

Eventually Josh heard the sound of the internal locks being undone. It was at that point that Fred hurried across to stand closer to Josh.

The door swung open and Fred quickly grabbed the guard and pushed him back inside. Josh picked up the suitcases and followed, feeling a sense of calm returning as he closed the door behind him. As he now turned to face the guard he took something from his pocket.

It was Mike's gun and he brandished in front of the guard's nose. Josh suggested that the man should make no sound and a nod of the head showed that his words had been understood. Fred then tied the guard into a chair and soaked a cloth in chloroform. He held it over the man's face and seconds later, he was unconscious.

The two men checked their pocket-watches; it was a little after six o'clock. They knew that Mike and Reynolds would be only a few minutes away.

Reynolds had planned this job down to the last detail. With the help of Janet he felt confident that he had covered all eventualities once they were inside the building.

Another knock was heard at the door. Josh checked that it was Reynolds then opened the door. Moments later Mike arrived as well. He took the gun from Josh and took up his position at the back door. He would remain there in case someone really did turn up with a delivery.

The other three left their suitcases with Mike. They did, however, take a couple of smaller bags with them. These contained items that they would need in the course of their work over the next couple of hours. They set off up an ornate staircase to the levels above.

Each step was taken slowly and with care. All the time they listened for signs that one of the mobile guards might possibly be coming in the opposite direction. They reached the first floor without incident and found the doors on that level unlocked. They continued through in to a large work area with neat rows of desks lying with their surfaces clear of items and highly polished. The whole room looked spotless no doubt thanks to the efforts of a particularly house-proud cleaner.

They made their way through the room of desks to a door on the other side. Reynolds opened it slightly only to hear movement in the room beyond. He signalled for the others to step back. They had just enough time to duck behind a desk before the guard came in.

He started to walk through the room. However, the minute he passed him Fred leapt to his feet and forced the chloroform soaked cloth over the man's face. He too slumped to the ground almost immediately. Josh took some more rope from his bag and gagged and tied the guard into one of the nearby chairs. They then continued on their way.

They crossed the hall and through the door on the other side. They then followed a short corridor before taking the next set of stairs up to the next level.

The three men now found themselves in another corridor. The door to the Manager's office was first on their left. They knew this door would be locked, but only by a bolt on the inside; there was no lock to pick from the outside. That meant they had to gain access to the Manager's office through Janet's office. Josh had picked that lock in seconds.

Reynolds knew that a guard would be stationed in Janet's office. He had stood and pondered for a second on how best to tackle this guard and eventually decided to go for the direct approach. With the door now unlocked, Reynolds simply opened it and walked in.

The guard leapt to his feet with shock and surprise on his face. His hand went for a whistle that was lying on the desk in front of him but Reynolds had reached him before he could do anything and the single punch that was landed on the guard's chin was enough to drop him to the floor in a dazed condition. Fred held the cloth across the man's face and he sank in to unconsciousness.

The three men now entered the Manager's office and Fred hurried over to where the safe was situated. He looked down on it for a moment and smiled.

"You okay with this?" Reynolds then asked.

"Piece of cake," came Fred's reply as he knelt down and undid a belt he had been wearing around his waist.

"You keep an eye and ear out for any movement," Reynolds then said to Josh. "I'm going to try and find that other mobile guard. It wouldn't do it he found any of his drugged mates before we were out of the building."

Reynolds backtracked the way they had come, reaching the main staircase back down to the ground level. At the top of the staircase he paused as he heard movement below. He carefully looked over the banister and could see another of the guards making his way slowly up the stairs.

Reynolds moved back in to the room of highly polished desks and waited silently for the guard to arrive. As he stood in silent anticipation it became evident to him that the guard would see his colleague tied in to one of the chairs as soon as he opened the door. Reynolds knew he would have to act quickly.

He looked around for something that he could use as a weapon. There was a paperweight lying on the desk to his left so he picked that up and held it in his hand. He took up a position to the side of the door and waited for it to open.

Time seemed to stand still as Reynolds stood there tensed for action. Eventually the door started to open and the guard stepped in to the room. As soon as he did so Reynolds brought the paperweight down on the man's head with as much force as he could. There was a sickening thud as the paperweight made contact with the man's skull. The skin burst open and blood started to pour from the cut as the man slumped to the floor.

Reynolds dragged the guard over to the corner of the room and left him lying behind a desk. Reynolds then checked for signs of life as he had thought, for a moment at least, that he might have killed the man. There was a pulse but it wasn't very strong and at the rate the man was bleeding, his chances of survival were slim at best.

There was no time for compassion, however, as there was a job to be done. A job that was heavily dependent on time not being wasted.

He continued on his way downstairs. They had now accounted for four of the guards. He went to the back door to check that all was still well with Mike

Twenty minutes in to the raid and everything was going according to plan. Reynolds explained to Mike that they would collect him once they had taken the key from the manager's safe. All four would then tackle the remaining guards.

Reynolds went back upstairs to where Fred appeared to be praying in the corner of the room. He had laid out his tools in front of him and he was now intent on finding the correct sequence of numbers that would open the safe.

"Problems?" Reynolds asked as hovered over where Fred was working.

"No," Fred said with some annoyance in his tone," but it just takes time even when you know what you're doing."

Reynolds looked out the window while Josh was sitting in the Manager's chair with the look of a man who did not have a care in the world.

Time passed. More time than Reynolds had allowed for and the fact that it was getting busier outside might have had some effect on their departure from the building later. He could feel his stress levels rising and yet there was nothing he could do to help Fred.

Eventually Fred pushed the handle down and the door of the safe swung open. It was nearly seven o'clock. At least now they could push on with the next part of the plan, which would require Fred having to crack the three vaults.

Fred was pretty confident that the main vaults would not take so long to crack. The combination element was nothing more than back-up to the two locks. The key to one of those locks was in Muir's safe and the other key would be with one of the guards in the main hall.

Although the combination to the vaults was changed weekly, Janet had at least been able to tell them that they followed a three-number code rather than the five-number code attached to Muir's safe. Once they had both keys safely in their possession, Fred was firmly of the opinion that he would have the vaults open in no time at all. Reynolds could only hope that that confidence was not misplaced.

They hurried back downstairs and picked up Mike on route. This was to be the most dangerous part of the plan in terms of something potentially going wrong. They had to hope that they would disable the three vault guards without the guard at the front door being aware that anything was amiss. Again Reynolds decided that the direct approach was probably the best. He took the gun from Mike and led the way in to the main hall.

The three guards were sitting at a table in the middle of the hall. They had been chatting casually and had initially paid little attention to the door opening as they had assumed it was one of their colleagues returning. By the time one of them noticed that it was not another guard coming through the door, Reynolds had managed to show them the gun and to quietly make it known to them that he would use that gun if necessary.

The three guards instantly decided that they were not paid anything like enough to give up their lives so they all surrendered to being tied up and gagged. They were then sent in to a peaceful chloroform slumber.

Reynolds took the second key from one of the guards and he and Fred went to check the vaults whilst Josh went to the back door for the suitcases and Mike went to deal with the last, remaining, guard stationed at the front door.

Fred studied the vault locks for a few moments and then grinned.

"This shouldn't take long," he said.

"Why so confident?" Reynolds asked.

"Look at the wheels," Fred said. "See how rubbed many of the numbers are? I'm guessing they don't actually change the numbers, they simply change the sequence in which those numbers are used. There can only be a few combinations I need to try."

"Good man," smiled Reynolds.

Thirty minutes later and all the vault doors all lay open. Each man set about filling his own suitcase. Reynolds reckoned that each suitcase now held around two thousand five hundred pounds. Now all they had to do was to casually walk to the railway station, climb aboard the London train and disappear forever.

They took their cases to the back door and one by one, over a half hour period, they left the building. Crowds of people were already starting to form on Union Street and the four men were able to blend in perfectly.

Although probably going unnoticed to the casual passer-by there was one thing that did connect all four men. They were all smiling.

TWENTY-THREE

Thursday 27th September - late morning onwards

The morning train to London pulled out of the Aberdeen Joint Station on time. There were fewer than expected passengers on board but this was the day when more people would be coming in to the city rather than be going out. The sun was shining, the King was coming and everyone had a day off work to celebrate.

On board the train, however, seated in various carriages were four men, each with a suitcase in the luggage rack above their heads and each watching with some pleasure as the city of Aberdeen disappeared behind them.

As the coastline of Nigg Bay slipped by the four men relaxed in to their seats and started to think about how they might spend the money. Mike had notions of opening a shop and starting to make some legitimate money. Fred wanted to retire. He had had enough of the criminal life and having recently met a loving woman called Ada, who had just agreed to become his wife, it now seemed the right time to sell his safe breaking tools to someone else.

Josh expected he would blow most of his on getting drunk and bedding whores. The rest he would invest in poker. He knew he could now afford to sit round the table with the big boys and he looked forward to adding to his fortune through lady luck shining on him now and again.

As for Reynolds; he had other plans.

***

By the time the train had pulled out of the station the centre of Aberdeen had filled with excited crowds eager for the best view possible of their King and Queen. The sky was a deep blue and the sun shone down with a warmth that belied the fact it was late September.

Also on the streets of Aberdeen were a large number of the eight hundred and ninety-five police officers who were on duty that day. Aberdeen would normally have had one hundred and seventy-three officers to deploy on the streets so this was indeed a massive undertaking to bring so many other officers in from other Forces and run them as an efficient and coherent unit.

Inspectors Forbes and Simpson had charge of the activities on the street and Inspector MacKay was in the main office at Lodge Walk. With the bright sunlight shining off the granite buildings and all the banners and bunting adorning walls, columns and posts around the city centre, Aberdeen was looking at its best. The city certainly had a smile on its face to greet the Monarch.

The King and Queen arrived at Holburn Street station and were escorted to their carriage. The royal legs were covered with a tartan blanket and then the carriage set off along Gray Street through the ceremonial arch that had been erected. The message on the arch was simple; *Welcome To Bon Accord*. Military cavalry and mounted police officers accompanied the Royal Carriage. As soon as the King and Queen were safely away from the station Jake climbed on to his bicycle with the aim of staying just ahead of the procession.

Where possible he took quieter routes staying clear from the worst of the crowds. Instead of taking the route planned for the King and Queen, which would go up Forest Avenue and then down Queen's Road, Jake cycled further down Great Western Road and turned left into Ashley Road. He then carried on up St Swithin Street until he reached Queen's Cross.

The pavements were particularly busy at this junction and it took Jake a little time to make his way through the crowds and back on to his route, which would take him down Albyn Place to Holburn Junction. He eventually paused at the Junction and waited, with one of his team, until the carriage passed by and the cheering crowds made more noise than ever. All seemed to be going smoothly. The procession seemed to go on forever such were the sheer number of various uniformed individuals astride beautiful horses. Everyone in the procession was cheered as they passed but the volume always rose noticeably as the King and Queen went by.

They carried on down Union Street, which was lined with cheering masses who stood, a dozen and more deep, down either side of the route. Those of means were dressed in their Sunday best whilst those less fortunate, although shabbier in appearance, had appeared to have still found what was best for them to wear. All the faces, visible to Jake as he passed, looked clean and happy with each one wearing the broadest smile possible. The whole scene was one of a sea of flat caps and ladies' hats.

Those people who knew the city of Aberdeen well were taking care to ensure their wallets and bags were not removed by some optimistic, street-urchin whose only source of income was to try and sell items they had picked from various pockets. Even with the main street swarming with police officers there was still every chance that these urchins would be operating as usual. There was no such thing as a Public Holiday for petty thieves.

There was even a small group of people gathered on the balcony of the Queen's Rooms, which lay on the corner of Back Wynd. Jake remembered seeing the advert offering space at the windows and balcony for an undisclosed cost. The building was draped in crimson cloth with a gold fringe. Between the windows of the building now hung stag's heads and it looked as if they too were cheering as the King and Queen passed by.

Other windows were now open and people hung out from them waving and cheering as the procession passed below them.

Every open window was seen as a threat by Jake and he always sighed just one more sigh of relief when the people at the window wanted to do no more than enjoy the fact the Monarch had come to their city. The procession reached Broad Street and the carriages turned left and continued along until, one at a time, they stopped outside the entrance to the university and their passengers stepped down.

At just before one o'clock the King's carriage pulled in to Broad Street and under yet another ceremonial arch that had only just been finished the day before. Waiting for Their Majesties at Marischal College were various dignitaries of the city and of the university. The King and Queen stepped down from their carriage and the King paused to remove his coat, which was returned to the carriage by one of the valets. The Royal couple were then led in to the building. Whilst they were inside the security arrangements could be relaxed slightly.

The arrangements for those who had been allowed to be inside with the King and Queen had been watertight and there were few fears that anything would happen whilst the Monarch was inside somewhere. Invitations had been sent and all those turning up for the more formal side of the day were checked and then checked again before they would be allowed in to any of the buildings.

Everyone attending did so under the utmost security. Cabs and carriages received numbers as did their occupants; thus the two could be matched on departure as well as arrival. Most people had arrived and were inside the building by half past eleven where they had been entertained by the Band of the Royal Scots Greys.

There had been a university in Aberdeen for four hundred years with the first building being King's College, which was situated in the Old Town. However, throughout the Reformation period it was felt, by many in Aberdeen that King's College was failing in its teachings.

By 1593 George, fifth Earl Marischal, had published his charter founding a second university, this time in New Aberdeen. Land previously owned by the Grey Friars of Aberdeen was made available along with the buildings originally used by the Friars. Although these buildings were added to and redeveloped over the decades they always remained slightly unsuitable in their design.

In 1860 the two Colleges merged in to what was to become Aberdeen University.

The building, in which the King and Queen now stood, had been erected by 1844, from plans drawn up by Archibald Simpson. Due to the increasing need for expansion work was undertaken to increase the area occupied by Marischal College. It was the official opening of these new buildings that had brought the King and Queen to the city, along with the fact it was the Quatercentenary of the University.

The ceremony took no more than forty minutes at which time the King and Queen left the university and climbed back in to their carriage. The horses moved off and the carriage was taken the short distance down Broad Street and round the corner in to Union Street where it once more stopped outside the ornate entrance to the Town House.

The police officers posted there now stood to attention, their eyes scanning the surrounding area for any worrying activities. The King and Queen climbed down and shook hands with the Lord Provost and his wife. The small, official group then went in to the Town House for lunch.

By the time the King and Queen had entered the Town House Jake was no more than thirty feet behind them. He had a huge sense of relief that everything had gone so well and that there had been no incidents of any kind, short of a few people getting slightly over-exuberant as the Royal Couple passed.

The masses had started to break up, with many of them seeking out a cafe for some lunch. Most of the shops had elected to close but the cafes always saw big business on public holidays so most of them were open. Jake let the police officers at the Town House go and have some lunch whilst he stood under the canopy and kept guard on their behalf.

By the time the King and Queen emerged after their lunch everyone was back at his post, all eyes once more looking for any sign of criminal activity. The Royal Couple climbed in to their carriage and set off for the main railway station. The crowds had gathered in their masses along Schoolhill, Union Terrace, Bridge Street and round in to Guild Street. Jake had gone on ahead and he was actually standing at the entrance to the station when the procession arrived.

Half an hour later the King and Queen were on the royal train back to Balmoral and the city of Aberdeen could return to business as usual. It had been a day of joy and celebration with no hint of anything else more sinister. The Royal Couple had only been in town for a few hours and yet the security arrangements had taken months of careful planning.

Jake returned to Lodge Walk where the Chief Constable had called all his senior officers together to say a few words on how the day had gone.

"Gentlemen, may I begin by offering my thanks for all the hard work that you and your teams have put in to the success of this day. I know that the King was delighted with the welcome he received from the people of Aberdeen and he even commented on the fact the weather had been nice as well. Obviously our fears about possible anarchist activity were unfounded and I am grateful for that. It appears that everything, up until now at any rate, has gone as smoothly as we would have hoped including the little matter of getting all those police officers fed. I shall be personally writing to the Manager of the Imperial Hotel and thanking him for all the hard work that both he and his staff have put in to today as well. The first luncheon began at two o'clock in the beautifully decorated muster room and service will continue through the afternoon until all the men have been fed. As for yourselves, gentlemen, you will be able to go to the upstairs hall, once I've said a few more words and get your luncheon there. I, myself, will be dining with some invited guests a little later. The main issue of the day, gentlemen, had always been the safety of the King and Queen and we have successfully ensured that this day will be remembered for all the right reasons and hopefully everyone will be able to look back on it with happy memories. I won't hold you back from some food any longer. Please ensure that your teams have received my personal thanks for the work they have done today."

Jake went to the Officer and Sergeants' Hall with Sandy Wilson where they received an excellent lunch and perhaps more importantly, an hour away from duty.

It was then back to their desks and the mountain of paperwork that awaited. Jake was still sifting through his papers when Sergeant Turnbull walked in to the room with a look of concern on his face.

"Your needed, Inspector," was all that he said.

Jake looked at his pocket-watch; it was nearly five o'clock. "What's happened?"

"It looks as if someone has raided the North of Scotland Bank," Turnbull explained, "we have one of their guards at the front desk calling for assistance."

Five minutes later Jake and Mathieson were being let in the back door, by the one guard who had regained consciousness in time to free himself from the rope that bound him and then make his way, as quickly as possible, to the police office. The Police Constable, whom Jake had collected from the muster room was asked to remain at the back door.

 The police officers were now shown through to the public hall where some of the other guards had managed to free themselves and were now tending to their colleagues. Five guards had gathered in the public hall and were already showing concern for their missing colleagues.

Jake surveyed the area. The three vault doors lying wide open; the keys still visible in the lock of one of them. The vaults low on money but not completely empty. The thieves had taken what they could carry and had not been driven by greed to try and take any more.

"Has anyone checked the rest of the building for the two missing guards?" Jake then asked, but it was clear from the response he got that, apart from the one who had run to the police, the guards were still in a state of shock and were not thinking very clearly.

Jake asked Mathieson to do a quick tour of the building and hopefully find the other guards.

"I'll go with you," said the one guard who appeared to be thinking with clarity," it's a bit of a rabbit warren in here."

Jake spent a little time surveying the area around the vaults. There was little for him to see but he wanted to give the guards a few more moments to recover from the effects of their ordeal. Eventually he crossed to where they were all sitting and asked if one of them might be able to explain what had happened.

There was a continuing silence for a few moments whilst the men sat and looked at each other. One of them finally began to speak.

"There were four of them .They came in here waving a gun around. They tied us into chairs and then knocked us out with chloroform. One of the men was youngish, maybe late twenties, early thirties. Another two were a little older, probably in their forties. The last one had such a bushy beard and moustache covering his face that it was impossible to judge age or anything."

"I note there are keys in the vault door," Jake then said," where did they come from?"

"I had one of them," another guard now said, "and they took the other one from Mr Muir's office."

"Is it common knowledge that Mr Muir kept a vault key in his safe?" Jake then asked.

"We knew about it, I can't answer for the other staff," the same guard replied.

Jake went to the back door and instructed the Constable to go back to the police office and gather enough men to allow a search of the building to be undertaken. He also asked the Constable to arrange for medical staff to attend as all the guards had suffered from chloroform inhalation and he also wanted someone to go and collect the bank manager and to bring him down to the branch.

"Do we know where the bank manager lives?" the Constable enquired.

Jake told him to ask Sergeant Turnbull as he would be able to find the bank manager's address. Once the Constable had hurried on his way Jake then went back to the main hall.

By the time he re-joined the guards, Mathieson was there. Jake could tell by the grim expression on his Sergeant's face that all was far from well.

"One of the guard's has died," Mathieson said. "He seems to have bled to death from a serious head wound."

"What of the other guard?"

"He should be on his way down, sir. I had to untie him and he was checking the upper rooms before joining us."

"I presume the Manager's office has been broken in to?"

"And the safe opened," added Mathieson. "However, it appears that nothing other than the vault keys was taken."

"Clearly these men knew exactly what had to be done," Jake commented.

Jake went across to the open vaults once more. He then turned back to face the guards.

"Do you have any idea how much money was in these vaults?"

The guards looked blankly back at Jake with just their odd shake of a head to convey that they did not know the answer to that particular question.

Jake looked back at the open vaults. There was money left in each of them though how much was difficult to tell.

"I'm guessing the gang is away with the lion's share of the money," Jake then said, "and I'm also guessing that they are long gone from the city as well."

It was another half an hour before Mr Muir came scurrying through the door, a look of horror etched on his face.

"Do you know how much money was in the vaults?" Jake asked again.

"They certainly knew the best day to do something like this," was all that Muir said at first.

"I'm presuming you were carrying more money than would normally be the case?"

"Tomorrow is pay day for both weekly and monthly paid workers throughout Aberdeen. With today being a public holiday we had no other option than to take the money in last night and leave it in the vaults throughout today. We did draft in some more guards but, to be honest, it never crossed my mind that anyone would be planning something like this."

"So, I ask again," Jake said, "how much money do you reckon was in there?"

"Close to sixteen thousand pounds."

"I note that they needed two keys to open the vaults," Jake began, "but they would have also needed the combination. How do you think they got that?"

Muir thought for a moment. "Most of the staff knew about the arrangement we had with the keys. The one in my safe was for my use only. The guard has a duplicate of the key that my Chief Clerk usually retains. As for the combination, well I really don't know how they knew that. I change the combination every week and no one, apart from myself and my Chief Clerk, know what it is."

"How complicated is the combination?"

Muir suddenly looked very sheepish. "The fact that the keys are needed to open these vaults has always meant that the combination has never been anything other than a final security measure."

"So the combination is not complicated at all, is that what you are trying to tell me?" Jake pressed.

"We use the same three numbers all the time. It is only the sequence that changes."

"So anyone with the necessary expertise in opening safes could probably work it out?"

Muir could not make eye contact. "I expect so."

Jake looked around the main hall again.

"These thieves seem to have been well informed."

Muir's outrage rose to the surface. "Are you suggesting that the thieves may have received help from someone who works for the bank?"

"I'm just saying they appear to be well informed, Mr Muir, now whether that was through inside participation or just good homework, I really don't know."

"I can't believe that anyone would betray the trust that the bank places on them in such a way."

"Money, Mr Muir, plain and simple. Everything eventually boils down to money and most people would do anything for the amount of money that you had in your vaults."

Jake left Mathieson and the other officers to collect all the statements and to piece together what little there was in the way of evidence. The gang had been professional and they had left no clues as to who they were.

The raid had been a complete success apart, perhaps, for the death of the guard. Jake believed that, unlike Mabel Lassiter, this death had not been planned.

Jake also wondered, as he made his way back to his office, if he would ever get the chance to meet any of this gang, especially the brains behind their activities. At that particular moment it seemed highly unlikely but then the case was still new and anything was possible.

TWENTY-FOUR

Thursday 27 September - nearly midnight

The train from Aberdeen had been sitting at Kings Cross for twenty minutes. The passengers had disembarked and the cleaning staff were climbing aboard.

At the exit to the station a young man was organising the transfer of his luggage from porter's cart to taxi-cab. Having seen all the cases safely placed on the cab, the young man climbed inside and they set off.

The young man sat back with some satisfaction. The plan was now complete. There were no loose ends and only Janet Lindsay could say anything about the Aberdeen bank raid. However, what she thought she knew amounted to nothing at all.

As the cab left the immediate area of the railway station one of the cleaners on board the train from Aberdeen was finding the first body. It would not be long before the other two were found. Each man had been killed with what looked like a stab wound through the heart.

None of it made any sense to the cleaners and the first police officers on the scene struggled to make sense of it either. There seemed to be nothing to connect these men and yet it seemed ridiculous to think that someone would kill three complete strangers on a train travelling down from Aberdeen.

Eventually, the young man knew that the connection would be made between the bodies on the train and the bank raid in Aberdeen. He also knew that Janet would realise she had been duped when she was told about her brother's death. She would know who had committed the murders but would be in no position to tell the police anything very meaningful. The man she had known had never existed. Reynolds had never existed he was simply the creation of a fertile imagination.

Of course until the police did tell her that her brother was dead, that poor deluded would be thinking that one day she would be going to London to meet up, once more, with her lover. He briefly thought about her as the cab clattered through the streets of London. She had been very helpful in terms of the bank information that she provided but beyond that he had struggled to play his part as her lover. The woman had been hopeless in bed; there had never been any excitement there, at least not on his behalf.

The young man was grinning by now as he reached inside his pocket and took out a pack of cigars. He placed one in his mouth and lit the end of it from a Vesta case that he had produced from another pocket. He puffed contentedly on his cigar and now started to think of the future. With ten thousand pounds all to himself he could now plan a future safe in the knowledge that money would be no object.

He thought about Elizabeth. She would be wondering where he had disappeared to this time. He was always disappearing but she knew that he would always come back. He had been away a bit longer than usual this time but then he was back with more money than ever. He'd soon spin some story to Elizabeth that would have her accepting him back in to her life without further question. He had always been able to tell women anything and they believed him. There had been so many over the years and hardly any of them actually knew the real him.

Elizabeth did. He had not hidden everything from Elizabeth, only the criminal parts.

He now had thoughts of settling down with Elizabeth. Maybe he should forget about future criminal acts and just buy a nice cottage somewhere and effectively retire. He could think of worse things than spending all day in bed with Elizabeth. In his mind's eyes he could see her lovely body stretched out on the bed, her eyes looking at him enticingly.

Maybe there was no longer a need for him to show the police how clever he was. He had proved that already so why continue?

Then again, it was the challenge of constantly proving himself to be better than everyone else that kept him going. It wasn't just about the money, it was about coming up with that master plan and then seeing that master plan run like clockwork. It was a game really and he loved every moment of it.

However, for just now he would go home and get some sleep. Then, tomorrow, he would visit Elizabeth with his story and by tomorrow evening he would be back in her bed; back in her arms and back between those long, parted legs. He was getting excited just thinking about it.

In keeping with his constant attempt to remain difficult to trace the young man took the cab to a hotel in Mayfair. With the assistance of the hotel staff the four suitcases were carried up to one of the rooms. The young man signed in for the night and then went up to his room. He allowed half an hour to pass and then went downstairs and out in to the early morning air. He hailed another taxi and took it to a large and imposing house situated about a mile away.

He let himself in to the house and went through to the lounge where he poured himself a drink. He then picked up the telephone and made one call. It was to a good friend who helped him out at times and arrangements were made for them to meet later that day so that they could carry the suitcases from the hotel to the house. The good friend knew better than to ask what might be inside the suitcases.

The young man then returned to the Mayfair hotel and got ready for bed. It was nearly time for him to go back to Elizabeth. It was nearly time for him to be William Rogers again; it wasn't his real name, of course, but he was always William Rogers to Elizabeth.

At around the time the young man was pouring himself a drink Jake arrived back at Esslemont Avenue at the end of a working day that had lasted just short of eighteen hours. It had been a long and tiring day but at least the King was now on his way back to Balmoral unharmed.

Jake opened the door and stepped inside. He went through to the back room and lit a lamp that he kept on the table. He then turned around to go through to the front room with his jacket. As he stepped in to the hallway he noticed a piece of paper lying on the mat behind the front door.

He picked it up and made his way in to the front room where he dropped his jacket on a chair and then sat down on the settee to look at the paper. It was a note from one of his neighbours informing him that someone had been sneaking around the back garden earlier and the neighbour was of the opinion that it had been Mary Thomson's cellar that had been of main interest.

Jake knew it was too dark to investigate but decided that, before he went to work in the morning, he would check the cellar and all other areas of the back garden. Clearly the search for some valuable piece of evidence, which Tommy had had in his possession, went on.

TWENTY-FIVE

Friday 28 September – All Day

Jake was up and on the go just before seven. After he had dressed and drank a cup of tea he locked up the flat and went in to the back garden, taking the key to the cellar with him.

The cellar door was found to be forced but there was very little inside and Jake felt sure that the mystery man would have left empty-handed again. At least it confirmed that whatever it was they were seeking, they still hadn't found it.

Jake closed the door as best he could and then set off to work. After the excitement of the previous day, Aberdeen would need to return to normal again.

Jake got in to the office at half past seven and sat down to begin another day. The bank raid was to be his number one priority that day and he had only been at his desk a matter of moments before the bank raid took a dramatic twist.

The message was brought to Jake by a young Constable.

Police in London had been called to Kings Cross station in the early hours of the morning to deal with what had turned out to be a triple murder. Three men, apparently unconnected, had been found stabbed to death in different parts of the Aberdeen to London train.

Police at all points along the route had been notified in the hope that they might be able to shed some light on this bizarre event. The London police had been able to identify all the victims from their fingerprints. The Metropolitan Police had had a Fingerprint Bureau since 1901 and as all three men had criminal records it had been fairly easy to find them amongst the many records held in the Bureau.

The names provided by the police in London meant nothing to Jake, although the name *Lindsay* did ring a bell with him; the only problem, for the moment, was he couldn't remember why.

However, as soon as Jake read the message he knew exactly why those men had been on the London train. The only person missing from the list provided was the brains behind their operation. He was the cold-blooded killer whom Jake now sought. He was the mastermind who clearly did not believe in leaving loose ends behind him. This was the man whom Jake knew would have to be stopped, before he committed further acts of violence and murder.

How exactly Jake would achieve that, given that he was in Aberdeen and his killer was now in London, was something that would have to remain an unresolved problem for the time being.

Mathieson came in to the room and Jake handed him the message. Mathieson read it then looked up.

"The murderer of Mabel Lassiter has struck again," he said.

"I have absolutely no doubt about that," Jake added. "He now has all the money and can lie low in the vast metropolis of London, safe in the knowledge that we don't even know his name. This man is clever and he is very professional in how he approaches his trade. He would have my respect if he weren't such a cold-blooded killer."

"We'll never see him again," Mathieson then said.

"That may well be the case," Jake agreed.

"With ten thousand pounds in his bank he'll not need to do anything but sit back and spend it?" Mathieson suggested.

"Some men might be able to do that but, somehow, I don't think this one will. He is a first class egotist above everything else and he gets a thrill from proving himself to be of a far higher intelligence than the likes of you and I. This man must be caught or else he will most definitely kill again. To that end we need to provide our colleagues in London with as much information as we can piece together. We have much to do, Mathieson."

At that moment there was a knock at the door and another Constable came in.

"Another message has arrived from London, sir."

Jake took the paper from the Constable and read it quickly. The police in London had discovered that Mike Lindsay appeared to have connections with Aberdeen. They had found a note of an Aberdeen address, which had been provided in the message, whilst searching a London address known to be connected to him.

That name *Lindsay* continued to bother Jake; he felt sure he had heard it recently.

The Aberdeen connection with Lindsay suddenly gave Jake an idea. It might be a bit of a long shot but were it to be successful then it would give Jake that chance he sought to bring his cold-blooded killer to justice.

"Maybe we will see our killer again after all," Jake then said and hurried out the door.

Mathieson stood in silence for a moment. He just knew that Jake had something in mind; the half smile on his face had given that much away.

Jake hurried upstairs in the hope that the Chief might be able to spare him a few moments. Luck was on his side and within ten minutes he was seated across from the Chief Constable explaining his idea.

Once Jake was finished talking the Chief showed little optimism as to the success of the idea but he did admit that it would be a feather in the cap of the Aberdeen City Police if they were the Force to arrest this murderer. The Chief agreed to make certain arrangements, on Jake's behalf and Jake returned to his office to make some arrangements of his own.

One hour later and Jake was back in the Chief's office only this time he was being presented with a telephone and informed that on the other end of the line was a Chief Detective-Inspector Potter of the Criminal Investigation Department at Scotland Yard. Jake had never had much use for the telephone system, up until now and he approached the implement with some apprehension.

With the main body of the telephone in his left hand and the earpiece held to his ear with the other Jake, rather tentatively, said hello. A cheery, though distant sounding voice responded almost immediately. It was still a marvel to Jake that he could not only talk to someone who was not in the same room but he could also talk to someone who was sitting in an office hundreds of miles away.

Wherever would technology go next?

Having established that first names would be used, Jake began to explain his suggested plan to Les who listened intently, saying nothing until Jake had finished.

"The man who murdered those men on the Aberdeen to London train is also wanted for two other murders he is believed to have committed whilst he was recently in Aberdeen. Not only did he kill two people in Aberdeen but he also led his merry little band of crooks in a rather daring bank raid in which they were able to walk away with several thousands of pounds. It goes without saying, Les that I would like to catch this man, hopefully before he can kill again. To that end I would like to make a suggestion as to how we proceed with the investigation. I would like to release a story to the Press, both in London and Aberdeen, that one of these men survived the attack on his person. That man will be Mike Lindsay. We will also say, in this story, that Mr Lindsay is being escorted back to his home city of Aberdeen where it is hoped he will recover enough from his wounds to be able to help the police with their enquiries in to a bank raid that took place there on the twenty-seventh of the month. Our murderer is a man who does not like loose ends, which is why he killed his accomplices in the first place. If we can plant that element of doubt in this man's mind; if we can make him think that there is still a loose end and here in Aberdeen, then maybe we can force him out of hiding. Maybe we can force him back to Aberdeen, even though he won't really want to do so. Once I have him back on my patch then I believe we can catch him, even though I don't know what he looks like nor what he is called."

There was a silence before Les Potter realised that Jake had stopped talking and was presumably awaiting a response of some kind.

"It sounds like a plan fraught with problems not the least of which might be the fact that there were many of the railway staff who saw the bodies. They'll know these men were dead and they are less likely to believe anything the Press might say. If your murder, therefore, was to come asking questions here then I fear your plan would fail at the first hurdle."

"Is it likely that any of the railway staff saw all three bodies together?" Jake then asked.

"Highly unlikely, I should have thought."

"So they can't be sure that all three men died. They'll assume the Press must be referring to one of the men that they didn't see. No doubt, in time, they will talk to each other about it and they may start to question the story then, but I'm hoping at least in the short term that we can get away with planting that seed of doubt."

"It's certainly worth trying," agreed Potter.

"Excellent. In that case we will release our story to the Press on Monday morning. Just to ensure that we issue the same misguided facts I will draw up a note of what I intend to release and if you are in agreement, you might issue something similar?"

"It's your plan, mate, so I'm happy to go along with anything you suggest. However, in the meantime we'll continue looking for him down here so if you discover anything that might be of help to us please let me know."

"Catching this man is my main priority at the moment," Jake then said, "so we will help you in any way that we can."

"Great. We'll maybe speak again, Jake?"

"It would be so much easier face to face," Jake then commented, "I'm really not sure about this telephone system."

Les was still laughing as the line went dead. Jake put the earpiece back on its hook and then put the telephone back on the Chief's desk.

"We have an agreement," he then said to the Chief. "It seems, therefore, that I have much to do, sir."

Jake returned to his office where he started on the story that would be released to the Press. It was essentially true up to the point where Mike Lindsay survived and was being returned to Aberdeen. The story spoke of two police officers being sent down to London to escort the wounded man back to Aberdeen. As he wrote it, Jake could only hope that the mysterious Reynolds would actually read it and more importantly, believe it.

By the time that Friday afternoon had all but finished Jake's plan was well underway. He had completed his press release and arranged for a copy to be wired to Les Potter in London. He had also spoken to the Chief again and with his agreement arranged for the two officers to go to London on the pretence of escorting the injured Mike Lindsay back to Aberdeen. It was also arranged that a third officer would travel separately to London. He would be 'Mike Lindsay' for the journey back.

Jake also found time to seek out Sandy Wilson and update him on the visitor he had had to the cellar at the back of the Esslemont Avenue property.

"Are you sure you are safe living there just now?" Sandy had then enquired.

Jake smiled. "I'm guessing they've checked everywhere now so I don't believe they'll be back again, especially as I am sure they will know by now that there is a police officer living in the property at the moment."

"Maybe Tommy had more than just a bank account under the name of Tom Anderson?" Sandy suggested.

"Something in their safe, do you mean?"

"It would be the safest place to keep something of value."

"You can check it out but somehow I don't think you'll find anything at the North of Scotland Bank round the corner," Jake then said. "Whatever Tommy had on these people it had to be significant to their potential downfall. I'd expect someone like Tommy to bury that deep somewhere; to put it where no one was ever likely to find it until the time was right. I'm guessing it's in a vault somewhere but under another name. If he could create Tom Anderson to hide his illegal income then he can create someone else to hide the other items."

Sandy Wilson looked dejected. "In which case we'll never find whatever it is."

"We may not find it in a hurry," conceded Jake, "but we will find it, one day."

TWENTY-SIX

Saturday 29 September – lunchtime onwards

At lunchtime the list of those people who had checked in to the Putney address provided by the fictional Basil Statham, arrived from London. Neatly copied out in handwriting that left Jake's looking like a chicken had walked across the paper, was a list of all those people who had spent at least one night at the address.

In the quiet of his own office Jake checked through the list and was not at all surprised to see that both Mike Lindsay and Mabel Lassiter had been there at some point of the last six months. Mike Lindsay had spent a lot of time at the address, appearing to almost live there permanently for the month of June. Mabel Lassiter had stayed at the address for three nights during that month as well.

There was, as Jake already knew, no mention of Basil Statham though it was highly likely that amongst the list of names laid out before Jake was yet another creation by the killer.

It now seemed possible that this guest house had been used as a meeting place for the gang. What better cover than to appear to be random individuals thrown together for the night by the simple fact that you all booked in to the same place on the same night.

In short, for the moment at any rate, the list was of no help at all. Jake felt that rising sense of frustration that always seemed to surface when he devoted some thought to this case. He felt like he was chasing a shadow in the sense that no sooner did he feel he was getting closer than everything seemed to disappear in front of him. Every potential lead continued to go absolutely nowhere.

Jake now knew that the three officers were on their way to London and that they would return on Monday. He could only hope that the murderer he sought would not be too far behind them.

Jake then gave some thought to Janet Lindsay. He knew he would have to arrest her at some stage of the investigation but he continued to hope that she might become a point of contact should the man she knew as Reynolds return to the city. He then wondered how she might cope with an event like that. She did seem to be the strongest person he had ever met and it could yet be the case that her love for this man would rule the day and she would warn him of her involvement with the police.

He took his pocket-watch from his waistcoat and checked the time. It was a little after one. His thoughts turned to Margaret. They were due to meet again in six hours and just thinking about her brought a smile to her face. Margaret had the ability to make Jake feel happy even when she wasn't in the same room. That had to mean something.

He was looking forward to seeing the film of the Royal visit and also to the reaction of the audience. There were many people who had still to see one of these moving picture shows and Jake felt sure that, particularly due to the fact the film was about the King and Queen, there would be a big crowd at the Music Hall that evening.

He dragged his mind back to work activities and continued to clear as much paper work as he could. He was relieved at the fact no new business came his way as the afternoon progressed. Another check of his watch then informed him that it was time to go home and prepare for his night out.

He put his jacket on and left the office. He said farewell to Sergeant Turnbull and made his way out on to Lodge Walk. He passed a number of people going about their business as he made his way up through Rosemount to Esslemont Avenue. He was relieved to find that the door was still intact as he turned the key and let himself in to the flat.

Jake boiled the kettle and used some of the water to make himself a cup of tea and the remainder went in to a large bowl so that he could wash and shave. He then put on his best suit and even took his hat, which he rarely wore, out of its box and tried it on. It had been an afterthought to even take the hat to Esslemont Avenue as he never felt totally certain that it even suited him.

He stood in front of the mirror turning his head from right to left and studying how he looked. Some men could look so sophisticated when they wore a hat, Jake however, always ended up feeling slightly silly. He eventually decided that he would wear the hat at least as far as Margaret's flat. If she laughed at him then he would leave it there.

Jake locked the door and went out on to Esslemont Avenue. He walked at a brisk pace down through Leadside Road and onwards to Margaret's flat. There were already a large number of people milling around and Jake wondered if many of them might be going to the Music Hall as well.

He arrived at Margaret's door at ten minutes to seven. He knocked loudly and then stood back. A moment or two passed before the door opened and Margaret stood, smiling, before him. She was dressed in a red jacket and skirt with a white blouse beneath. She also wore a hat. Jake immediately thought that she looked a lot better wearing a hat than he ever would.

"I like the hat," Margaret said.

"I never know if it suits me or not, that's why I rarely wear it," Jake explained.

"It does suit you; you should wear it more often," Margaret added as she stepped in to the hallway and turned to lock the door.

They walked through North Silver Street and in to Golden Square. A crowd had already gathered on the other side of the Square outside the Music Hall. Jake and Margaret joined the queue where they moved slowly, for the next twenty minutes, towards the front door, which was around the corner on Union Street.

Once inside they made their way through to the main hall at the back where rows of chairs had been laid out. On the stage they had set up a large, white screen and situated in the middle of many of the chairs was the machine by which the film would be shown.

Standing around this machine were three men, all looking very pleased with themselves. Although films had been shown at public events for ten years there was still a sense of magic about them and no doubt some of the men presenting the films saw themselves as some kind of magician. Jake and Margaret found a couple of spare chairs, which seemed well positioned for seeing the screen and sat down.

A quarter to eight came around and one of the gentlemen, who had been standing by the projecting machine made his way up on to the stage. He then said a few words about how the film had been made and that it would last for approximately fifty minutes. He then hoped that the large audience that had gathered would enjoy the experience and tell their friends.

At five minutes past eight the film began. In the darkness Jake reached across and took Margaret's hand in his own. They sat like that through the entire film. There was no sound other than the clicking of the machine as they fed the film through it. Jake looked around and in the light being cast from the screen he could see faces wide-eyed with wonderment. Though the people of Aberdeen were getting more accustomed to watching moving pictures it was still a novel experience to watch something that they themselves were in.

Here they were, just two days after the event, sitting watching it all happen again. For those people who may have missed the events as they had happened this must have been an amazing experience but equally for those who *were* there then the fact they might now see themselves on screen was very exciting.

Jake started to wish that the cameras had been nearer the end of Lodge Walk then maybe they would have captured, on film, the gang members as they had made their way to the station. Maybe someday film would play a part in catching criminals?

The film finished and the lights in the hall went up. There was a moment's silence as everyone took a second or two to realise it had actually finished. There was then a spontaneous burst of applause and one or two cheers of approval. Another of the men presenting the film then went on to the stage and thanked everyone for coming. He again wished they had all enjoyed the show and hoped they would all have a safe journey home.

Jake and Margaret walked out on to Union Street. Jake felt that the experience had been well worth the two shillings he had paid for each seat. Margaret turned to face Jake.

"I have a piece of cold pork and some beer in the flat if you would care to join me for an early supper?"

"That would be very nice," replied Jake and they started to walk back towards Rosemount Viaduct.

Margaret's flat was bigger than anything Jake had seen before. She had a sitting room, bedroom, kitchen and bathroom; all coming off a large entrance hall. Margaret showed Jake in to the sitting room, which had a large, curving window that afforded a view down Schoolhill.

"We would have had a great view of the Torchlight Procession had we been here on Tuesday," Jake commented.

"We had a good view where we were," added Margaret. "It's always good to see something like that in a crowd. Now, please sit down and I'll organise the food."

"Is there anything I can do to help?" said Jake.

Margaret paused in the doorway, a look of surprise crossing her face. "It's very good of you to offer, Jake; thank you. However, I have everything under control so please be seated and I'll be right back."

From her reaction it seemed clear to Jake that Margaret was not accustomed to having men make offers of help in her direction. Jake drew the drapes before he sat down. While he waited for Margaret to return he looked around what was a large room with a high, ornate ceiling. As well as the window that faced down Schoolhill there was another, of the same size, that faced across to the library. Jake could certainly appreciate the view from the windows but not the height. He had never been a fan of high places and this flat was very high.

A few minutes passed before the door opened and Margaret came back in to the room carrying a tray on which she had a plate of cakes, two cups, two saucers, milk jug and sugar placed upon it. She took the tray over to a small table that lay between the two easy chairs that created two-thirds of the suite. She smiled at Jake, checked that he would drink a beer and then turned to leave again.

It was fully twenty minutes later before they were both sitting in the room with their food and drink laid out in front of them. Margaret had a glass of water whilst Jake drank his beer. The pork was delicious as was the bread Margaret had cut to go with it. Little was said initially as they both realised they were a lot hungrier than they had realised.

Eventually conversation returned to the room and they discussed their views on the film of the King and Queen. They then chatted about films in general as Margaret thought the idea of going to a local hall and seeing pictures of events that you may have missed, was a good one. All the time they were talking Jake could not stop thinking about his conversation with Alan MacBride and the fact that some men were intent on turning the budding world of moving pictures in to something sordid.

An hour later Jake thought it would be best if he left. Margaret stood up and he moved across to stand in front of her. This time nothing was said the simply moved closer and kissed. Again there was an intensity to the act that seemed to betray that here were two people with real feelings for each other. As the kiss concluded and Jake stepped back Margaret spent a silent few seconds simply looking at him.

"You must come here for lunch next Sunday?" she then said. "We can have a little more than just pork and bread."

"I enjoyed my pork and bread, Margaret and I would be delighted to come for lunch next Sunday."

"Excellent," Margaret concluded with another smile.

They kissed once more before Jake put on his hat and left.

TWENTY-SEVEN

Sunday 30 September   afternoon

Jake didn't have to but he went to work on the Sunday. He had enjoyed his night out with Margaret but he had never completely been able to forget about how he might catch Mabel Lassiter's murderer.

He didn't expect he would achieve much in the office but he felt happier being there as an alternative to simply hanging around the house all day. He spent some time looking at the list he had received from London as if he hoped that the more he looked at it the more something helpful would jump out. It didn't happen.

He was still thinking about the case when a Constable came in to the room to tell Jake that there was a young woman asking for him. She had been given a seat in the interview room.

"Do you have her name?" Jake enquired.

"Myrtle Abbot."

Jake wondered what this woman could possibly have to tell him as he hurried along the corridor and in to the interview room. Myrtle Abbot looked even prettier with her hair down and the fact she was wearing proper clothing made Jake feel a little more relaxed.

"Miss Abbot, what can I do for you?" he said as he sat on the other chair.

"I've spent a lot of time thinking about poor Mabel since you last spoke to me and I eventually remembered something that I thought might be of help."

Jake sat forward with interest. "And what might that be?"

"You asked if anyone ever paid Mabel more attention than other men and at the time I was thinking purely of our time in Aberdeen as I assumed you were looking for an Aberdeen connection of some kind. However, once I started to think of possible Aberdeen connections in other cities I suddenly remembered a man who got to know her very well in London."

"Mike Lindsay?" Jake suggested.

Myrtle looked a little deflated. "Oh you know about him already."

"His name has come up in our enquiries as has a man called Reynolds. Do you ever remember meeting a man called Reynolds?"

Myrtle thought for a moment. "I never knew the man's name but I do remember seeing Mable leave the show one night with Mike and this other gentleman."

"Can you describe the other gentleman?" Jake asked hoping that this time it would not be the usual description of a bushy beard and not much else.

"He was young, handsome and looked as if money had been a part of his life for a very long time."

"Clean shaven?" Jake then asked.

"Yes."

"Would you be able to describe this man to our police artist?"

"It would be from a distant memory but I'll do the best I can, Inspector."

"Good girl," Jake concluded and hurried to the front desk. He arranged for someone to go and collect the police artist from his home and take him down to Lodge Walk. He then arranged for tea to be taken through to Myrtle and Jake then remained in her company until the artist arrived.

The drawing that was completed at least gave Jake a different image to work with. It was always possible that this new man wasn't Reynolds but Jake had a strong feeling that it was. He thanked Myrtle for her help and noticed most of the young officers, standing at the door, turning to view Myrtle with admiration as she passed and headed out the front door.

It wasn't much but at least Jake now felt that in Myrtle he had at least one possible witness who could confirm the identity of Reynolds were they ever to catch someone in the first place.

Jake returned to his office feeling a little more upbeat about the case. His plan was now firmly in place and Monday would see the release of the story to the Press. He could only hope that the plan would work and that Reynolds, or whatever he was calling himself now, would hurry to Aberdeen to check on Mike Lindsay.

September was drawing to an end and a new month was about to begin. For all that he had achieved in September Jake still needed to catch Reynolds; still needed to help Sandy Wilson find Tommy's murderer and now needed to keep an eye on pornography possible raising its ugly head in the world of moving pictures.

Such a lot for Jake to do but, for the moment at any rate that could wait for another day. Tomorrow would see the start of October and hopefully the arrival of some much needed answers.

Jake put his jacket on and went back to Esslemont Avenue. He had an evening meal and then read a book until tiredness got the better of him and he went to bed. He fell asleep with his head full of thoughts for Margaret.

He hoped that October would also see their relationship continue to blossom. He expected so much from October but, for tonight, that would be another story.

***

1906 – October

ONE

Monday 01 October – Morning

The weekend was over and a new month had begun. Detective Inspector Jake Fraser, of the Aberdeen City Police, was at his desk particularly early that morning. He was excited at the prospect of launching his latest plan on an unsuspecting world and seeing what came from it.

During the month of September Aberdeen had seen murder and robbery on a grand scale. One of the murderers had been caught and brought to justice but the other had escaped across the border and was now hiding somewhere in London. This man had not only murdered Mabel Lassiter, a young dancer whose only crime had been to get caught up in a plan to raid a bank, but had also then murdered the other members of the gang who had carried out that raid.

The senseless murder of Mabel Lassiter had really got under Jake's skin, probably more than any other case he had been involved in. It had annoyed him that her murderer had been able to make good his escape, greatly helped by the fact that the police neither knew his name nor what he looked like. Everyone who had met him, while he had been in Aberdeen, appeared to describe a different person using a different name.

Jake had set himself the personal target of catching this man and to better achieve that he had devised a plan that might bring the murderer back to Aberdeen. Jake had agreed with colleagues at Scotland Yard, to release a story to the Press that only two of the three men knifed on the train from Aberdeen to London had actually died.

One of the men, the story would continue, had been returned, under police guard to Aberdeen; this being his home city. The man's name was Mike Lindsay and the story would suggest that Lindsay would be helping the police with their enquiries in to a bank raid once he had recovered from his injuries. This would be the day on which that story was given to the Press and then it would be a matter of waiting and seeing if the murderer took the bait.

The fact that Jake had neither a name nor an identity was always going to be a problem but he was now fairly confident that one of the bank's staff, Janet Lindsay, had to be related in some way to Mike and if that were the case then there was every chance that she might also know the murderer and would become a point of contact for him on his return to Aberdeen.

It was only a matter, therefore, of persuading Janet Lindsay to cooperate. Jake did not believe that that would be too difficult a mission for him as the only alternative to not helping the police would be imprisonment for Janet Lindsay were they to prove that she had played an active part in the bank raid.

Sergeant Mathieson, Jake's right-hand man, had gone to the North of Scotland Bank to collect Janet Lindsay and bring her back to the Central Police Office in Lodge Walk. It would be a short journey for Mathieson as the back door of the bank was almost visible from the front door of the Police Office.

Jake took his pocket-watch from the left pocket of his waistcoat and checked the time. It was nearly ten o'clock. He wanted to have his Mike Lindsay story in the hands of Alan MacBride, a young journalist with the Aberdeen Daily Journal who had recently been of some help to Jake, by lunchtime so that they could print the story slightly ahead of the Free Press who would not get the story until the middle of the afternoon.

That meant he had around two hours to talk to Janet Lindsay and try to ascertain her part in this whole sorry business. There was a knock at the door and a young Constable came in.

"Sergeant Mathieson and a young lady are waiting for you in the interview room, sir."

"Thank you, Constable Strachan, I'll be there in a moment."

As Jake made his way along the corridor he was already beginning to work out in his own mind how he would conduct the interview with Janet Lindsay. She needed to be kept in the dark with regard to Mike Lindsay but equally she had to be brought on-board the search for the man she had known as Reynolds. If Reynolds reappeared in Aberdeen Jake had to know, for certain, that Janet Lindsay would play along and not go and do anything stupid such as telling Reynolds that the police were on to him.

Jake stood outside the interview room and gathered his thoughts. When he finally felt comfortable with what he would say to Janet Lindsay he opened the door and went in. The outcome of the next few moments would be crucial to the success of his plan.

Jake entered the room and closed the door.

....to be continued.

Printed in Great Britain
by Amazon